FORBIDDEN NIGHTS

Lauren Blakely

**BOOK #5 IN THE
SEDUCTIVE NIGHTS SERIES**

Copyright © 2015 by Lauren Blakely
LaurenBlakely.com
Cover Design by © Sarah Hansen, Okay Creations
Photo: Scott Hoover
Interior Layout by Jesse Gordon

ALSO BY
LAUREN BLAKELY

The Caught Up in Love Series (Each book in this series follows a different couple so each book can be read
separately, or enjoyed as a series since characters cross-
over)

Caught Up in Her (A short prequel novella to
   Caught Up in Us)
Caught Up In Us
Pretending He's Mine
Trophy Husband
Playing With Her Heart

Standalone Novels (Each of these full-length romance
novels can be read by themselves, though they feature
appearance from characters in Caught Up in Love)

Far Too Tempting
Stars in Their Eyes
21 Stolen Kisses (March 2015)

The No Regrets Series (These books should be read
in order)

The Thrill of It
Every Second With You

The Seductive Nights Series

First Night (Julia and Clay, prequel novella)
Night After Night (Julia and Clay, book one)
After This Night (Julia and Clay, book two)
One More Night (Julia and Clay, book three)
One Night With Her (A short prequel novella about
     Michelle and Jack, this story is also included in the
     ebook of *Nights With Him*)
Nights With Him (A standalone novel about Michelle
     and Jack)
Forbidden Nights (A standalone novel about Nate
     and Casey)
Sweet, Sinful Nights (A standalone novel about Brent
     and Shannon, Summer 2015)

The Fighting Fire Series

Burn For Me (Smith and Jamie)
Melt for Him (Megan and Becker)
Consumed By You (Travis and Cara, Summer 2015)

DEDICATION

This book is dedicated to all my readers. Thank you for loving words and romance and sexy stories as much as I love writing them. And, as always, this book is for my dear friend Cynthia.

FAMILY TREE

Dear Readers:

I'm thrilled to share a family tree with you for the first time! This tree was made by Brandi Hughes and depicts the key connections between my books. Enjoy!

Xoxo
Lauren

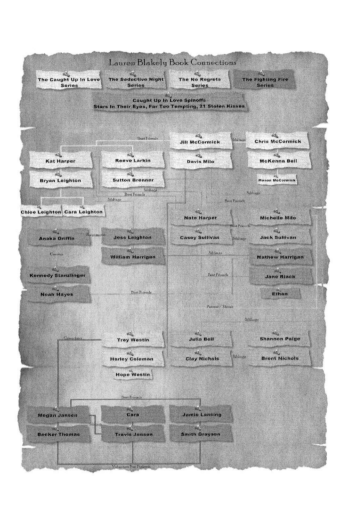

Lauren Blakely Book Connections

The Caught Up In Love Series   **The Seductive Night Series**   **The No Regrets Series**   **The Fighting Fire Series**

Caught Up In Love Spinoffs
Stars In Their Eyes, Far Too Tempting, 21 Stolen Kisses

Jill McCormick   Chris McCormick

Kat Harper   Reeve Larkin   Davis Milo   McKenna Bell

Bryan Leighton   Sutton Brenner   Mason McCormick

Chloe Leighton   Cara Leighton

Anaka Griffin   Jess Leighton   Nate Harper   Michelle Milo

William Harrigan   Casey Sullivan   Jack Sullivan

Kennedy Stanzlinger   Mathew Harrigan

Noah Hayes   Jane Black

Ethan

Trey Westin   Julia Bell   Shannon Paige

Harley Coleman   Clay Nichols   Brent Nichols

Hope Westin

Megan Jansen   Cara   Jamie Lansing

Becker Thomas   Travis Jansen   Smith Grayson

CHAPTER ONE

New Orleans, noon . . .

All his rigorous training over the last few years had paid off.

Nate was now officially a certified expert at looking Casey square in the eyes, and he could sustain a full five minutes of conversation without staring at her legs, breasts, or ass.

Okay, five minutes was a bit of an exaggeration. Maybe it was closer to three minutes, tops. But in his defense, he'd worked his way up from lasting only ten seconds without roaming his eyes up and down her beautiful body.

Today, he was slated to earn his general stripes on this account because the blue-eyed blonde looked absolutely stunning as she stepped off his plane at the New Orleans Lakefront Airport, her long, shapely legs on display in a red skirt and black heels. Damn, the woman was tailor-made for her job as the head of a sex toy company. She radiated sex appeal.

She adjusted the strap on her shoulder bag as she scanned for him, a hand above her eyes to shield the June sun that was shooting balls of fire. The small executive airport was relatively quiet today; there were only a few other guys in suits meeting passengers here. Nate was a guy in a suit too, but he'd ditched his jacket, loosened his tie, and rolled up the cuffs on his sleeves. When she spotted him, her lips curved up in a big smile and she waved. She walked over to him, and damn, did she look fantastic from top to bottom.

Eyes up, eyes up.

When she reached him she planted a quick kiss on his cheek, and the citrus-y scent of her hair that was so very *her* drifted into his nose. "You've completely spoiled me, I'm afraid. I can't ever fly commercial again after this kind of treatment," she said.

"The full treatment?" He arched an eyebrow. "And to think, I've told the flight attendants time and time again to stop all the naughty play on my jet, but they must have been unable to resist you," he said dryly. She swatted him on the arm, then laughed as he took her suitcase and rolled it behind him as they headed across the tarmac, the mid-day heat and omnipresent humidity pelting them from above.

"I was *actually referring* to the high-speed wireless in the sky you've got going on, which I made ample use of, as well as the risotto for lunch and Perrier," she said, pointing her thumb back in the direction of the Gulfstream Nate had acquired full use of when he'd been wooed, courted and won in a search two years ago for a new Chief Executive Officer of The Luxe line of luxury hotels.

When they reached the terminal, they were greeted by a blast of arctic air from the overactive AC units that were operating at full throttle in New Orleans these days.

"Damn," he said in a low whistle, shaking his head. "Makes me so sad to think you worked the entire flight. You're such a workaholic."

"Takes one to know one."

"Touché," he said because they were equally addicted to their jobs. They both logged long hours and late nights, their midnight emails to each other almost always answered within minutes, and took countless cross-country and transcontinental flights. "Speaking of, are you ready for your meeting?"

She nodded, pushing a few loose strands of hair off her shoulder. "Absolutely. I freshened up on the plane, and brushed my teeth. Want to smell my minty-clean breath?"

He rolled his eyes. "I was *actually referring* to your proposal for the lingerie company," he said, slinging her previous words back at her.

"Oh, the partnership proposal for Grant. That teeny, tiny little thing?" She waved a hand as if it were no big deal. But he knew how important it was to her. She turned serious. "I reviewed it a few more times, and practiced my pitch on the plane. I've got it down pat and I'm hopeful," she said, holding up her hand as she twisted her index and middle finger together, "that he's ready to play ball."

"If you were a ballplayer, I'd give you a good luck smack on the ass as you ran onto the field."

She raised her eyebrows and wiggled her ass, and yup. There it was. He'd made it three whole minutes before he dropped his gaze fully to her backside, which was so damn

tantalizing. Round, firm and tempting. As they left the airport, he held the door open for her, enjoying the view
while she walked ahead of him. Hell, if she was going to
wiggle that smackable rear, he was going to stare freely.

She tipped her forehead to the black town car, gleaming
and polished, that waited by the curb in the broiling heat.
"Yours?"

"But of course," he said as the driver scurried around to
open the door. Once inside, she smiled like she had a secret. "Want to hear my pitch?"

"You know you can always practice your pitches on
me," he said. He settled into the leather backseat, only
vaguely wishing she wanted to practice other things with
him. But that was never in the cards because their friendship was too important. As they'd both risen to CEO posts
in the last two years, he at the hotel, her at Joy Delivered,
they'd leaned on each other more. She was his sounding
board, and he was hers. Though they both traveled fre-
quently, they were based in New York, so they got together
regularly to bounce ideas, discuss concerns, and provide
advice and insight that benefitted their respective companies.

As they drove away from the airport she launched into
her proposal for Grant Abbot, a lingerie magnate who ran
a line of upscale boutiques around the world. "Let's talk
about all that the LolaRing can do for Entice," she began,
and Nate was glad he was a good multi-tasker. Being close
friends and confidantes with a smart, beautiful, clever
woman who he also wanted to nail had turned him into
the consummate juggler. However, keeping his focus on
business turned far more complicated when she started to

discuss the off-the-charts pleasure her new product was sure to deliver. Words like *delicious, stimulation,* and *molten desire* fell from her tongue and landed right in his lap.

"We're talking about the ultimate pleasure on a path to prolonged orgasm," she continued, her stormy blue eyes fixed on him as she rattled off all the benefits of one of her company's newest products. "And our intensely arousing toy, paired with your sleek and sultry new line of lingerie would make the most fantastic gift package for the sexually adventurous couple."

Okay, he was promoting himself to full lieutenant general stripes today. It was like pulling teeth to keep his mind anywhere but on imagining using this intensely arousing new product on her. Clenching his hands in tight fists, a massive dose of restraint coursed through his bloodstream as she waxed eloquent on the number of all-consuming, toe-curling, star-seeing climaxes she expected the LolaRing would serve up.

God, he was being tested *so fucking hard* today.

"So what do you think?" She shifted closer, her eyes wide and eager.

He breathed out roughly, considering his response before he opened his mouth. The thing was, Nate Harper had been hot for Casey Sullivan for years, but when he answered her, he wasn't speaking from below the belt. He was speaking from the brain. He was speaking as a businessman. As someone who was on the receiving end of pitches all day long. "You nailed it, Casey. I have no doubt that we'll be celebrating at dinner later," he said, since he'd already made a reservation at the hottest new fusion restaurant on Bourbon Street.

She flashed a big, bright smile, her eyes glittering with excitement. "Here's hoping we'll be toasting to lingerie and dildos tonight," she said, as she dipped a hand into her purse and reapplied her lipstick. They pulled up to her destination in the downtown business section.

She grabbed the door handle, ready to head to her meeting. Then she stopped and turned to look at him, a softness in her eyes. "By the way, thank you for doing this for me. The plane, the car, the room at your hotel. . ."

"It was nothing. I'm happy to help. I'll make sure your suitcase gets to your room."

She nudged his shoulder. "Guess what? I even remembered to bring my shampoo. No hotel shampoo needed this time. Though I'm sure yours is fabulous."

He laughed. It was a running joke. She was particular about her shampoo, but always packed in a rush so she often forgot to bring it along.

Minutes later, he walked across the cobblestone courtyard of The Luxe, lush with greenery and a fountain playing a lazy rhythm, then through the gilded revolving doors and into the marble lobby. Within seconds, his hotel manager rounded the corner and marched over to him.

"Good to see you again, Mr. Harper," Daniel said. The man had a homing beacon installed, but then, that's what a good manager should do—zero in on the boss. He'd done so nearly every time Nate had stepped through the front doors the last few days. When he'd arrived earlier in the week, Daniel's first words had been: "We weren't expecting you 'til next week, but we're always glad when you take the time to visit."

That was because Nate had rearranged his schedule so that his trip to visit his company's recently renovated French Quarter property intersected with Casey's New Orleans venture. He had no notions whatsoever of acting on his attraction; he'd learned to live with it and tamp it down. He simply knew this potential deal was important to her so he wanted to make sure he did everything he could, from the private ride through the sky, to the room on the top floor. She deserved it. He'd never met a harder worker than Casey, and if he could deliver a few perks for her, well hell—that was why he was in the business of delivering perks.

CHAPTER TWO

New Orleans, afternoon . . .

"Think about the Rabbit. That's become the rare product that's known by one word now. Say *the Rabbit* and everyone knows it means the world's best kind of vibrator," she said, as Grant Abbot wrapped his long fingers around a glass of bourbon, knocking back a swallow of the amber liquid. Casey loved that his eyes were on her the whole time. The man was focused—he was interested in what she brought to him. "And I believe the same can be true of the LolaRing."

He took a beat before responding. He liked to take his time, it seemed. He wasn't in a rush.

"Interesting," he said, his smooth voice a perfect complement to the jazz music that piped through the bar from the overhead speakers, as a handful of waiters and bartenders refilled the drinks of nearby patrons. It was only four in the afternoon, but Happy Hour had started early, and Grant had insisted they take their meeting to his favorite watering hole. "Such a better location for the conversations we'll have about silk, satin and vibration, don't you think?" he'd said with a flirty wink when his receptionist had shown her to his office, a corner suite in a nearby building with a view of downtown through its floor-to-ceiling windows. But she'd barely caught a glimpse of his 9-to-5 habitat because he'd placed a hand on the small of her back, and guided her down the elevator, around the block, and through the cranberry-red wooden doors of Velvet. The establishment was bathed in low lights and cool music, and had an upscale ambiance with its couches that were stitched from the same material as the name.

Casey hadn't let the switch in venue throw her off. Nor had she let herself be affected by her long-simmering attraction to the man. He was only a few years older than her thirty-two, and ever since she'd met him at a conference a year ago, she'd let her mind wander from his crystal blue eyes to his dark, close-dropped hair, to the way he wore a suit so damn well. Not to mention that accent. That Big Easy, Southern drawl that would likely sound delicious if he spoke low and sexy in her ear. Then there was the way he wore a shade of mystery, and chased it with a dash of intrigue.

But she pushed all those other thoughts of him into the far corners of her mind. Because business was business was business. They'd been talking about the "synergies" between their two companies since they'd met—they were both purveyors of pleasure, after all. They were a natural fit, she reasoned, especially since she'd been guiding Joy Delivered down an expansion road in the last year and a half since her brother Jack had stepped down as CEO.

Though she and Jack had founded the company together several years ago after she'd graduated from business school, he'd run the ship until the woman he fell in love with was offered a job in Paris. The romantic that her older brother was, he'd given up his post and moved overseas to be with Michelle. Their wedding was at the end of the month.

Joy Delivered had already been thriving when she became the woman in charge. Under her care she'd turned it into an even bigger and more profitable business with her new focus on partnerships with like-minded companies. She'd been relentless in her pursuit of success since taking on Jack's role. She wanted to prove to the business world and to herself, frankly, that she could guide the company as well as he had.

Being a woman had never held her back, but she knew she had to work that much harder. When Casey wanted something she went after it passionately, with everything she had. It was ironic that the strategy had worked well at her company, but her approach hadn't gone as swimmingly in her rather dismal personal life. A string of bad luck in relationships trailed behind her. Yup, laugh it up. She was the Sex Toy Princess who didn't get any action beyond the battery-operated kind.

It wasn't that she chose badly, or liked jerks. She didn't. But there were two issues working against her. One, men didn't ask her out that often, and when she did ask out a guy, he'd often admit her profession scared him. "Do you have any idea how terrifying it is to approach a woman who sells sex toys?" one guy had said. He hadn't lasted long. The other issue was that she had a notorious habit of speaking her mind, and, it turned out, that didn't always work for the guys she had dated.

"You intimidate me," Scott, her ex, had told her, when he'd said sayonara the same night she'd been planning to ask him to move in with her. "You're fun as hell, but I can't see myself getting serious with an alpha female."

Ouch.

She'd bristled at the designation. "Alpha female?" she said with narrowed eyes. "What are you talking about? That's a term for a dog."

"You're great at business, Case. But your relationship skills are kind of lacking. You never let me decide anything. You want to be in control of everything. You want to make all the decisions, from dinner to movies to what position in bed."

"I didn't hear you complaining about any of those positions when we were in them," she pointed out.

"It's not hard for a guy to get off," he said in an admonishing tone, and the message was loud and cruelly clear—*I'm not into you in the bedroom.*

Later, after the soreness at being left again had abated, and after she'd turned a few hairbrushes into projective missiles lobbed at the door, she was able to call a spade a spade. She *did* like control. She did enjoy picking and choosing, whether they went to an art gallery or a film, and she absolutely loved telling a man how she liked it— *harder, faster, there, right there, don't stop.* What was so wrong with that? Hell, this was the field she worked in. She marketed sex toys, for goodness' sake. Her days, and her late, late nights were spent finding new ways to communicate all the joys her toys could deliver. And yet, something about Scott's condemnations had stung because they'd hit home. They'd touched down and felt true. She was an alpha woman. Strong and confident, driven and ambitious, and absolutely unafraid of saying what she wanted. It scared some men. It scared *most* men.

Good thing she and Grant were communicating then about business. She could be as direct as she needed to be.

"What do you think about such a partnership? We're keeping the toy under wraps until we roll it out later this summer with our key retail partners, and I'd very much like to have Entice as one of those partners," she said, then took a drink of her French martini as she waited for his response.

He draped his arm across the back of the royal blue couch, tracing a line absently with his fingertip. The thought briefly flicked through her mind of him running that same finger against her shoulder, her neck, her leg . . .

"I've often thought we'd make good partners," he said, with a slight quirk of his lips, and a certain look in his eyes. A look that almost said there was an undercurrent of interest. Then he wiped his hand across his brow, as if it had gotten too hot in here. "And now you come to me with this sultry talk of a LolaRing," he said, clearly enjoying the naughtiness of their professions. "What's a gentleman to do?"

God, the man was a flirt, and such a fine specimen. The head of his company, surely he wasn't one of those guys who'd be bothered that she was strong-willed, that she was in love with work. Because she was in love with love, too. She was a believer in happiness, in possibilities, in two people who fall madly in love. The kind of love her brother had with Michelle. The kind of love she was determined, bad luck be damned, to find.

She leaned her head back and laughed. "Then what do I need to do to get your bras and panties in bed with my hot new toy?"

He laughed, a sexy rumbly sound. "Why don't you let me tell you how I see this working?"

"Please do."

His eyes seemed to light up when she said *please*.

As they discussed all the possibilities of working together, she could taste the sugary-sweet flavor of a deal coming together. She wanted this one badly; she'd been chasing it for months.

And then, there it was at last—he extended a hand. "Let's make my lingerie customers even more satisfied," he said, as he wrapped his fingers around hers. Excitement coursed through her and she wanted to pump her fist, to shout a victorious yes to the sky. Instead, she tamped it down. She knew how to behave like a grown-up.

"I'm thrilled, Grant. Truly thrilled."

"As am I. However," he said, and her heart dropped because words like *however* had a way of tanking deals, "we need to wait a month to dive in. I'm going to be in Vietnam for most of June visiting my factories, and then Hong Kong for business, and I want to personally oversee our partnership. Which I can do properly when I return."

Ah, well that wasn't such a bad *however.* "I like that idea," she said with a smile.

"I want to give this my full attention."

"I would love that, too."

He reached for her hand, and gently pressed his lips to her skin. Holy hell. Her insides fluttered from his touch. "You are a brilliant woman, Casey. I love how you pursued this deal. Your ideas and plans have been fantastic. It'll be a pleasure to work on the business of pleasure with you."

"That's my favorite kind of business." She held up her glass in a toast.

"I'll work on the papers and send them over to you, so everything will be signed before I leave."

"Excellent," she said as he took a drink.

Then she noticed his glass was empty, and she signaled the bartender for another round.

When she turned her attention back to Grant, the flirty look was absent. Instead, he stared at her, an intense and somewhat chiding look in his inky blue eyes. "I like how you operate in business. But now I want to focus on other things, and as we do, you should let me order another round. I'd like to be the one to do the . . . *ordering*," he said, taking time to enunciate that last word. The way he said it made it sound suggestive, a hint at something other than drinks.

"Ordering?" she said carefully.

"Yes. Ordering," he said, his eyes blazing darkly at her, kicking off a fresh wave of heat inside her.

He raised a hand, snapped his fingers, and called the waiter. "This beautiful woman will have another martini. Make hers dirty this time. And I'll have a gin and tonic."

Damn, he wasn't joking when he said he liked to order. He liked to pick and choose too, and that was exactly what Scott had said she should let a man do. So Casey didn't protest the second martini, even though she preferred them of the French variety.

"As you wish, sir," the waiter said and scurried off.

Grant flashed a smile at Casey, a lopsided grin that was full of charm and something else . . . something strong and commanding. "You should know that I will be thinking about you when I'm in Asia."

She swallowed and blinked. He'd been flirty, but now he was downright direct. Perhaps her luck was changing. "You will?"

"When I return, I hope we can not only do business, but also finally spend more time together. Would you like that?"

"I would," she said, looking him straight in the eyes.

"Excellent. Let's make it a date in July. You can come back here, and we will have dinner together." He moved closer, reached for a lock of her hair, and twined it around his finger. "But, let me pursue you," he whispered.

Let me pursue you.

The words rang in her head, along with his earlier ones. Like *ordering,* and *why don't you let me tell you how I see this working?* Then the way he liked it so much when she'd said *please.*

The message was loud and clear. Grant Abbot liked his women to be demure. He didn't want an alpha female. He didn't need a mirror to his dominant side.

Casey had no clue whatsoever how to be that woman.

She didn't have a submissive bone in her body.

CHAPTER THREE

New Orleans, evening...

All through dinner she hadn't been able to get Grant Abbot off her mind. Not as she and Nate shared an appetizer of oysters. Not as she worked her way through a delicious niçoise salad while he ate the Chilean sea bass. And not even through a round of celebratory champagne he'd ordered for them during dinner at Poisson, a small French bistro in a white, two-story house with large picture windows that looked out onto the bustling and busy Bourbon Street. Inside, a torch singer crooned in the corner of the restaurant.

Casey was half present, and half hanging out four hours ago.

She hadn't gone into the meeting with Grant expecting anything more than the chance to close a deal. Sure, in the back of her mind she'd hoped for more. Now she had a . . . well, a potential *someone*. A beau, maybe? A prospective love interest? At the very least, she had a date on her calendar a month from now.

But her suitor spoke a language she barely understood, and it was one she was sure Nate could decipher. She was dying to tell him all about Grant. They'd shared plenty before, and he knew the ins and outs of her stalled romantic life. Still, she'd been looking for the right moment to spill the strange details.

Perhaps over dessert, because the waiter appeared with a chocolate lava cake that looked so delicious her mouth watered.

"Your Molten Pleasure," he said, using the official name of the dessert while grandly setting it on the white linen tablecloth, before returning to the kitchen.

"My chef said this is the best lava cake in town, and that's saying something, because the one we have at the hotel is pretty damn fantastic," Nate said.

"You're getting me all excited now," Casey said as she picked up her fork, ready to dive in. She pointed to the cake as he finished off the remainder of his champagne. "You're going to have some, right?"

He laughed and nodded, his amber eyes even warmer than usual when he smiled. He had one of the best smiles she'd ever seen. Plus, he had great teeth—straight and white, the best kind to have. "Yes. I'm going to have some. I just wanted to finish my drink first."

She dipped her fork into the soft cake and brought it to her lips. But before she bit down, she flashed back to Grant's words, and the way he'd ordered her drink. Taking control. Wanting to decide. Could she truly do that? Could she hand over the reins like he wanted? As Nate dug into the cake, she sniffed an opportunity. An odd one, but an opportunity nonetheless.

She set down her fork.

He eyed it curiously. "I thought you were excited to eat it?"

She swallowed, then spoke softly. "I have a request," she squeaked out.

"You want me to ask her to play the Pina Colada song?" he said, gesturing to the sultry singer in the slinky cream-colored dress, gripping a microphone tight as she sang about love gone wrong.

Casey laughed and shook her head. *Just woman up and ask him to do it.* She called on her best demure voice. "Would you feed me a bite of the cake?"

He furrowed his brow. "Feed you?"

She nodded quickly, before red flared in her cheeks. "You know, because we're celebrating," she said, even though she really wanted to say *I'm trying a different tactic.*

"When in New Orleans," he mused as he shrugged and dug into the cake, then offered it to her, his arm stretched across the table. The sleeves on his white cotton shirt were rolled up; his strong forearms on display. Nate was an exercise fanatic. He'd played soccer when he was in college, and he put a premium on fitness now, too. She'd still be friends with him even if he weren't so easy on the eyes, but it sure as hell didn't hurt being fed chocolate by someone so . . . gorgeous.

She parted her lips. She was poised. Waiting.

Tense beyond belief.

Everything about this felt off to her. But she told herself to just let go as he fed her the cake—delicious, sinful, chocolaty cake that melted on her tongue. She rolled her eyes in pleasure. "Mmm," she said in a low moan as she finished.

Something dark flared in his eyes ever so briefly. "You like being fed that much, Case?" he joked, shifting back to his playful side.

"No, I actually hate being fed. This cake is just fantastic."

"So why'd you want me to do that?" he asked as he took a forkful for himself.

She took another bite, savoring the chocolate once more before setting down her utensil. The songstress warbled a tune about longing, while outside the window a group of women in short dresses teetered on high heels as they held hurricane glasses. Returning her focus from the action on the street to Nate, she decided to do what she did naturally —be straightforward.

"Okay, confession time," she said in a conspiratorial voice, wiggling her fingers for him to come closer. He scooted his chair near to her. They were inches apart, and she was vaguely aware of how he smelled. Clean, and freshly showered, and he looked handsome in his dark jeans and white shirt. He wore suits well all day long, but at night he could rock the good-looking casual vibe like no one she'd ever known. He had the tousled hair, the warm honey eyes, and the slightest bit of scruff on his jawline to pull it off.

"Confess," he said, like he was luring it out of her.

She held up her hands. "I don't get it. I don't get the whole 'let it go' thing."

He shook his head as if her words didn't compute. "What whole 'let it go' thing?"

"The whole let go of control."

"Is this about cake?"

She shook her head.

"Yeah, I didn't think it was about cake. What's it about?"

She took a deep breath, grateful she'd had a glass of champagne tonight to take the edge off her own inhibitions. Her drinks from this afternoon had worn off as she'd returned to the hotel, finished some other work, taken a shower and then slipped into a flouncy dark pink skirt and a silvery silk tank for their dinner. She'd refueled though, and the little dose of liquid courage was what she needed to forge ahead.

"We're friends, right?"

"Obviously."

"And you know about Scott."

He nodded resolutely. "The douchebag," he said, narrowing his eyes.

"Is Scott Nixon really a douche?"

"He let you go. I'm going to assume that makes him a douche."

She couldn't help it. A smile took over her features at his sweet words. Instinctively, she reached out her hand, and rested it on his arm. A friendly gesture. But it was odd that he hitched in his breath as she touched him. His muscles tensed under her hand. "You know what I mean. You know what he said to me when we broke up."

"That you were too headstrong," he said, a touch of anger in his tone. For some reason, that anger felt protective, and she kind of liked it.

"He also made it clear he wasn't that into the sex. That I was nothing special," she said, looking down.

"Again, the guy is a complete and utter ass," he said, acid in his tone.

"Be that as it may, you know I've kind of had bad luck with men for that reason. The whole *too headstrong* thing."

"I disagree about the reasons. But go on."

"And I know all about you and your women."

He threw his head back and laughed.

"I don't mean Joanna," she said quickly, and he looked away at the mention of his ex-wife. She'd never met Joanna, but she'd have to be an idiot not to know how deeply the woman had hurt Nate. He didn't talk about her often, but Jack had shared some of the details from their marriage and then their divorce four years ago. Joanna's betrayal was the reason Nate played the field like a professional ballplayer. The man practically had a three-dates-and-out rule. He had a more meaningful relationship with his regular dry-cleaner than he'd had with a woman since Joanna. "I mean the fact that you are . . ." she paused, considering her words, "the opposite of me. You're very lucky with the ladies."

He blushed, a sliver of a smile appearing on his face.

"My point is we know each other," she said. "We trust each other. We have no agenda." She took a deep fueling breath, then ripped off the Band-Aid. "And that's why I need you to give it to me straight. Am I too controlling? Do I need to learn to let go? Am I just too alpha?"

* * *

It was a good thing he had finished the last of his champagne, because he would have spat out his drink at the absurdity of her question. "What are you talking about?"

She dropped her head and pushed her hands through her hair. He missed her hand on his arm. He wished she'd wrap those slender fingers around him once more. When she lifted her face, she seemed both sad and frustrated.

"Here's the thing. Grant Abbot indicated that he's interested in me, and well, I've kind of been into him for a while," she began, and his gut tightened when she said that. Sure, she told him now and then about an occasional date she had in New York, and he'd even met the infamous Scott, who he wanted to punch for making Casey feel like shit about herself, but hearing her say she was into some other guy when he was so damn close to her that he couldn't get the sweet citrusy-scent of her shampoo out of his mind, pissed him off. Especially because that smell was driving him wild.

"You're interested in him?" he asked, as if he were tasting dirt. Jealousy pulsed through his veins. He had no right to be jealous. He was all wrong for Casey. She wanted love, and tenderness. She wanted commitment and the possibility of forever.

Those were notions that had no appeal to him. He'd been there, done that and had the ugly scars to prove it. A few years after earning his MBA and landing his first job in management at a startup, he'd met the woman of his dreams—a gorgeous artist, dark and beguiling, with haunting eyes and a wild spirit. He and Joanna fell fast and hard into love, the all-consuming, raw and passionate kind that becomes your oxygen. They relied on each other.

They desperately needed each other, in every way. He would have done anything for her, and so he did. She was a struggling young sculptor aiming to return to graduate school, and since he had moved up quickly in his career, leaving the startup for a job in the hotel business, he paid for her MFA.

And boy, did he ever pay when he learned she'd been having an affair with her sculpting professor, some supposed world-renowned artist named Claude who Nate only thought of as a world-renowned prick.

Never again, he'd vowed. Never again would he put his heart on the line like that. It was far easier and a hell of a lot more fun to play the field, to bounce back and forth with women, never settling, never giving anyone his heart again. Call him a playboy. He was fine with that. There wasn't a more fitting title for his relationship approach. Casey knew it, Jack knew it, his own sister, Kat, happily married and with twin daughters, knew it too, and Nate didn't try to hide it from anyone.

The one thing he hid well was his desire for Casey, but that was proving exceptionally challenging as she went on about this simmering mutual attraction she'd felt for the lingerie guy. "And I've been into him for so long, so when he said he wanted to get together . . ." she said, continuing her recap.

He closed his eyes briefly as she talked, wishing this conversation didn't bother him so much. There was no earthly reason why jealousy should be raging like white waters in his blood. He hadn't put himself on the line for her. He hadn't told her he wanted to crush her lips to his, to taste her kiss, to capture her moans and sighs in his mouth, because he could give no more than that. He had to keep his desires in check and focus on the friendship.

"So what's the problem then, Case?" he asked, doing his best to be dispassionate as he looked her in the eyes. "You like him, he likes you, you'll make beautiful blue-eyed babies who grow up to run an empire of lingerie and sex toys. Sounds perfect." He flashed her a smile so she knew he meant it. At least, he tried to mean it.

"Here's the problem," she began, stopping to take a drink of iced water. "I want what I want. You know, in bed. I like to be on top. I like to say what I want; I like to be direct," she said, and his head was swimming with images now. He'd take her on top. He'd have no problem whatsoever with her riding him, wild and free, her blond hair loose and tumbling across her shoulders, her perfect breasts bouncing.

He spread the napkin further across his lap.

"But Scott didn't like that enough. And I don't think that's what a man like Grant wants either. And maybe that's my problem. Maybe that's why I've had such bad luck with men."

"Because you like to be on top?" He furrowed his brow. "You're not even dating him yet. Why are you worried about what position he likes?"

She shot him a look that said *you can't be serious.* "C'mon. We're not in high school. If I date him, chances are we'll get to the bedroom soon enough."

The jealousy ran wild now, stampeding through his body. "There's nothing wrong with you. Casey. Don't you get it? If some guy doesn't like who you are, you don't need him."

"Thank you," she said, then lowered her voice more. "But maybe it's time to change. I want more from this life, Nate. I want to have a chance with Grant, and maybe I'd like letting go. Maybe I should try giving up control. I mean, do you like your women submissive? Are you a dominant?"

He laughed at the fact that they were discussing *this*. He was fantasizing about her naked body and she wanted to know if he was dominant.

She laughed too. "See? You know I'm direct. I speak my mind. I just asked if you were a Dom!"

"Are you? Are you Mistress Casey? Is that the deep, dark secret of what you do after hours? Admit it, you're a card-carrying member of that BDSM club you and Jack supported a couple years ago," he said, egging her on.

"No. I swear. I mean, hey, leather is great. And I would have no objection to wielding a crop and giving orders now and then, but no. I am not a Domme, and I'm not a member of a BDSM club, and I'm not a mistress. I'm just a woman who sells sex toys and loves to be in control. And evidently, that's my problem. I'm not *wild and free* enough in bed or something," she said, slapping her palm on the table in emphasis. Her champagne glass rattled slightly, and he grabbed it before it spilled. She took it from him and downed the rest of it. "What about you?"

"You want to know if I'm dominant in bed? If I like whips and chains?" he asked, and this was a much more pleasurable direction than discussing her desires for other men. Especially when she used words like *wild* and *free*.

She nodded, an eager look in her eyes. "I do want to know. Do you like to be in control? Do you need a woman to call you Sir or Master?"

He leaned back in his chair, savoring the moment, enjoying the question. Even if they never did more than *talk*, this was a hell of a fun way to spend the evening together. "When it comes to women, you could say I'm an omnivore," he said, his lips curving into a grin.

"What do you mean?"

He stretched out in the chair, gesturing widely with his arms. "I like everything. I'm equal opportunity. I like a woman on top, I like to be on top, I like a woman on all fours, I like her bent over, I like her up against the wall. I'm good with reverse cowgirl, sixty-nine, inside, outside, upside-down," he said, and her eyes widened with each suggestive term. Oh, he was having too much fun rattling off all the things he liked, because he was being one hundred percent truthful. Everything rocked when you were into a woman. "Blow jobs, hand jobs, going downtown, spankings, ropes, scarves, handcuffs. Fingers, toys, beads, blindfolds—you name it, I'm your man. If it happens naked with a woman I want, I like it, and chances are, I'm making her cry out in pleasure," he said, arching an eyebrow playfully at the last line. It was cocky, and he knew it, but let her have an orgasmic image in her mind.

Casey grabbed at the neckline of her tank and tugged it away from her chest. "Whew. Someone get me a fan," she said with a wink, and he laughed.

But one thing he didn't like hearing about was her trying to change for some guy. Because this guy didn't deserve her if he wanted her to be someone other than herself. He was about to tell her when she moved even closer, and grasped his hands, sending electric sparks through him. God, the slightest touch from her was such a turn-on. When he was alone later in his room, he'd be thinking of all the omnivorous ways he could consume her. He'd be picturing running through every option on the list he'd just shared.

"I have a crazy idea," she said, her blue eyes lit up with mischief.

"Is it feeding you cake? Because we tried that and it didn't work."

She shook her head, and bit her lower lip briefly. "Teach me," she breathed out, and all the air swept out of his lungs. He froze, as shock spread through his body in a nanosecond.

"Teach you what?" he asked in a wobbly voice as he began to recover the power of speech.

"Teach me how to let go. Teach me how to give up control."

He shoved a hand roughly through his hair, and swallowed. His throat was dry. He grabbed for a glass and downed the rest of his water. "Are you kidding me?"

"No. I'm not kidding. I know it sounds crazy. But maybe it's not crazy. I'm the head of a damn sex toy company and I don't know how to give up control. Maybe because I'm surrounded by all these toys. Because I've learned every detail of my own body and what I like, and how to turn up the setting higher, or adjust the vibration lower, or thrust harder, or tease more, to yield the result," she said, laying out her pleasure-seeking clinically like it was a math problem, when to him it was a vision of sensual beauty—

her on the bed, legs spread, learning the intricacies of her own body, a territory he longed to explore intimately. "And now, when I'm with a guy, and God knows it's been a long time since that," she said with a scoff, "it's so hard for me to let go of the reins I've been holding onto for so long. But I want to learn. And we're friends. I trust you completely, and it would never ruin our friendship because there would never be anything more."

"You want me to give you lessons in seduction?" he asked, making sure he wasn't imagining this. Because he'd had these sort of dreams before.

She straightened her spine and shook her head. "I don't want lessons in seduction. I want lessons in submission."

Holy shit. Screw the New Orleans heat wave. It was a certified scorcher in this small little bistro. His neck was hot, his jeans were tight. His mind was operating in overdrive. He started to open his mouth to speak, but everything was a jumble.

She brought her hand to her mouth, covering it. "Shit," she muttered. "That was a ridiculous thing to ask. Completely presumptuous. You're probably not even attracted to me. Forget I said it." She backpedaled as she clearly misinterpreted his silence.

"I assure you, my attraction to you is not the issue. I think the bigger issue is—are you attracted to me?"

"You're handsome," she said, her lips curving in a sweet smile as she locked eyes with him. "You're very, very handsome, Nate."

Handsome was good. He could work with handsome. And because he didn't even want her to ask the question about herself, he preempted her. "And for the record, Casey, you're absolutely fucking gorgeous."

She beamed. "Thank you. So will you do it then? Will you teach me? Or is there some bro code you won't cross because of my brother?"

He laughed at the notion of Jack Sullivan having a problem with the two of them. That simply wasn't Jack's style. He didn't issue hard and fast rules about anyone's love life, or say things like *don't touch my sister*. He wasn't that kind of guy. "Jack's not like that. You know that as well as I do."

"I know. He's not a rules guy."

Hell, Nate wasn't either. He wasn't even that ticked off when his college buddy Bryan had hooked up with his own sister, Kat, especially since those two were happily married now. Not that marriage was on the table in this scenario with Casey. Nor was a real relationship either.

Sex was on the table.

Sex was what he wanted.

He wanted nothing more than to teach her, to take her, to please her. But something nagged at him. A relationship that was far more important than a bro code would ever be —his relationship with her. "I don't want to ruin our friendship," he said because as much as he wanted her, he didn't want to lose her.

"I don't either. That's why this is perfect. We're friends, and we're not trying to be anything more. You're in be-tween women. I'm not dating Grant yet and won't even have dinner with him for a month because he's going out of the country. So we have this little block of time, and no one gets hurt because we know exactly what it is. And when we're done with your . . ." she stopped and tilted her head coquettishly, ". . . *tutoring,* we go back to being just friends. You're not the committed type, so this is perfect. It can never be more than it is, and therefore neither one of us can get hurt. Perfect. Business. Arrangement." She finished by brushing one palm neatly against the other.

He shook his head, impressed with her negotiating style. Direct and downright enticing.

Still, were they really going to attempt this? His analytical mind began to turn it around like a Rubik's cube. On the one side was their friendship. On the other was his desire for her. But if they went in with eyes wide open and expectations clearly laid out from the start, they'd be fine, right? She was a woman who deserved a man who could commit, but she wasn't asking him to be that man. She was asking him to show her how to get down on her knees.

Fuck analysis.

With that image in mind, there was only one answer, because this was heaven—this was his chance to have his hands and tongue on the woman he'd lusted after, fantasized about and dreamed of, and *still* keep her in his life as a friend. This was the chance to drive her wild with pleasure and know that the next night, next week, next month they'd still be in each other's lives. This was having your cake and eating it too.

"You want this, Casey? You really want this? No feelings, so strings, just lessons?"

"Yes. There's no reason this won't work perfectly. I mean, except for the fact that it's one-sided. I'd be getting a lot more out of it than you would. What can I do for you?" she asked, so damn earnest and cute.

He laughed once more. "Trust me. I'll be getting plenty out of it."

Namely, he'd be getting her out of his system, and once he did it would be even easier to be around her. Maybe he wouldn't be in a state of constant arousal every time they went to the movies or dinner.

"Are you sure?"

"Casey. You're going to need to stop questioning me," he said in a commanding tone. "That's your first lesson. The next one starts now."

CHAPTER FOUR

New Orleans, evening . . .

He threw the napkin on the table and reached for her hand. Her expression was one of complete surprise. "Dance with me."

Her lips quirked up and she seemed to understand what he'd done. Given her an order. She nodded demurely and he led her to a small sliver of a dance floor, near where the woman with the microphone was singing a Billie Holiday number. He pulled Casey in close. She tensed briefly, as if unsure where to rest her hands, whether on his shoulders or waist. He planted them firmly on his shoulders, and wrapped his arms around her sexy, slim waist that fit perfectly in his hands.

"Just relax and let me lead," he said, whispering in her ear, a waft of her tropical scent drifting by his nostrils. She shivered briefly against him, and that nearly did him in. He stayed strong, swaying gently, guiding her in slow, sensuous moves. "I'll show you how to let go, but you have to trust me. And that's where it starts. With trust. I'm not a

Dom, you're not my Sub—we're not going to join a BDSM club, or sign a contract. But I *can* show you how good it will feel when you give up control."

She breathed in sharply, as if acclimating to new air on a distant planet. "Why do men like a woman to give up control? What is it about the lack of control that men like so much?"

"It's not that they like a lack of control. But a man wants a woman who gives herself to him. He wants a woman to melt into his arms, to get aroused from a kiss on the back of her neck," he said, and traced a fingertip gently under her hair, watching her reaction as she drew in a breath. "It's the hand on her arm." He trailed his fingers down her bare skin to her elbow as he leaned in to whisper, "Or warm breath near her ear." She gasped, and he kept going. "He wants a woman who's so turned on, she'll nearly beg for it. He wants her abandon. He wants to be the only one to make her feel that way."

She parted her lips to speak, but he shushed her with his fingertip against them. God, he was so tempted to let her suck on his finger right now, to watch her simulate a blow job, to let her show him what she could do. But that would come later. He needed to kiss her first.

That is, after he teased her.

"At some point soon, some point very, very soon, I'm going to kiss you," he said, watching the expression in her eyes shift to a heady kind of desire. Her fingers curved into his shoulders, holding on tightly to him. "You're going to close your eyes," he said, and then her lids fluttered closed. "And you're not going to know when it's coming. You're going to want it. Your body is going to be crying out for a kiss," he said, his voice husky and raw as her chest rose and fell, and she moved closer to him as they swayed. He cupped the back of her neck, watching her response to every touch, from the way her lips parted as he threaded his hands through her hair, to how she leaned back into him, almost relishing the way his fingers ran slowly through those soft, wavy strands. A sigh came next, a desperate needy sigh, and a barely-there arch of her back, her body seeking out more contact. "But I might not kiss you yet. I might run my hands down your arms," he said, then did just that. "Or maybe I'll stop telling you what I'm going to do."

He swore she murmured a *no*, but then her sounds were swallowed by a sexy gasp as he dipped his mouth to her chest, kissing her above her breasts. Immediately, she reached for him, her hands shooting around his neck.

He tsked her, moving her hands, gently but firmly, to his shoulders. Then he yanked her closer, so their bodies were snug and neatly aligned. He pressed his groin against her hip, letting her know how immensely turned on he was. A small moan escaped her lips, and her reaction thrilled him. Gently pushing her hair off her shoulder, he pressed his lips in a soft, sweet kiss on her collarbone. She wriggled closer as he mapped a path up her neck, the tip of his tongue tasting her as he found her ear, then nipped on her earlobe.

"And only then, after I've teased you, after I've made you think the kiss might come at any second, will I actually kiss you. But you'll need to say please."

"Please," she whispered and her voice was so barren, so strung out with need that he knew he'd succeeded at his first mission. Not a lesson, but rather his driving goal to turn her arousal meter way past high.

"I need you to keep your hands on my shoulders, Casey. Can you do that for me?"

"Yes."

"No place else. Got it?" he asked, and it pained him to ask her to hold back. But this was what she wanted. To learn how.

"I promise to be good," she said, on a sexy smile as she dug her fingers into his shoulders to emphasize that she was listening.

"You're such a good student," he whispered.

She licked her lips once, and he took his time, wanting to memorize every second of his first kiss with the woman he'd lusted after for years. Her cheeks were flush, her lips were open, and her expression was so damn inviting. He ran a finger against her lips, eliciting another small gasp from her. He couldn't wait any more. Their lips met, and for the first few seconds it was soft and sweet, a gentle taste and tease. It was an exploration—her lips, her mouth, her breath that ghosted over him. She tasted like chocolate cake, and he relished every millimeter of her lips, tugging on her bottom one, then nipping the top with his teeth, making her want him. Making her want so much more. His hands trailed down the bare flesh of her arms, and he felt the goosebumps rise on her skin, all from the teasing, taunting kisses. The swell of her lips, the curve of her mouth, the sweetness of her breath—all of it collided in his senses, along with his heightened awareness of this intensely sexually aware woman who was now asking him to take her to new places and explore unchartered territory.

It never occurred to him that they wouldn't kiss well. It had only ever occurred to him that they would kiss excellently. Passionately. The kind of kisses that demolished your grip on the here and now, that sent you spinning into blissful oblivion.

"Do you want me to kiss you more?" he whispered hotly.

"Yes," she said on a hypnotic nod.

"What do you say?"

"Please," she murmured, as she pushed against him and he felt the heat between her legs.

His mind took off, imagining how silky hot she'd feel when he touched her. "I only have one goal now. To give you the kind of kiss that makes you hot and wet and desperate for more."

"Oh God," she said, then his tongue found hers, waiting, ready, so fucking eager.

There was no pause. No transition. The speed simply shot to the stratosphere. Their mouths united in a hot and hungry fusion. Part of him wasn't thinking at all; he was only feeling all this desire that swamped his body. Then another part of him was thinking intensely about how he was finally kissing her, and it was better then he'd imagined as their mouths crashed and their lips came together in a greedy union that overpowered his brain and took hold of his mind. He didn't care that they were in a bistro, and others might be watching. He *couldn't* care because she kissed him back hard and passionately in a sweet devouring of the senses. He stopped controlling her and let her go wild as she laced her hands into his hair, grasping, pulling, tugging. She was so fiery, so intoxicating, and it was like being buzzed on the kind of kisses that only spelled one thing, flashing like a neon sign advertising *hot sex, coming soon.*

She ran her fingers through his hair, her hands curling around his skull. She rocked her hips against him, and soon this was about to become a very indecent public display of affection on the tiny dance floor in the bistro. He barely cared though as she moaned into his mouth.

It wasn't going to be easy to teach her to let him lead all the time when he wanted this kind of wildness from her too, this kind of abandon as she grabbed at his hair, her fingers greedily diving in and holding on.

But he was determined to give her what she'd asked for, so he reached for her hands, gripped them tightly and brought them down to her waist.

He stepped away. The look in her eyes was hazy. She was panting.

The loss of contact with her lithe, eager body was a cold glass of ice water thrown in his face. But he had a better plan.

"You stopped," she said, on a pout.

"You're not learning if your hands are all over me. So you'll need to get down on your knees," he said, and her eyes flared with a wild awareness of what he was asking. "My room. Now."

CHAPTER FIVE

New Orleans, night . . .

He slammed the door shut behind them in one firm push. The sound of it clanging signaled a change in him. The dark look in his eyes and the stony set of his lips thrilled and scared the hell out of her too. She'd never seen him like this. *Of course* she'd never seen him like this. But she never even knew he had this side—a man staring down the woman he planned to claim.

He didn't speak. He simply pointed. *To the floor.* Holy shit. He was serious. "You want me on my knees?" she asked, her eyes wide.

"You *want* to be on your knees," he corrected, his confident, sexy voice sending a hot spark through her. She'd been on her knees. She'd given blow jobs. She wasn't inexperienced. She knew sex inside and out and upside-down. She'd read books on kink, quirks, fetishes, and Kama Sutra. But never had she asked a man to take control like this. And never had she thought she'd like it. But her body didn't lie. Not when the aching between her legs intensified as his hands moved to his belt, and he slowly, purposefully, took his time taking it off. Loop by fucking loop.

Like a man in control. He could do anything with that belt. He could tie her hands, swat her with the non-buckled end, or none of the above. She didn't know and that was part of the allure.

She watched him take it off.

Oh God, her mouth was watering. This was Nate. This was her good friend, and he was stripping off his belt and flicking the leather on the floor of his hotel room.

A suite on the top floor of the hotel he operated, this room was designed for pleasure and luxury. The white bed cover was pristine, but so enticing, and the sliding doors to the bathroom were mirrored. She caught a brief glimpse of her reflection. Her blond hair was loose and curly already; the humid June weather hadn't been able to work much voodoo magic on her tresses that were naturally on the wild side. The strap on her tank had slid down her shoulder. She looked like herself, except for one thing—the desire in her eyes. She knew her own body intimately, understood precisely what made her tick, tingle and heat up, but she'd never seen her own eyes when she was this turned on. She wasn't sure she'd *ever* been this turned on. But when he'd kissed her at the restaurant he'd set her heart to flames, scorching a path of pleasure from the center of her body all the way to her fingertips.

Somewhere inside her lived the slightest morsel of fear. She wasn't afraid of Nate, but perhaps she was afraid of herself. Unsure how she'd feel if she liked submitting as much as she'd liked the way he'd kissed her, as if he owned her pleasure.

Completely.

The room was near silent—the only sound the faint hum of the air conditioning.

She stepped backwards. He moved closer. She continued towards the bed. He stalked over to her. She felt like prey. Judging from the intensity in his gaze she was the most succulent meal he'd ever wanted. She stopped when the back of her legs hit the bed.

"Where are you going?"

"You told me to kneel," she said, her voice wobbly.

"I told you to kneel. I didn't tell you to move."

"Oh," she said on a swallow. She wasn't sure how far the game went.

He pointed to the floor. "Here."

She began to kneel, but he grabbed her, pulled her to him, wrapped his arms around her, then tucked his fingers under her chin so she was looking at him. "Hey, this is us now. Are you okay?"

She breathed a sigh of relief, so glad that he'd asked. And admittedly, a bit more turned on that he had. "Yes."

"Do you still want this?"

She nodded. "I do."

"No questions? No worries?"

Her natural instinct to be direct overtook her. Feeling brazen and dangerous, she grasped his hand and guided it between her legs so he could touch the damp heat of her panties. She was soaked through the cotton panel. He hissed the second he made contact. "Fuck," he muttered, then slid his fingers across the thin fabric. She arched into him, wanting so much more. He dipped his mouth to her neck, mapping a hot trail along her skin until he reached her ear. "See how turned on you are now? You're going to be so much wetter after you take me in your mouth for the first time. Do it now," he said, and she felt a rush of heat that began proving his point.

She kneeled, and looked up, waiting instructions.

He raised an eyebrow appreciatively. "Unzip my jeans," he said as he worked on his shirt, starting from the top button. She wasn't sure where to feast her eyes, whether on him systematically undoing each button, revealing inch by inch his strong, broad chest, or on the throbbing hard length right there behind the denim.

She couldn't look away from his hands though, especially when she saw his chest for the first time—his strong pecs, his flat and hard belly. She was tempted to stand so she could trail her long nails across his skin and watch him hitch in a breath, watch his reaction to her.

Uh-oh.

Old habits died hard. This wasn't about what she could do to him. It was about what he was doing to her. With her eyes and fingers on his crotch, she popped open the button on his jeans, and slowly unzipped his fly, the teeth of the zipper spreading.

Did he wear boxers or briefs? White or black or blue? She was about to find out.

The answer nearly knocked her to the floor when his cock sprang out, long, thick, hard and completely riding free. She stared at the glorious sight. She might even have gawked, slack-jawed, because he was stunning.

As she tugged down his jeans, she looked up at him. "You go commando," she said with a grin as she stated the obvious. But the obvious needed to be stated, and admired.

"I do."

"Have you always been totally naked under your jeans every time we've gone out?" she asked, as he unbuttoned the final button on his shirt, then pulled it off and tossed it on the floor.

"Yes."

Casey's eyes widened. To think, the whole time she'd known him, he'd been naked under his jeans every single time. Every time she'd had dinner with him, gone to the movies, a baseball game, a comedy club, or an art gallery, he'd been one layer away from nudity.

"All the time?" she asked, craving some kind of final confirmation of this mouth-wateringly gorgeous vision of his free-range cock.

Ready at a moment's notice. Every second of the day.

"Yes, I go commando all the time. Every time you've seen me I've been riding free. Now, I need you to stop talking and put that mouth of yours to a better use. Suck me now, Casey."

There it was again. That rough, commanding tone. The order that sent an unexpected rush down her spine. Then his hands were on top of her head, his fingers digging into her hair, as he tugged her closer so her mouth could meet his hard, hot cock. She curled a hand around the base. He groaned from her first touch. She hadn't even wrapped her lips around him yet. A thrill raced across her bloodstream from his reaction. She brought the head to her lips, swirling her tongue and tasting him like he was candy.

His fingers gripped her hair harder, digging in through her strands to her skull. She drew him in more, licking and lapping him up, but keeping up a teasing pace, only letting him in so far. She knew how to give a hell of a blow job. She was skilled in driving a man crazy and to the brink of lust-fueled insanity. She'd take her sweet time with her hand curved tightly as she stroked him, and her lips giving the head the special treatment. From the way he rocked his hips into her, he liked it. *A lot.*

"No teasing," he growled. "Take me all the way in."

Okay, so maybe a change of pace was called for. She opened wider, and brought him deep, the head hitting the back of her throat.

She heard a sharp breath, then a groan as he grasped her harder and rougher, spearing her hair with his strong fingers. "That's better. Keep it up like that, sweetness. I'm not going to be gentle. I intend to fuck your pretty little mouth."

His dirty words were like some kind of switch in her sex drive that he'd tripped. They sent the temperature inside her from scorching to inferno. She'd never suspected Nate was like this. She knew he was strong in business, commanding in the boardroom, but she hadn't let her mind imagine what he'd be like in the bedroom. Now, she was discovering a new, dominating, dirty side to him. On the surface she was in control, with her teeth millimeters from his most sensitive flesh, but he so clearly had all the power as she sucked him to the base as he'd demanded, her mouth becoming a warm tunnel for his shaft. He tasted delicious, the perfect mix of clean and musky.

Opening wider, she gave him total use of her throat. He took every inch of the real estate, filling her all the way to his balls that she stroked and tugged as she sucked.

"Lift your skirt up," he said roughly. "Pull it up to your hips so I can watch you."

She yanked it up, revealing her wet lacy panties. "Beautiful," he said in an appreciative growl. "Spread your knees more."

Feeling terribly vulnerable, but terrifically naughty, she widened her knees on the navy blue carpet of his hotel room. Thank God, The Luxe had soft carpeting. She hated rug burn.

"Pull your panties to the side. Let me see how turned on you get from sucking my dick," he told her as he continued his thrusts in her mouth.

Heat rushed between her legs, and she ached there, a deep and exquisite hollowness crying out to be filled. With one hand on his balls, and his cock rendering her incapable of any speech, she yanked the panel of her panties to her thigh. She was glistening between her legs. She was coated in wetness, the kind of silky dampness that would make for a fabulous, frictionless fuck. Oh lord, her body was demanding to be touched. Begging. She desperately craved his hands, his fingers, his mouth, and his cock.

"That's a gorgeous sight," he murmured and she sneaked a peek at him. The scene was so surreal. Nate standing up, jeans at his ankles, his tall, strong body revealed to her for the first time. She on her knees, loving his delicious dick with her mouth as she spread herself for his viewing pleasure. His hands were wrapped around her head, restraining her, controlling her, as he stared so hungrily between her legs. His eyes were wild, like a feral animal.

She'd never felt so craved in her life.

Then he leaned his head back, closed his eyes, and groaned so loudly she was sure he was about to come, that she would taste his saltiness sliding down her throat any second. The possibility electrified her, arousing her more than she'd ever expected. She wanted it. Badly.

Instead, he stopped abruptly. He pulled himself out of her mouth, leaving her on the floor with her legs and her mouth wide open.

"Take off everything but the shoes, and bend over the bed."

Her natural impulse was to talk. To say something. To ask what he wanted next. She didn't know what he planned to do, but as she stood, she realized that was the point. He *hadn't* told her. The anticipation was its own aphrodisiac. He kicked off his shoes and jeans as she stripped down. As she reached for the clasp on her bra, the reality of what they were doing reared its head again. She was about to be naked in front of him. She wasn't ashamed of her body at all, but this was another turning point in their relationship. From this point on, he'd always know what she looked like naked.

Carpe diem, she told herself, as she unhooked her bra and tossed it on the floor.

His lips parted as his eyes roamed her body, his gaze finally hooking on her breasts. She dipped her thumbs into the side of her panties, and was about to pull them off, when he placed his hands over hers.

He dipped his head to her neck and pressed a soft kiss to her collarbone. That seemed to be his favorite spot on her. "You're so beautiful," he murmured against her skin, and a sweet rush of tingles spread through her from his tender words. Cupping her breasts, he whispered, "I can't resist touching them."

Desire ricocheted inside her. "I like it," she said, fully aware that they were breaking character, but she knew he was okay with it, because he'd broken first. And truth be told, she loved his unfettered reaction to her body. She loved that he simply had to give in, and hell, did he give in as he squeezed and kneaded her breasts so expertly that she was about to shout *take me now.*

That would defeat the purpose of this lesson, so she simply let herself exist in the exquisite pleasure of this moment, and of Nate worshipping her body.

Until he returned to that voice he'd used before.

"Now turn around, put your hands on the bed and bend over for me."

"But you told me to take off my underwear, and it's still on."

"I changed my mind. I want to take it off. Turn around now."

She did, placing her hands on the edge of the bed, bending her back for him, her ass in the air. So many words started to take shape on her tongue—*are you going to fuck me, are you going to touch me, are you going to taste me . . .?*

She shut her mouth, trying to truly free her mind of the need to know everything.

"Close your eyes," he told her, and she did. Now it was all in the waiting. The room was dark, there was no music —it was only the two of them, and the possibilities.

His hands traced a warm path on her back, making her tremble. When he reached her ass, he cupped her cheeks and groaned. Then she felt a whoosh of air between her legs, his warm breath as he blew. Oh God, what was he doing to her? She was throbbing between her legs, hot and damp and absolutely aching for him. His fingers curled into the band of her panties. He inched them over her cheeks, down her thighs, to her knees. She started to step out of them, but he grasped her ankles firmly in place, a reminder that he was in charge. He left the panties at her ankles.

"Stay like that. I want to look at you."

She didn't move. The image of him, naked, erect, and so fucking handsome as he stared at her body turned her insides molten. She was so aroused she could feel a bead of wetness slide down her thigh.

For the briefest of moments, she was embarrassed, but any worries were quelled by Nate. Or more precisely, by his mouth that captured that drop on his tongue. She gasped at the feel of his lips on the inside of her legs, and then again at the realization that he'd been watching her so closely that he saw everything, every response in her body.

"You taste so good," he murmured as he licked her thighs. He pressed a palm on the inside of each leg, and gently guided her to a wider stance. "More. Spread them more and raise your ass higher," he told her, and she bent lower, leaving herself completely open to him. Shoes on, panties at her ankles, not a stitch of clothing covering her body. Turned on beyond any and all reason.

She cried out. His tongue. Oh God, he'd flicked his tongue once against her clit, and then stopped, and she was dying for more.

"I need more of you in my face," he said, and it was half a command, and half him simply giving a play by play as he took the matter into his own hands, using his thumbs to spread her open for him. "Perfect," he said, then returned to her heat, pressing his lips to her and diving in. Her vision went fuzzy. Her world turned into a black and silver blur. The feel of his mouth was breathtaking, and in an instant pleasure engulfed her body. The sweet oblivion of desire radiated throughout her entire being as he licked her like a ravenous man.

"So fucking delicious," he whispered as he flicked his tongue against her swollen clit. She moaned so loudly she was sure someone would hear if they were anyplace but a hotel with soundproof walls designed for this kind of play.

His lips were soft, his tongue was divine, and he ate her pussy like he'd never had anything he wanted so much. Pleasure forked inside her, spinning from her belly to the tips of her fingers. He gripped her hips harder, holding her firmly in place, restraining her with his big hands as he consumed her wetness. He lapped up every drop of her, sending her spiraling into such a state of bliss that all she wanted was to come. The pressure built to a crescendo. She wanted to crash on through to the other side.

"Oh God, Nate," she cried out. "I'm so—"

He cut her off. "You're so close, aren't you?"

"Yes," she said, aware somewhere in her mind that this was part of the control. That he was in charge of everything.

"Work for it," he said, then returned to her pussy, licking, teasing, but still resisting that final push.

She rocked back into him, desperate. "Please. Please, give me more."

Another lick. Another deep, consuming kiss. She was so damn close to ecstasy.

"Please," she cried out, desperately seeking orgasm.

"Please what?" he said on a quick pause.

"Please, don't stop."

"I like that you said please. Now be as loud as you want. I'm not going to stop 'til you're coming on my lips."

She moaned and lifted her hips higher, dropping down onto her elbows, giving him all the access he needed, making herself one hundred percent vulnerable. Giving in to him. Handing over all her control.

"I'm so close. Oh God, it's so good."

He licked and kissed her in a heated frenzy, his own moans so damn sexy that his sounds of pleasure set her off.

She shouted his name.

Her body detonated. Her climax swept through her, crashing over every square inch of her mind and body. She panted and moaned, and practically sang out with joy from the sheer intensity. She didn't think it would ever stop as wave after wave spread through her, bathing her in ecstasy. He slowed as the orgasm ebbed away, giving her one final sweet kiss before he rose, pulled her gently up on the bed, and wrapped his arms around her, spooning her.

She brushed her hair away from her face, her bones still humming, her body awash in the afterglow. "Wow."

He kissed the back of her neck, and she turned to meet his gaze. He looked, quite simply, happy.

"That was . . ."

". . . amazing."

She trailed her finger along his stubble. "Are we going to have sex now?"

He shook his head, and she dropped her jaw in surprise. "But I thought—"

He cut her off. "I want to. I want nothing more than to take you. But waiting for it is part of letting go."

* * *

That was true. It was completely true. If she wanted to learn to give up control, he had to withhold. But that wasn't the only reason he planned to wait for another time.

Because it ensured another time.

CHAPTER SIX

35,000 feet, midday . . .

The black, white and brown beagle mix wagged its tail at his feet.

"No more begging, buddy. Back to your seat," Nate said, pointing to one of the back rows in the plane where a year-old French Bulldog, a middle-aged Terrier, and some kind of Dachshund-mix lounged on a blanket spread across the seats. The Dachshund had been particularly well-behaved and Nate was thrilled for that, given the home that was picked out for him.

The Beagle didn't listen. He kept wagging his tail, waiting for scraps from the chicken salad that had been served for lunch. Nate was sorely tempted to feed the little guy, especially when that tail started thumping wildly on the carpeted floor of the plane. But the dog would be better off in his new home if Nate didn't indulge him in bad habits now.

"C'mon. Time to get back to the pack," he said gently, gesturing once more to the dog's companions.

"Psst," Casey whispered, tapping his shoulder. "I think he might not understand English yet."

Nate laughed, set down his nearly empty plate on the lacquered brown table, then scooped up the dog and carried him to the rear of the plane where a row of cushy seats had become the temporary quarters for the hounds on the flight. "Go back to sleep with your friends," he said, gesturing to the other four-legged creatures who'd been conked out most of the ride. He stroked the dog between the ears and scratched his chin 'til he settled, curling up in a tight ball. The canine quartet of traveling companions was hitching a ride on his flight on their way to New York. The local shelter in New Orleans didn't have room for all the dogs, and had made plans with a no-kill rescue in Brooklyn that had already matched these four pets with homes in the metro area, since New Yorkers often preferred smaller breeds. Nate was an animal lover and had grown up with dogs, so he regularly arranged to be an "escort" for animals in need, ferrying them from various locales around the country back to the Brooklyn shelter that served as the matchmaker.

One of the dogs—the Dachshund—was en route to his sister, Kat. She lived on the Upper East Side with her husband, his buddy Bryan, and the small dog was a gift for their twin daughters. Nate would have liked to have a dog himself, some kind of scrappy breed like a Border Collie that could catch Frisbees in the park and go for long runs along the West Side bike path with him. But he traveled far too often to be able to give a dog a good home. He did this instead; chauffeured pets in style to their new homes. His small contribution to the world.

He returned to his seat, the flight attendant having cleared their plates. Casey was wearing a short jean skirt and high-heeled sandals. He didn't try as hard today to refrain from staring, but he did give himself a three-count for a quick perusal before returning his focus to her eyes.

"Some day, I'll have a mutt of my own." He nearly dropped his hand on top of hers, and clasped it, like they were on a date. He resisted, and, not for the first time on this flight, he wondered if she was refraining too. Not from holding hands, but from talking about the night before and the mind-blowing physical connection they'd shared. Neither one had mentioned it this morning. She'd rushed out of his room to shower and pack. He'd had early meetings on the property. While his trip to New Orleans had started a few days before hers had, he was done with business by mid-morning, so he'd simply made a few final calls and then they'd taken off for the airport.

The dogs had distracted them most of the flight. They'd barked on takeoff, then needed, understandably, some petting and comfort once airborne. Still, he wasn't entirely sure what to say next to Casey. Or if anything needed to be said. He knew his way around women, but this project with Casey was a little . . . unconventional. Should he ask when their next lesson would be or simply tell her the time to arrive and what to wear?

Tight leather skirt, no panties, and heels. Oh hell, there went any semblance of concentration.

"When you get this mutt of your own someday, what will you name him?" she asked, twirling a strand of her hair around a finger. Maybe she was nervous, too. Wait, was he nervous? Hell no. Nate didn't get nervous.

"Fred," he said dryly.

She rolled her eyes. "How about Paul?"

"Or maybe just Mark. I always thought it would be funny to give a dog a completely human name, and then when you're in Central Park to call him back to you. Not with C'mere Fido, or C'mere Max, but *C'Mere Mark. Come on now, Ethan.*"

Casey smiled and laughed, kicking her leg back and forth, like a pendulum. Okay, she was nervous. He needed to say something.

Instead, his brain tripped on the name he'd just shared. *Ethan.* "That reminds me. I haven't seen Ethan Holmes in a while."

"Ethan at the Victoria Hotels, right?"

He nodded. "Yeah. We worked together at the Luxe, back when I was VP of biz dev. He was in operations, and we were both up for the top job. Good guy, but I haven't talked to him much since he left when he didn't get the CEO gig."

"I hear Victoria is trying to revamp its image a little. That the chain is seen as a bit stuffy, and they want to appeal to a younger crowd."

"Yeah. I heard that too. I should check in. See if he wants to catch a Yankees game. We had a vendor who gave us tickets to his box seats. I'll have to give him a shout when I get back."

"So Ethan's a no-go then for your future dog's name," she said with a wry smile.

He snapped his fingers. "I know what to name my future dog. Jim, after the comedian," he mused, and her eyes lit up.

"His show was so great. Remember?" she said, nudging him. "We were laughing all night when I took you to see him."

For his birthday last year when he'd turned thirty-two, she'd taken him to a Jim Gaffigan stand-up show, and they were nearly doubled over during his Hot Pockets bit. It occurred to him then that he was hunting for any sort of connection, and that even suggesting he'd name a dog someday after a gift she'd given him was his roundabout way of tying this conversation back to them.

But he didn't plan to psychoanalyze the fact that he wasn't sure what to say to the woman he'd made cry out his name last night. Deep down, he already knew why he was struggling to broach the topic. Because he could talk to her about anything—about dogs, and books, and business, and women, and men, and he'd been able to do that long before he'd seen her beautiful body bared just for him. He didn't want last night to have messed up their ability to talk.

"Casey," he said, turning to look her in the eyes.

"Yes?"

"About last night . . ."

Her eyes widened in fear. "You didn't like it?"

His heartbeat quickened. That was the last thing he needed her to think. "Don't even go there," he said, scooting closer to her on the smooth leather seats in the plane. The big jet hummed quietly as it soared through blue skies. The attendant had retreated to the front of the cabin, giving them privacy.

She brought her hand to her chest and breathed out hard. "Good. Because I thought . . ."

"You thought what? That I was going to say you were too forward? Too direct?"

Red inched across her cheeks. She nodded.

"But you weren't either of those," he said, his lips curving up as he raised his hand, brushing a finger down her cheek. "You did great."

"I did?"

He nodded. "Yes. What did you think? Did you enjoy yourself?"

"Yes. So much."

"How did it feel to let go?"

"Honestly?" she asked, narrowing her eyes.

Uh-oh. Now it was his turn to worry. Maybe he should have finished things off last night because what if she didn't enjoy the kind of sex she wanted to try? What if last night had been his only chance to be with her and he'd blown it by waiting? Fucking idiot. What kind of guy denies a woman who's hot for a no-strings one-night stand? *This one.*

"Yes. Honestly," he said, steeling himself.

She brought her face closer, their foreheads nearly touching. His chest tightened, and his nostrils flared as he inhaled her scent. Her sweet lips were so close to his ear, as she whispered, "Nate Harper, you gave me the best orgasm of my life last night. It was better than any of my toys, and that's saying something, because those bad boys are top-notch."

A bolt of lust tore through his chest, like lightning heating up the sky. Desire and pride surged in him, and he was ready to go again. Now. Tonight. Anytime. He wasn't going to miss his chance.

But when she inched away from him, that sexy lustful look was gone and had been replaced by a studious, business-like one. "What about you? I mean, I know you didn't come and all. But was it good for you?"

"It was spectacular, Casey."

A smile lit up her face, and the moment turned oddly surreal again. "I think we should do it again. I did a little research this morning on things we can try." She was the eager student, ready for more teaching.

He arched an eyebrow. "You did?"

"Yes. I thought it would be smart to prep if we're going to do this. To do it properly," she said and grabbed her mini iPad from her purse, snapped open the cover and tapped on the notepad icon. "Christian and Ana ran through a checklist in advance. It helped them," she said, and when he scrunched up his brow, drawing a blank at the names, she added, "Christian Grey."

"Ah, but of course. I should have been on a first-name basis with him."

"Anyway, I grabbed a list from a website on kink and submission, and since we're doing lessons, I thought perhaps we should discuss the curriculum in advance."

He reined in a laugh. At least she was keen to continue. "Oh well, if Christian and Ana did it this way, we should too," he said dryly.

"They're the leading experts. But no red room of pain for us. And we don't even need to discuss caning, whipping or flogging, because those are not going to be on the menu."

"I won't even try to order them a la carte," he said, slashing his hand through the air.

"Let's begin with . . . spanking," she said, reading the list.

"I'm good with it. You?"

She nodded. "Absolutely."

He peered at the list on the screen. "How about ropes?"

"I believe I won't mind being tied up with you," she said, raising an eyebrow at her double entendre. He nodded approvingly, both at the pun and the prospect of her restrained.

She pointed to the next item on the list. "Ball gag?" She cringed. "That's not ever going to happen."

"We'll send it the way of the cane."

She nodded vigorously, then dropped her voice to a confessional whisper. "But I might be open to a riding crop. I'm not sure, but I'd like to try."

The situation in his jeans was getting tight. "I'd like to use a crop on you," he said in a low and dirty voice. She gazed back at him, the look in her eyes saying she was willing.

"Hair pulling, biting, scratching. I'm pretty sure I'd like all those," she said, miming checking them off the list.

"Always good to test them out to be safe though. What about handcuffs?"

"Only if you wear a cop uniform."

He groaned appreciatively, then tapped the list. "Which gives me the answer to the next one. Role-playing. That's a yes."

"Definitely." She gestured to the next item, and made a pout. "Orgasm denial? I don't think I'd like that."

"Oh, but I bet I could make you love it."

She narrowed her eyes, then spoke in a sultry, suggestive tone. "But Nate, I love coming."

Heat ran rampant in his body, like wildfire. This woman was going to be his undoing. She was flirty and dirty, and eager to give him the reins to her body. He was a lucky son-of-a-bitch.

"I don't know what man would not want you to be direct. Because when you say things like that—direct and insanely sexy things—it just makes me want to make sure you come over and over," he said.

She drew a quick breath, pushed her hair off her shoulders and mouthed *thank you*.

"Now, onto blindfolds," she said, returning to her workman-like attack of the list. "I think I can handle a blindfold. We sell them, you know."

"Good. Why don't you see if you can get the CEO discount? How about candles?" he asked, reading off another kinky option.

"Yeah. About that one," she said, tapping her finger against her lips. "Do I want hot wax dripping between my breasts? Yes? No? Yes? No?"

She glanced down, then ran a fingertip along her cleavage, checking how it might feel. A groan worked its way up his chest as she traveled across her skin. She was driving him wild. So clinical, so logical, when all he wanted was . . . to drip hot wax between her breasts. He reached for her hand, the thing he'd wanted to do earlier, then laced his fingers tightly in hers, guiding her hand along her breasts, down her belly, and to her lap.

"I'll do the testing," he said as he let go of his grip. "But what I really want to know is this…"

He threaded his fingers through her hair, grabbing a fistful. He waited 'til she moaned softly, then he tugged hard, yanking her head back in one quick move. A muffled cry of pleasure gave him the answer.

"Now I'm picturing you on your hands and knees, your spine bowed, your hair spilling down your back. I won't be able to resist pulling it hard then either," he whispered roughly, as he gripped tightly in demonstration.

She shivered in response, and breathed out sharply. With one hand firmly in her hair, he dragged his other hand down her chest, trailing a finger from the hollow of her throat to the valley between her luscious tits.

"Now let's address some other questions, Casey," he said, as he continued his exploration, dropping his hand inside her powder blue bra to stroke her breast. "You like it when I play with your breasts. I learned that last night," he said squeezing a dark pink nipple. She gasped in surprise. "But the one thing I'm not sure of is whether you like them to be sucked. Let's find out," he said, unbuttoning the top two buttons on her short-sleeved shirt, freeing a gorgeous globe of flesh. He groaned greedily, eager to taste her as he dropped his mouth to her hard nipple, drawing it between his teeth.

He bit down.

Instantly, her hands flew to his hair, tugging him closer. She arched into him, and he heard a hiss in her breath, as if she were trying to be quiet so the flight attendant up front wouldn't hear. He flicked the tip of his tongue against her delicious nipple until she moaned so loudly he feared she'd wake up the sleeping dogs. He pressed his hand to her mouth, covering it tightly, shushing her as he sucked and tasted each breast until she was wriggling in the seat. He finished with a quick bite on each nipple.

When he stopped, her wild untamed gaze told him everything he needed to know. "Yes, you like nipple play a hell of a lot, and that tells me you'll love it when I drizzle hot wax between your breasts. It'll get you so wet your panties will be useless, and you'll be begging me to strip you down to nothing and take you," he said, then grabbed her waist, and moved her on top of him. "But right now, we have another lesson."

"What's the lesson?" she asked as she straddled him, knees tucked up on either side of his legs.

"This one is called Don't Wake the Dogs," he said, then clasped one hand on her mouth yet again, and dipped his other hand underneath her skirt, sliding his fingers across the slick wetness on the panel of her panties. God, there was little he loved more than the evidence of a woman's arousal. He slid his fingers inside, gliding across that silky wetness that made his whole body feel electric. Touching her at all was such a privilege; touching her in this heightened state was a gift.

Her eyes glittered with lust as she rocked against his fingers. He couldn't resist—he drew his hand away from her legs, brought his fingers to his mouth and sucked off her wetness. Her eyes flared as she watched him.

"All morning, I could still taste you on me. I *had* to taste you again," he said, then returned to her slick flesh, sliding through her slippery wetness that told him exactly how much she'd enjoyed having her breasts sucked.

So much that his fingers were coated in her. She was some kind of live wire right now, and he intended to make her body sing. He ran his fingers across her heat, then ze-roed in on her swollen clit. She muffled a moan against his palm. She wasn't going to take long at all. My God, the things he could do with her body. The pleasure he in-tended to give her. The possibilities were endless.

"Let me feel you all over my hand," he said, his eyes on hers the whole time as he slid a finger into her, crooking so he could find that magic spot. She bowed her back in re-sponse to the penetration. Her slick walls gripped his fin-ger, and he added one more, all the while rubbing his thumb across her clit. "Rock into my hand. Do it hard," he commanded.

She did as told, riding him, humping his fingers, fuck-ing his hand furiously. She was a gorgeous sight, all wan-ton and naughty, and his lungs burned with desire for her; his dick ached to fill her. His body craved her climax. He wanted it badly, wanted her to fall apart for him in the sky.

She tensed all over, her thighs gripping him, and her eyes squeezed shut. "Come quietly," he whispered, urging her on. "I want to watch you come quietly."

She shuddered and dug her teeth into his palm, her body shaking before she collapsed into his arms.

He held her.

"Can I touch you now?" she said, her sweet voice melt-ing him. He loved that she offered, that she seemed to want to, even if it wasn't part of her "training."

He raised her chin so she could meet his eyes. "No."

She frowned. "Why? Are you into orgasm denial? That is no fun."

"Not in the least. But the answer is simple—I don't want to be quiet. And I don't want to wake the dogs, or annoy the flight attendant. That's why I said no. But rest assured, when we're back in New York we'll get through some other items on your list."

She sighed happily, then wriggled against him, as if she wanted to be closer. Not wanting to deny her a thing on this earth, he roped his arms around her.

"You're amazing," she whispered, her breathing still erratic as she floated down from her orgasm. Her praise sent a wicked thrill through him. Call it masculine pride. Call it ego. When a woman turns to you to teach her a new type of fucking, there's nothing a man wants to hear more than *amazing*. Though, come to think of it, *best orgasm of my life* was just as good.

"So are you," he said softly, stroking her hair. He couldn't believe she thought she needed to learn anything.

"I can tell why women adore you," she said, continuing her compliments.

He tensed at the reminder of his playboy status, then told himself not to bristle. He was what he was. She hadn't asked him for help because he batted ninth. He was a clean-up hitter, and so far with Casey he'd been belting home runs.

"I'm just glad you enjoyed it. And, by the way, you take direction exceedingly well, so I don't know why you're fixated on this idea that you—" but then he stopped short before he finished the thought—*can't give up control*. He wanted her to still need him, so he edited himself. "Need to change, but you're doing a great job learning how to give up control. So we'll just keep teaching you."

She moved off him, grabbed her iPad, and returned to her list. "Hmm," she said, as she studied it. "I'm not sure which of the items I'm supposed to be checking off. What do you consider what we just did?"

He gritted his teeth, annoyed with the idea of being an item on a list. But hell, he was the one who'd brought up the list a minute ago. "Ball gag. Consider that an impromptu ball gag, since you couldn't speak," he said, rising. He turned to face her. "Oh, and in case this helps you on your list, you can check that you liked it. Now if you'll excuse me."

After a quick restroom trip to wash his hands, he visited with the dogs, giving each a soft pat, then returned to Casey. She was scrolling through an email.

"There's a note from Grant about getting together in a month," she said, a happy look on her face as she read the message. He was ready to grab the iPad and smash the damn thing.

"That's great," he said, closing his eyes, willing himself to not be irritated that she was excited. Grant was a man she could have a future with. Nate was a man who lived for the present.

CHAPTER SEVEN

New York City, afternoon . . .

Casey ran her thumb over the LolaRing, absently flicking it on as she chatted in her office with one of her top executives, Nelle O'Connor.

The miniature vibrator buzzed against her thumb as Nelle shared the updates on the various partnerships Joy Delivered had struck in the last year—a deal with a high-class boutique in Stockholm, a partnership with a leading department store in Paris—courtesy of Jack's new European contacts—and even a pair-up with an upscale pharmacy called Sofia's in London that Casey had a meeting with in two weeks. Sofia's was a first in England—not many high-end pharmacies carried pleasure toys, but Sofia's took a chance, adding a few Joy Delivered products to its shelves, and the partnership had been a runaway success. Those retail outlets had also been carrying The Wild One, a twelve-speed vibrator introduced two years ago that had won legions of fans.

Next up was the LolaRing.

"Did you and Abbot hammer out any of the positioning details last week?" the no-nonsense Nelle asked, and Casey nearly dropped the toy in surprise from the unintended double meaning.

"Not in great detail, but we'll be doing that once he returns from Vietnam and Hong Kong," she said, and was tempted to add *among other things*.

Well, she was getting ahead of herself thinking of *other things*. They'd need to start with dinner, with more getting-to-know-you before they got to *other things*. She certainly hoped they had a good time at dinner. And that he was a good guy too. And, *of course*, that he treated her well. Would it be too much to also want him to be well hung?

Like Nate.

Who knew he'd been packing that kind of heat all along? She was a lucky lady to be able to turn to a man like him for her bedroom makeover project. Because that man did not have a textbook dick. His dick was so beautiful it needed a nickname. Like JackHammer. Or Plow Me Now. Or Mouthwateringly Delicious. Or Long, Tall Piece of Man Candy.

Actually, those sounded more like marketing slogans that other sex toy makers might use, like her friends at Good Vibes. She loved that company and was in regular contact with the top execs, but they approached the market differently. Joy Delivered tried to operate at a cut above, but Nate had her stooping to all sorts of low levels. Like on her knees. Or maybe on her hands *and* knees next.

Okay, time for her wandering mind to get out of its down and dirty gutter, and focus on catching up with her top employee on Monday afternoon.

Nelle peered at Casey over the top of her fuchsia glasses. They were camped out on the purple couch in Casey's office, the one she'd chosen for her brother when he was CEO, then reclaimed when he left for Paris.

"I've got some ideas I'd like to share with you for how to promote the partnership. Perhaps they'll come in handy as we prep. Contracts told me the paperwork has already been sent over, so we might as well get moving," Nelle said. The woman was both efficient and creative. Those twin qualities rarely resided in one body, but they did in Nelle, who'd been overseeing the rollout plans for the LolaRing.

The new toy had received through-the-roof reviews from The Happiest Ladies in the World, the product-testing group at the company. The toy marked an evolution in one of Joy Delivered's most popular vibrators, the Lola, that simulated oral sex. It was an amazing device, and truly felt like the world's most talented tongue. The LolaRing was a two-person toy, because it paired the Lola with a cock ring. Being man-free for the last year, Casey hadn't been able to take the LolaRing for a test drive herself, but the Happiest Ladies had said in their product write-ups that it was "like being licked and fucked" at the same time. "Translation: Heaven, Absolute Heaven," one of them had written.

Casey was jealous as hell when she'd read those reviews.

She tried to picture a man like Grant wanting to use this toy with her, but the image didn't compute, and she wasn't entirely sure why. She couldn't put her finger on it. Maybe because she was putting the cart before the horse to think of him that way. She didn't know if they were physically compatible, or emotionally compatible, for that matter. She didn't even know how he kissed. And here she was, trying to change her ways for him.

Was she crazy? Foolish? Or just plain stupid?

But, she reasoned, even if Grant Abbot was a bust, she needed to try a different approach with the opposite sex in general. Her romantic life had been sorely in need of a shake-up. And that's what she was giving it. These lessons with Nate would be useful whether she and Grant were a match, or she and the next guy.

Right? Right.

Funny how giving up control with Nate wasn't as hard as she'd expected, but maybe that was because he knew her inside and out. She trusted him completely. Grant was a step up from a stranger. And that was all the more reason to keep up the lessons. She needed to be thoroughly schooled in how to let go.

A hand waved broadly in her face. "Earth to Casey."

She snapped her attention back to Nelle, with her piercing dark eyes and straight black hair. "Sorry," she said.

"You went in space cadet mode there," Nelle said with a smirk. "Worn out from New Orleans?"

Worn out from great . . . almost sex. "Yes. Sorry. It was just such a quick trip. One night-turnaround and all," she said, even though that was no excuse. She'd been back in New York for two full days now. She wasn't known for zoning out during a one-on-one meeting with her right-hand woman. She pushed all men from her mind.

When they finished the meeting, Nelle headed out, stopping briefly in the doorway. She rapped her knuckles on the wood. "Knock, knock."

Casey rolled her eyes, but happily replied with "Who's there?" This was the side of Nelle that wasn't no-nonsense. Her knock-knock side.

"Ben Hur," Nelle replied, deadpan style.

"Ben Hur who?" Casey asked as she sank down into her desk chair.

"Ben Hur over the table," Nelle said, then doffed an imaginary top hat and bowed deeply before leaving on a trail of Casey's amusement.

Later that afternoon, Casey plowed through her emails, pleased to find a note from Grant.

"Glad to see everything is moving along smoothly with our deal. I'm taking off for Asia this evening, so let me simply say I hope the next month flies by."

She grinned and the teeniest spark tried to light up in her chest at the thought of Grant. She concentrated on that small flame, tried to will it to flare, but it quickly died out. There'd be time for flames though, for roaring fires and burning heat. These were the first tentative steps. Clicking through her inbox, she stopped at a message from her brother that had arrived a few minutes ago, which was after midnight, his time. He'd always been a night owl, but he and Michelle had taken to the Paris lifestyle, dining out at 10 p.m. on most nights. They'd probably just returned from dinner.

Michelle is calling you about your dress. Whatever she says, YOU LIKE IT.

Casey tapped out a quick reply. *But I DO like it!*

Moments later, her phone rang from the France country code.

"Hi Michelle," Casey said, as she swiveled around in her chair, giving herself a better view of her favorite office scenery—a replica of a Roy Lichtenstein painting, a comic book style rendering of a couple kissing. She had another one from the series at her home.

"How did you know it was me, and not Jack?" Michelle asked curiously.

"He just emailed and told me you were calling. He also told me to tell you no matter what that I like the dress. But I LOVE the bridesmaid dress, so I don't have to fake it. And you should tell him he doesn't have to say those things."

"*Jack,*" Michelle shouted. "You're in so much trouble."

She heard him respond with, "The good kind of trouble?"

Michelle laughed, then returned to the call. "Anyway, does it fit? I'm sorry it took so long to get it to you, but I wanted to find a perfect dress for an island wedding."

Casey scoffed. Loudly. Pointedly. "Island wedding? That's what you call a wedding in Hawaii. Or the Caribbean. Your wedding is a *paradise wedding*. That's what you call a wedding in the Maldives."

She swore she could hear Michelle smiling through the phone. "Well, can't wait to see you in paradise then, in three weeks."

"Me too. Can you put Jack on?"

There was a rustling sound from Michelle handing the phone to Jack, then his voice. "Thanks for getting me in trouble."

"You do it to yourself, Jack Sullivan. Whenever are you going to learn that the women in your life can see straight through you?"

"Never. Probably never."

They chatted more, and she caught him up to speed on the latest news with Joy Delivered, then he told her about some projects he was working on. He'd become a strategy consultant for many European companies, advising them on the U.S. market. He'd started in related businesses to Joy Delivered, but had now expanded, and even had begun working with some investors who specialized in high-end goods, from diamonds to vintage cars to art.

"You're so fancy now," she teased.

"That's me."

She told him she'd see him soon in the Maldives, and said goodbye.

Soon in the Maldives.

The words slammed her in the chest, like a linebacker knocking out the opponent's air, as she connected all the dots that were in front of her.

The wedding was taking place on the property of one of Nate's hotels in the Maldives. He was the best man, and his wedding gift had been to arrange for a discounted block of rooms for the guests, friends and family. She'd be at her brother's wedding, standing beside the bride and groom with the man whose hands and mouth and tongue had been exploring her. The man who was teaching her how to let go. How to give in. How to *bend*.

She waved her hand in front of her face, like a fan. Hell, just the thought of him was turning her on. Grabbing her phone, she began to dial his number to find out when their next lesson was. But before she hit the final digit, a neon sign flashed through her brain, blaring: *Let me pursue you.*

She had to do the same with Nate.

Letting him lead this unconventional arrangement was part of her much-needed romantic transformation from intimidating to demure.

She set down her phone and focused on work, eagerly diving into her projects. Because here, in the office, over-seeing this company she'd loved and founded, she was al-lowed to be her true self—to pick and choose, to decide, to direct.

Even so, as she stayed late, burning the midnight oil, she couldn't deny that inside she was squirming, hoping he'd reach out soon. When she packed up to go, she stopped to consider the painting on her wall, a favorite of hers. She'd studied business in school, but had minored in art history.

She ran her fingertips lightly over the illustrated lips, then touched her own lips, as she closed her eyes, remem-bering how Nate had kissed her. Like a field course in kiss-ing. The kind of kisses scientists would study for years in an attempt to dissect all the elements of a perfect kiss. Sul-try, possessive, as if he were claiming both sides of her— the side that wanted a tender, lingering touch and the side that wanted it rough and hard.

* * *

"He's the perfect dog. The girls love him and he's so obedient," Kat said as she leashed up the Dachshund, who'd immediately burrowed into his sister's arms when Nate dropped him off Saturday after the flight, and now, two days later, had clearly made himself at home with his new family.

"He's a chick magnet already," Nate quipped and Kat flashed him a smile as they walked down the steps of her brownstone on Park Avenue.

"I already picked a name for him," she said as they reached the sidewalk.

"You didn't let Chloe and Cara name him?"

His sister shot him a stern look. "They're one, Nate. I'm not giving them naming rights to the first dog."

"Fair enough. What's his name?"

"Indiana Jones," she said, as if it were an obvious choice. But then, it dawned on him what she'd done and why. "Because it was *your* favorite movie growing up. Remember we went to see it when you won the election for class president in eighth grade?"

Nate nodded, the memories flashing by of their childhood, summer days at the shore, dinners together every evening, movie nights to celebrate special occasions. His home had been happy, his parents had been in love and still were, and they'd worked together in a tourist shop they continued to run in his hometown of Mystic, Connecticut. His mind flicked to Casey. Her parents had split the second she'd left the house for college, so eager to be divorced. It was ironic that he and Casey had the opposite experiences, and each veered in the other direction. Despite her unhappy parents, she hadn't soured on love; she still had faith in it. Meanwhile, Nate believed in un-love.

Thanks to Joanna.

Funny, how several years ago he'd have bet *this* would be his life now—two kids, the happy home in the city. He was drunk on love with Joanna then. The two of them spent late nights tangled up together in their Murray Hill apartment, drinking wine, playing slow, sexy music and coming together again and again. She'd even sculpted his hands once. She'd made a goddamn sculpture of them as a wedding gift to him. "The only hands I ever want touching me," she'd said, and it was so heady, those words falling from her red pouty lips that poured forth promises of being together forever. They swore they'd be wrapped up in each other 'til the end of time.

Their marriage had lasted two intense, and seemingly beautiful, years. Then he was divorced at age twenty-eight.

Love was a drug; it played voodoo tricks on your brain, and the chemicals bathed you in lies as you fell, tempting you to believe in crazy notions like happily-ever-afters, and houses, and families.

He clenched his fists, shoving the memories away. He was happy, quite happy, thank you very much, in life post-Joanna. There was no need to linger on the past. He'd learned his lesson. He was glad though that his sister was happy.

They talked more as they walked. The little brown and tan creature sniffed every stoop, every bush, every small tree on the handful of blocks between Kat's home and Fifth Avenue where they caught up with Bryan, who'd gone for a jog in the park with the kids.

He was running down the block, pushing a double stroller.

Nate clapped his friend on the back when he pulled up next to them, breathing hard. "Look at you. Dog, two kids, and the double wide. Such the family man now. I'd give you a hard time if you were married to anyone but my sister," Nate said, and Bryan rolled his eyes.

"Thanks man. I appreciate the un-compliment."

"Hey," Kat said softly to Bryan, then pecked him on the cheek before she bent down to coo at her daughters. Nate joined in, because his nieces, Chloe and Cara, were pretty much the cutest babies in the whole world.

"Why don't you boys take Indiana Jones for a walk and I'll get the girls fed," Kat said, switching places. Bryan handed off the stroller, and she gave him the leash then turned around. "Bye, Nate. Don't forget, if you get those tickets for the Yankees game, I want in. I'll get a sitter."

He saluted her his *yes*, since he'd been in touch with his contact who'd always snagged him box seats at the game. "Consider it done."

"Um, excuse me," Bryan said, holding up a hand. "I'd like to claim one of those tickets too."

"We'll see, buddy," Nate said.

Kat shrugged playfully at her husband. "What can I say, Bryan? He likes me better than you." She blew kisses in the air and walked off.

Bryan looked at the Dachshund, and shook his head. "I'm a man with a hot dog now. And my friend won't even score Yankees tickets for me."

"Hey, that's a prize dog. Don't put Indiana Jones in the middle of your mid-life crisis," Nate joked, pointing to the pooch, who happily trotted towards the park.

"So what's the latest with you?" Bryan said, wiping off the sweat on his brow with his T-shirt. "I trust you have stories to tell me of your trip to New Orleans? Regale me with your tales."

Nate laughed, but didn't plan on giving up any intel on the woman he'd spent the night with in the Big Easy. "Hardly."

"Oh, c'mon. You falling down on that score?"

"Never," he said, and his mind was right back to Casey, on the look on her face on the airplane yesterday. The way her eyes floated closed, how her breath hitched, how she bit down hard on his hand when she came. He glanced at his palm, almost wishing there were imprints from her. Evidence of her passion.

Nate's phone buzzed. He grabbed it in case it was an urgent work call. He needed to return to the office tonight anyway. The message was from Ethan, who he'd reached out to earlier in the day about grabbing a beer.

"*Beer is always good. I'm free tonight or tomorrow.*"

He gestured to the screen. "Ethan Holmes. I need to reconnect with him."

But he needed to reconnect with Casey too. And he'd been mulling over the best way to take the next step with her. Even though he wasn't wooing her or courting her, he wanted to rock her world with this sexual boot camp.

And that's when he realized what was needed next. Supplies for their training.

"Hey, I gotta take off," he said, and turned tail, texting Casey to let her know she'd need a new email address for him to use as her "teacher."

* * *

"You should ask for her number," Nate said later that evening, gesturing to the very pretty bartender at Speakeasy, the bustling midtown establishment where he and Ethan had knocked back a few beers and talked shop. Ethan was high up at Victoria Hotels, and had peppered Nate with some questions about how to tackle the image issues his company faced. The classy hotel was no longer cutting it on the gold-plated ambiance and needed to go younger, hipper, cooler, Ethan admitted. Nate offered his advice where he could, glad that the two were back in touch. They'd been work friends at The Luxe, but hadn't talked much when they were both candidates for the top job. That had been a tense few weeks, both men vying for one spot. When Nate had landed the coveted position after an exhaustive internal and external search, Ethan took him out to toast, but it had been a strained night, and the man had remained in a bit of a funk for the months that followed. Nate was glad that they'd both moved on now, and could chat again about work and women.

His friend peered at the woman behind the bar, pointing to a redhead with a round belly. He cocked his head to the side, looking at Nate as if he had grown horns. "The pregnant one? Pretty sure that belly means she's taken."

Nate laughed and shook his head. "Not Julia. The hot brunette who's been giving you the eye. Julia told me her name is Danya. She's been taking on more hours, since Julia's cutting back a bit in a few more months," he said.

"You think I should just go right up to her and ask for her number?"

"Just talk to her. That's what I'd do."

Ethan scoffed and pushed a hand through his blond hair. "I'm sure a beautiful bartender at a classy establishment in Manhattan doesn't get hit on very much at all."

"You never know if someone is game unless you try. I need to take off, so give it a shot," Nate said, and when Ethan shrugged, rose and walked over to Danya, he wanted to pump his fist. She shot him a wide smile, and they seemed to fall into conversation easily.

"Need another?"

Nate turned to Julia, shaking his head. "Nah. Closing time for me. I've got a laptop calling my name for the next few hours," he said, then slapped down some bills to pay for the drinks, leaving a sizable tip for her. He figured she deserved an extra twenty percent on top of everything else for managing a bar with a belly that big.

She scooped up the cash, and blew him a kiss. "Thanks for coming by. Don't stay up too late working. I'll tell Clay you said hi."

"And let him know I'll follow up soon about Brent and his clubs. I've got a trip to Vegas on the calendar, so I'll meet him then."

"Absolutely."

As she moved to a new customer, his phone buzzed, and a kernel of excitement tore through him like a comet flaring across the night. When Casey's name popped up in his inbox, his dick twitched, hardening instantly. Damn organ; her name already elicited a Pavlovian response in him. His dick saluted anytime she was near.

He tapped open the email, re-reading the note he'd sent her a few hours ago.

from: commandonate@gmail.com
to: learnsnewtricksgirl@gmail.com
date: June 6, 6:57 PM
subject: Tomorrow's Lesson

At some point tomorrow I will stop by your office. I will have a gift for you. I will expect you to not be wearing any panties. Do not disobey me.

from: learnsnewtricksgirl@gmail.com
to: commandonate@gmail.com
date: June 6, 9:03 PM
subject: Practicing Now

Removed. Ready. Waiting.

Those three words alone made him groan. But what was most intoxicating about her response was the attachment. She'd sent him a photo of her red lace panties on top of her desk.

CHAPTER EIGHT

New York City, afternoon . . .

Thank God it was June.

Summer was an easier time to go commando than the cold months.

Thank God she was buried in deskwork today too, with the majority of her meetings of the phone variety. Casey liked to wear short skirts and heels, or short skirts and boots. Today she'd opted for a tight, knee-length skirt, since she didn't need to perform any accidental Marilyn Monroe shows. She'd never dressed panty-free at work before, and she felt like she had a naughty little secret when she popped into the conference room to visit with the product team for a meeting. No one knew, of course, but the knowledge that she was bare had kept her thoughts on Nate all day long. Being naked down there also meant she was turned on all day. She was an electrical line, exposed and crackling, waiting to spark.

She'd even wandered past reception a few times, peering down the elevator banks for him. Each time, she struck out, and cursed under her breath.

The minutes ticked by, and she was sorely tempted to break out one of her products, to lock her door and spend a few minutes with The Wild One, since that magical device did the trick in mere minutes; sometimes in seconds. But she resisted. Even if no one would know, she didn't want to be the CEO of a sex toy company who actually *did* get herself off at her desk. Better to be a woman in control at the office.

Now it was past three, and that man needed to show up soon because she was getting pissed. She was turned on and she was frustrated, and that was not a pleasant combination. She didn't like games or being toyed with. Leaving her door open, she picked up her phone and returned a few calls.

Midway through a conversation with a retail partner, he appeared.

Wearing a dark gray suit, a navy tie, and his jacket slung over his shoulder, held with one finger, he leaned against the doorway. Her throat went dry. He was so damn sexy. He didn't even break a grin, just gazed at her with that same intense stare she'd seen in the hotel room. "I'll call you back," she said into the phone and hung up.

"Hi," she whispered, her voice sounding crackly and dry.

He nodded, then stepped inside, turned to the door and pushed it shut. He walked over to her, and when he reached her desk he set down a black box with a red bow on it.

"For later. But first, I need to know if you did as instructed."

She nodded, her eyes wide, her cheeks flush with heat.

He shook his head, and raised his finger to tsk her. "I need to *know*, Casey. That means," he said, stopping to take his time, as if he were tasting each letter like a meal, "show me."

Oh God. Her heartbeat sped up, and heat thrummed in her body.

He gestured with his fingers, signaling for her to move back. She pushed back in her chair, inched up her skirt, and opened her legs. She was so damn glad the only windows in her office looked out over the New York skyline, not the rest of the company.

His eyes narrowed, and he emitted a barely audible moan of appreciation. He walked around her desk, bent down, and cupped her chin in his hand. "Such a beautiful, bare pussy," he said as he looked her in the eyes, then brought his lips to her ear. "I bet you want my mouth on you right now."

"I do," she said, her voice feathery.

"Wait," he said. "Wait for later. Wait for me."

Then he dropped his mouth to her lips and devoured her. He claimed her mouth, kissing her so passionately it was as if kissing was making love, kissing was fucking, kissing was sex with their lips. Heat pooled between her legs, where she ached. When he let go of her mouth, her vision was still fuzzy, and she was floating above the earth on a cloud of lust. It took a second to register what he was doing. He was reaching his hand between her legs, sliding one finger through her wetness, then bringing it to his mouth to lick it off.

"That'll get me through the next five hours of meetings about our expansion into New Zealand. At eight o'clock, I will be at your apartment. Don't open the box until I arrive. Wear something unbearably sexy that you think will drive me crazy. Because it will. And have a drink ready for me when I walk in the door. Whiskey will do."

Shivers raced across her skin, lighting her up from his commands. No one had ever talked to her like this. He was so direct, so controlling, and so fucking sexy with his orders. She'd never expected to enjoy this kind of play, but as he walked out the door, she wanted to slam it shut and take care of herself, to slide her fingers across her wetness, and bring herself to release.

But she still had a modicum of self-control.

She would wait.

She would wait five hours. She would wait until he could take care of her intense, overwhelming need to come.

* * *

He hadn't told her specifically what to wear, but she was savvy enough to know what qualified as *unbearably sexy*. She donned a tight leather skirt that hit her mid-thigh, right at the top of her black stockings. A bit of lace from the stockings peeked out. He was a legs man, so she chose strappy heels.

Up top? A cherry-red bra.

That was all. She didn't wear a shirt. She smiled to herself as she appraised the outfit in the mirror. The lack of a shirt was her homage to her own need for control. She had chosen this ensemble because she wanted to open the door with only a red lace bra on top. It was her way of being true to herself. She hoped Khashi, her neighbor across the hall, wouldn't happen to return from work then. A sexy plastic surgeon, he kept odd hours between his job, and the ladies he entertained.

At 8 p.m. precisely the buzzer rang. Electricity sparked in her bloodstream as she buzzed him in. She didn't know what was in store for her tonight, but she couldn't wait to find out what he'd planned.

As she walked to the door, she fluffed out her hair and glanced around her apartment. He'd been here many times. He knew the kitchen with its exposed red brick walls, he'd lounged on her soft teal couch, and he'd seen the reprints of artwork on her walls. It was a warm and homey loft in the West Village. One window was open and the June breeze blew inside, along with the faint sound of traffic rattling through the Village on a New York night.

But never had she opened the door to him like this. Her fingers shook as she unlocked the chain and turned the knob to the right. The heavy door creaked, the soundtrack to her own nervous system and to her wildly beating heart.

Her breath caught in her chest. He stood in the hallway wearing charcoal slacks, a crisp white shirt, and the navy tie. Her fingers itched to unknot that tie. He was rolling up the cuffs on one of the sleeves. A businessman at the end of the workday—that's what she would've named this photograph of him that she took in her mind's eye.

"Did you open the box?"

She shook her head. He entered her apartment and she let the door fall shut behind them with a click.

He strolled casually to her kitchen, leaned against the counter, and tapped the wood.

She understood. The game was on. They were playing their parts. Joining him in the kitchen, she grabbed the bottle of whiskey and poured him a glass, doing her best to keep her hands steady. She watched his every move as he knocked back the amber liquid. She imagined the burn in his throat. He set the glass down. It was nearly empty.

She stood near him, keenly aware that it was his move next.

This was a chess game, and she barely knew how to play. She swallowed dryly. Waiting. Uncertain.

She wanted a burn in her throat too. That would be better than all these nerves. She grabbed his glass and finished it.

"Do you want to open the box now?"

She nodded, grateful to have been given his direction. "Yes. I do."

He tipped his forehead to the L-shaped couch in the living room.

She nodded briefly, and walked over to the couch. She sank down into the soft material, stretching her legs out in front of her on the lounge section, crossing them at the ankles. He joined her in the living room, choosing to sit on an ottoman, his knees spread, his hands resting on his thighs. "Open it now, Casey."

Leaning forward, she reached for the black box and untied the bow, letting it fall to the floor. Gingerly, with nervous fingers, she lifted the top, shimmying it off. In seconds, she'd know what he'd planned, and a ribbon of excitement unfurled inside her from the possibilities. She wanted to say something, but words escaped her at that moment. She wasn't sure how to vocalize all these unsteady feelings thrumming through her body.

Or if he would even respond.

Nate had always been easy to talk to. He'd always been chatty. But the man was wearing steely silence like a new coat. All his moves were measured, chosen carefully, designed to keep her guessing as to what he had in store for the evening.

She put the top of the box on the table, and the guessing game ended when she dipped her hands inside the box and withdrew a long, silky scrap of fabric—a blindfold. Next, she reached for a soft object, retrieving a feather tickler from his collection of goodies. Finally, there was a small riding crop, as if it had been made in miniature. Perhaps, so it didn't seem so scary. She glanced up at him. His eyes seemed dark brown tonight. Gone was that warm golden color, replaced with a heat, a sensuality and blazing desire for her.

She trembled. "What do you want to use first?"

He didn't answer her question. Instead, he issued an instruction. "Lie back. Close your eyes."

She did as told, scooting into the couch. She hadn't even turned on music, so she was keenly aware of every sound. Of the low hum from the refrigerator, of the far-off din of traffic, of the stirrings of a breeze. But there were no words from him. The silence vibrated between them as she waited, the world dark behind her eyelids.

His fingers found their way to the top of her stockings. Gently, he rolled them down, one by one, removing them, along with her shoes. "Don't get me wrong. These are un-bearably sexy, but I need your bare skin."

Her world went pitch black. He had pressed the silk blindfold over her eyes. "This is about you. About all the things you can feel if you let go. With this on, all you can do is *feel*," he said, low and husky, near her ear. Oh God, she *was* feeling everything. She was feeling the tight coil of desire deep inside her, and the fervent hope that he'd take her to the far edge of pleasure. That's what she was feeling.

She drew a quick breath at the soft fluttery touch from a feather running along the inside of her calves. The feather brushed across her knee. Goosebumps rose on her flesh. Her skin felt electric as the feather travelled across her body, visiting her belly, teasing her breasts, trailing along her sides. When the sensations stopped briefly she wanted to ask what happened, until she felt the feather once more.

He was tracing the shell of her ear, and she gasped.

Warmth spread inside her body. She had no idea that being touched on her ear would be such a turn on. She had no notion either that she'd arch her back, seeking closeness, willing him to touch more, when he ran the feather down her arm, inside her elbow and across her wrist. "Your whole body is a playground," he instructed. "For now, until you learn to thoroughly give up control, it will be *my* playground. Isn't that right, Casey?"

She nodded and moaned her agreement in a voice she didn't even recognize as her own.

"Then hike up your skirt for me," he told her.

Instantly, she responded to his request. She reached for the hem, pulling it up. Her skirt was now bunched at her waist. He stopped, and hissed in his breath. His audible reaction to her body drove her arousal. They were a feedback loop of desire. She'd move; he'd admire. He'd say a dirty word; she'd heat up. They fed each other with this fevered kind of lust. She pictured him drinking her in, memorizing the way she looked half-undressed on her couch.

Then, she was alone again as she heard him rustling through the box. She knew what was in the box: three things. She was wearing one of them. The other one he had already used. That left only the one she feared. She tensed, waiting for soft to change to hard. For tenderness to turn to a sting.

She emitted a small cry at the first smack. He had flicked the crop once against the flesh of her outer thigh. He shifted to the other, flicking her there. She let out a tiny yelp. Reflexively, she closed her legs. She wasn't sure if she liked the crop. She parted her lips to speak, but then his fingertip pressed softly against her mouth. "Shhh," he said. "I can tell you don't like it."

In a second, he was trailing the crop down her chest, underneath her bra, and along her rib cage.

Then it was gone.

He must have lifted it in the air again, and she waited nervously for him to swat her. But instead, she felt something hard against the wet panel of her panties. He was using the riding crop against her clit, like a toy, turning something she hadn't liked into something she enjoyed immensely now. He rubbed one end across her throbbing bundle of nerves, stroking her, sending the temperature inside of her through the roof. She sought more friction, more contact, lifting her hips closer. When he stopped, she heard a whooshing sound in the air, then a smack against the hardwood floors. He'd tossed it away.

Next was the weight of his body on hers, his soft voice in her ear, him whispering, "I never ever want to do something to you that you don't like. Do you understand that?"

"Yes."

"You should only feel pleasure with me. You should never feel anything less than desire," he said, and he was Nate now, the man she trusted inside and out.

The next thing she knew the blindfold was falling loose, dropping to her nose, giving her sight again. There he was, raised on his arms above her, and smelling like sex.

Tonight. God, she hoped he'd take her tonight. Reaching behind her head, he untied the blindfold all the way, then brought it to her wrists, wrapping it around them in a circle, and binding them together in a tight knot.

"I'm going to undress you now."

He laced his hands around her back, unhooked her bra, and freed her breasts. Then he unsnapped her skirt, tugged it down her hips, to her knees, and over her ankles, laying it neatly on the couch.

His eyes roamed her body, drinking her in from head to toe.

"The panties must go," he said, a clear command, now back into character.

She held up her bound wrists as if to say *you're going to need to be the one to take them off.*

In one swift move, his hands were on her hips, practically tearing them off, like a hungry, greedy man eager for the prize.

He stood and stepped away from her. He crossed his arms over his chest. "I want to watch you spread your legs for me. Do it nice and slow. Like a tease. Make me so fucking hard, harder than I already am, from the way you open your legs."

She breathed in deeply, letting the air spread all this electric fire to the far corners of her body. She was tingling everywhere, burning up across every square inch of skin. That burn narrowed between her legs, where it became an exquisite ache to be filled. Slowly, intending to torture him, she raised one knee, watching him as he dropped his hand to his crotch, stroking himself through his pants. She took her sweet time letting that knee fall to the side of the couch. He groaned, a rough and hungry sound. She lifted the other knee inch by inch, spreading for him.

Now it was his turn to strip and she never took her eyes away from him, not as he yanked off the tie, undid his buttons, stripped off his shirt, or as he skimmed down his pants.

There was no artful tease. No stage moves or strip show timing. He was a man in need. A man who was finally going to fuck her.

He climbed over her and straddled her waist, his knees gripping her, his rock-hard cock hitting the soft flesh of her belly, the blunt head nudging the silk fabric that held her hands in place. She wondered briefly where the condom was. He was down to his birthday suit, after all. She didn't really see where he could be hiding it. And she didn't intend to let him ride her bareback.

"Nate? Do you have a—"

He cut her off. "Lift your wrists above your breasts. Lift them up here," he said, tapping her cleavage, "So you can squeeze your tits together."

She did as instructed, her clasped hands scrunched by the side of her face, as her elbows squeezed her breasts.

He dipped his hand between her legs, and she cried out. At last, he was touching her. She needed it so badly, needed him. He slid his fingers between her slick heat, up, down, up, down, building speed.

Suddenly, he stopped, and his fingers were on her breasts, sliding the wetness across her cleavage.

Holy shit. It hit her fully what he was about to do. He must have seen the moment of recognition in her eyes.

"You wanted me to come, didn't you?"

She bit her lip, nodding.

"You still want me to?"

"Yes. God, yes."

"Good. Because I'm fucking dying to," he said, and thrust his hard cock between the tunnel of her breasts. His eyes closed in pleasure, his lips fell open, and he pumped. He fucked her breasts as her bound wrists held them in place, his dick sliding between the slickness he'd used to pave the way.

She watched, mesmerized as he moved on her, her mouth watering with each upstroke, each view of the shaft that she wanted to suck. She licked her lips.

"You want to suck me off, don't you?" he said roughly.

"Yes."

"You want me to be fucking your pretty little mouth right now?"

"Yes. God yes," she said.

Another stroke. Another pump. "You want to taste me coming?"

"Yes, please."

"I want that too," he said, panting as he thrust harder, faster. His jaw twitched. His breathing grew erratic. "But right now, I am in motherfucking love with your perfect tits, and I don't want to be anyplace else."

"Then fuck me harder," she said, her voice strong, guiding him on. She wasn't going to just lie here. She was going to have some fun too. She was going to be the woman she loved being. Dirty and direct.

"You like that, don't you?" he said, his lips curving in a grin as he thrust.

"I do. I do like it."

"You like talking back. You like telling me how much you want my cock. You've been dying for it," he said, as his hips began rocking faster, like a jackhammer.

"I love your dick, Nate. It's a work of art. I want to see you come on me," she said, her body heating to supernova levels as she urged him on. He stopped talking, and let her do the work. Gripping her breasts tighter, she guided him home. "Give it to me now," she said, like a command. "Give it to me all over my body. I want to feel you come on my tits."

"Oh fuck, Casey," he shouted, groaning loudly as he released himself between her breasts, the warmth spreading up to her neck. He drew a deep exhalation, his arms shaking, his whole face contorted with pleasure.

So fucking beautiful and dirty at the same time. She loved every second of watching him come.

He moved off her and walked to the bathroom to grab some tissues. When he rejoined her, he wiped the evidence of his orgasm from between her breasts. He brought the tissue to the trashcan, then returned to her once more and untied her wrists. She reached for him, eager to draw him near, wanting more from him.

"Will you please?"

He shook his head. "Show me."

"Show you what?"

"Show me how you touch yourself. If I left right now, I know you'd masturbate. I want to watch you get yourself off."

Pressing a hand on each knee, he gently guided her legs open for him.

"Look at you," he said, licking his lips as he stared greedily at her center, his strong chest rising and falling. He seemed to breathe her in. "So wet. So pretty. So pink. I want to see you run your fingers through that pretty, pink pussy."

Wetness beaded between her legs, calling out for her touch. God only knew, she'd be stroking herself something fierce tonight if he left, so she did it now. No point in waiting. Her body would launch a mutiny if she didn't give in to its demand.

She ran her fingers across her aching clit and closed her eyes, throwing her head back, giving in to the first possibility of sweet release from this mad desire that had been escalating in her all day long.

"Open your eyes," he told her and she did. "Look at me the whole time. Look at me. I'm the one you're getting off to. Tell me how good it feels."

She panted and moaned as she rubbed faster. "It feels so good, Nate."

"What am I doing to you?"

"You're teasing me, that's what you're doing," she said, speaking the truth.

He smiled. "I know. I love it. I love teasing you. But what am I doing when I'm *not* teasing you?"

"I'm imagining you entering me for the first time," she said, stroking faster. He groaned, and she saw his dick grow harder. She thrilled at his physical response to her, at the way he seemed barely able to control the lust she inspired.

"You have no idea how much I've thought about that," he said in a low and dirty voice.

Her fingers flew faster, her wetness spreading. "I want you inside me, Nate. I want to feel you fill me up," she said, locking her eyes with his. "I want you all the way in me."

She cried out, her belly tightening, her orgasm coming into view. There on the other side it raced closer, ever closer, and she concentrated, seeking it out desperately.

"I want to know how your body feels against mine," she said in between breaths as she arched her hips, bucking into her hand, her words turning into a chorus of cries as her back bowed and her body flooded with pleasure. In seconds his lips crashed down on hers, and he kissed her ferociously, incessantly, his hand dropping back between her legs, touching, stroking, rubbing, and somehow coaxing one more crest out of her as she cried out again, com-ing once more as he kissed her feverishly.

When at last he let go, he kissed her neck, her throat, her collarbone. "I want you so much," he said, and his voice was different this time. It wasn't the voice of the teacher, the dominating force who told her what to do. Nor was it her friend who she joked with and talked to and teased. It was the voice of a lover, the sound of a man, and it lit up her heart in a way she hadn't expected.

She wanted him too.

CHAPTER NINE

New York City, night . . .

The natural next step was to leave. To say a few nice words; to kiss her goodbye, to be on his way. But he didn't want to go. He wanted more of her. He wanted to *not* lose what they had before. As much as he was accustomed to the over-and-out of these kinds of nights, he feared that if he left, he'd be treating Casey as merely a sexual object, when she was so much more to him.

That's why he'd have to fight the temptation, the overwhelming impulse to slide into her, to feel her legs wrap around his waist, to take her to the heights she so desperately wanted. Even though he was absolutely certain sex with her right now, in the state they were both in, would be beyond spectacular, he also knew that she seemed to thrive on not knowing what was coming next. In their few short nights together, he'd learned that she responded quite nicely, oh-so-very-nicely, to being surprised.

He wanted that perfect chemistry of anticipation and wonder, of tease and heat, stirred in her to just the right temperature before he finally took her. He didn't know when that would be, but he was confident now that it would happen. That she was hooked on these lessons too. Maybe for different reasons than he; but still she'd been seduced by submission, and by her own natural wildness as well. She had a fantastically wild side and a dirty side, and he loved experiencing those parts of her.

All of her.

That meant now was not the night for *more*.

He pulled on his pants, and she cracked up as he reached for the zipper.

He tilted his head to the side, curiosity getting the better of him. "Why are you laughing?"

She pointed to his pelvis. "Because it's funny."

"My dick is funny?"

She shook her head, another giggle falling forth. "No, it's funny the way you have to put them on so you don't zip yourself up."

He glanced down at the practiced move. Obviously, he could do this without looking, do it from memory, but yeah, you had to tug the fabric *away* from the crown jewels to make sure you didn't catch them in the teeth.

"Ever get it caught?"

He rolled his eyes and suppressed a laugh. "Yes. Yes, I have. Years ago, as a younger man," he said, launching into a storyteller's voice, as if sharing a tale. "But, alas, I survived, and there are no scars." With that, he snapped his pants shut, and gestured proudly. "Voila. Impressed?"

"So impressed," she said, clapping several times.

"Wait 'til you see me juggle."

"You juggle?"

"I've never shown you my juggling skills?"

"I've always known you could juggle women, but didn't realize it extended to objects."

"Ha ha. Got any oranges or apples?"

"In the kitchen. There's a basket on the counter. You can grab them. I'm going to change," she said, standing up in all her naked glory.

He hated for her to take away the view. "But you look so good naked," he said. He briefly considered begging for her to stay undressed.

"So do you, and yet you put on pants," she said, then retreated to her bedroom.

He wandered into the open kitchen of her loft, and found the bowl of fruit on the island counter. Grabbing three oranges and an apple, he headed back to the living room and tossed the first orange in the air, then the next, then the next, finally adding the apple. He found his rhythm quickly and the fruit whirred in a circle before him.

Then she returned, and his jaw dropped, and the apple smacked the floor with a thud.

"Damn, Casey," he said, quickly grabbing the three oranges mid-flight, before they spilled to the ground too.

"What is it?" she asked, her eyes so wide and innocent.

"You're just . . ." he said, tripping on his tongue, barely able to form words around her. Because one minute she was the leather-clad woman in stockings, heels and a red bra, and the next she wore pink cotton panties and a white tank top, fresh-faced and all-American blonde, with her wavy hair pulled into a loose knot at her neck. He walked over to her, unable to resist touching her. With his free hand, he trailed his fingertips down her arm, then pressed a soft, simple kiss to her lips. "You're just so beautiful," he said, finally able to finish the thought, then he stepped back.

"So are you," she said softly, never taking her eyes off his, and the way she looked at him did funny things to his heart. Foreign things he hadn't felt in years. "But don't start thinking calling me beautiful is going to distract me." She snapped and pointed to the oranges and the fallen apple. "Juggle. Now."

She crossed her arms and tapped her foot, waiting.

He grabbed the apple, tossed it high, then threw the oranges and juggled them round and round for at least a minute, his full concentration on keeping the quartet in the air, and impressing her with this skill. He slowed, ending the whirl, taking a bow and returning the oranges to the counter. He dropped the bruised apple into the basket, grabbed another one, and walked to Casey. He tugged her arm, and gestured to the couch. They sank into the cushions, next to each other on the lounge section.

"Say it. Say you're impressed with my skills," he said.

"I am so impressed with your skills," she said as he crunched into the apple. He offered it to her next, and she bit into it, passing it back to him. He draped an arm around her shoulder, and she snuggled in close as they finished off the apple. He stretched across her to set the core down on the table, the same one that held the tickler and blindfold. The crop was still on the floor.

"Are you hungry?" she asked.

"For you? Yes. For food, the answer is also yes. What do you have in mind?"

"Food first. Want to order from the House of Nanking around the corner? I'm craving their moo shu pancakes."

"Of course. And you know what I like."

"I do," she said, grabbing her phone.

That's what was so odd between the two of them right now. As she ordered his favorite dish, sesame chicken, it occurred to him that she knew so many things about him. She knew bits and pieces of his past with Joanna, she knew his challenges and his triumphs in business, she knew what he liked to eat, to read, how much he enjoyed watching the Yankees, and she knew what he liked to do on the weekends. Oftentimes, the answer was *work*. They both had admitted how much they actually did love the siren call of the deal, the decision, and the chance to increase the profit margin. "I like working late," she'd once confessed. "I can't resist it either," he'd seconded.

Except now.

He had no desire to be anyplace but here. When she ended the call, he gestured to the artwork on her brick walls.

"You got a new print of one of Lichtenstein's kisses?"

She nodded. "Yeah, but it's not an original."

He laughed. "I know. I didn't think it was an original one. They're kind of pricey. I think one of them went for $6 million at auction."

She arched one eyebrow, giving him a curious look. "Since when do you know the prices of artwork?"

"There was a Lichtenstein lithograph next to one of Joanna's early sculptures at an exhibition years ago. I wound up knowing all about him."

She cringed, squeezing her eyes shut, saying, "Shit, I'm sorry. I should have known that would be the connection."

He placed his hand on her arm. "Hey, it's okay."

She shook her head. "Well, I shouldn't have brought it up."

"I swear, Casey. It's okay. I've gotten over it. It's not as if I can't be surrounded by the art world because of Joanna," he said, and that was mostly true. Joanna's star had risen quickly after she finished her MFA. Her works were featured, bought and sold at top galleries in Manhattan and London. He couldn't insulate himself from the imprint of her.

"I'm glad she hasn't totally ruined it for you. That woman did a number on you, though."

He simply curved up the corner of his lips in acknowledgement. "I won't deny that. But I also like to think I've moved on," he said, and that was true too. He had moved to a better place. A spot where he could never be hurt like that again. Trust no one, let no one in, and you're safe.

"I'm glad you feel that way, for you. And because it also means I can tell you that I'm going to an auction in London when I go there later this month to meet with my clients at Sofia's Pharmacy. I'm so excited," she said, her eyes twinkling. "I have my eyes on a few items in the lot."

"What are you hoping to bid on?"

"Nothing too fancy. I'm still just a working girl," she said, jokingly. Then, she turned serious. "There are some gorgeous paintings from a newer artist, Miller Valentina, and I want to get them to finish out my collection of kisses. But I suppose, if you think about it, you don't really

ever need to finish a collection of kisses. They can keep going on."

He looked at her, and she was gazing at the images on
her wall—an image of a couple in the rain curled together
in an embrace, then a black-and-white photograph of a
sailor kissing his girl, and also a movie poster of Rhett
locking lips with Scarlett from *Gone With The Wind*. "You
are such a romantic," he said.

"Yeah, I am," she said, nodding, and owning it. "I completely am. All the more ironic, considering my parents are
anti-romantic, isn't it? They couldn't wait 'til I left the
house for college so they could finally divorce."

"I like that they didn't sap the desire out of you."

"But aren't you glad you don't have to worry about
tending to the overly romantic side of me? You only have
to think about this side," she said, gesturing to her body, as
if she were presenting him with it.

Admittedly, there was a part of Nate that was immensely glad he didn't have to worry about the romantic
side of her. The evidence of her heart's true desire for love
was displayed on her wall for all to see—proof that she was
the opposite of him. And she didn't hide it. She didn't try
to deny it. She simply tried to live by it. Of course, now
she was trying to both live by it and add a few new tricks
to the mix in the proverbial quest to have it all.

But some small part of his heart lurched in sadness that
he could *only* serve the physical. He didn't have it in him
to be more. He wasn't prone to romance, or to the kind
she wanted. He'd made a choice to live on the other side,
and that was a damn good choice that had served him
well, and protected him. He'd stand by it, come hell or

high water. And since they didn't see eye to eye on this front, it was best for their friendship, and their future, that they be able to do precisely what they were doing right now—safely return to the friend zone after a session in the lover's lane. So he did what he'd done before, even if it pained him to bring up an ex.

"Did Scott tend to that side of you?"

She shrugged, a defeated look in her eyes. "As much as I hate to admit it, he did. I mean, it's not like he's some paragon of how to be a good boyfriend, but he was attentive, and took me to dinner, and bought me flowers and gifts, and candy on Valentine's Day. So really, it was clearly the other side of me he didn't like. He didn't like me in the bedroom."

Nate's jaw clenched. The guy was such an ass. "That's not romantic," he muttered.

She propped herself on her elbow. "Oh yeah, Mr. Not Romantic? Tell me what's romantic then?"

"You think I'm not romantic just because I don't get serious?"

She scrunched up the corner of her lips. "Well, kind of."

He grabbed her hip, playfully pulling her closer. "I'll have you know, Miss Casey, that I am excellent at buying flowers. I can whip out my platinum card like that," he said, snapping his wrist and mimicking slapping down a plastic card. "I can also—wait for it—use that same card to buy gifts. In fact, I did," he said, gesturing to the box.

"I know, and I liked your gift. But you know what I mean."

"I can do candlelight dinners too. Let me tell you, the way I book a restaurant is inspired. Only to be topped by my ability to order champagne and have chocolate delivered on Valentine's Day. "

She held up her hands in defeat. "Fine, fine. You win. What is romantic to you then?"

"*Romantic*," he said, lingering on the word as he stopped to finger a strand of her hair, "is taking care of a woman. It's being attuned to her needs. It's listening to her. It's making her feel beautiful, inside and out, because she is. It's knowing her favorite dish, and picking it up on the way home. It's giving her your coat when she's cold, and holding open the door, and it's making sure she has everything she needs before a big meeting," he said, and a flicker of recognition flashed in her mountain lake blue eyes.

It was as if they existed in a bubble right now, a sealed cocoon where they were dancing perilously close to admissions they should never make. The moment fueled him, spurring him on. "It's knowing what matters to her, whether it's her collection of kisses, or the way she likes to be kissed."

She brought her fingers to her lips, as if recalling a kiss. He couldn't resist. "Sometimes, it's just kissing her because she needs to be kissed, and because you can't help yourself when it comes to her," Nate said and kissed her once more. A soft, slow kiss. An unhurried one, as he explored her lips with tender moves, tracing her mouth with the tip of his tongue, gently brushing his fingertips along her face. Their bodies drew near to each other inch by inch, as if an invisible thread knit them together. The kiss became a sensuous journey across her mouth and her lips and her tongue. It was her melting into his arms, and him melting with her. Because he kissed her with all he had and she kissed him back the same way, spreading her hand across his chest, and hooking her leg over his. It was a full body kiss, heady and intoxicating, and it pulled him under, like a wave. He barely wanted to come up for air.

Then he stopped and looked her in the eyes. "Is that okay?"

"Is what okay?" she asked, sounding dazed. Looking dazed too. He loved that kiss-drunk look she wore so well after he'd touched her.

"If I just kiss you like that? For no reason? Or is that crossing a line in our agreement?"

"Oh, right. Yes, our agreement," she said, smoothing her hands down her shirt, looking away from him. She seemed to be . . . rebooting. When she returned her gaze to him, she had on that business-like face.

"I think as long as we know that there are lines we'll be fine," she said, in a cool and measured voice.

"Absolutely. The lines are clear. Hell, if you want, I can keep my hands off unless we're practicing a lesson," he said, perhaps more gung-ho than he intended. But he couldn't stop. He needed the reminders too. He laid on the bravado reassurances that he was cool with it all. "It's not a problem. I can easily just take a step back when we're not in the middle of things."

"Don't you worry," she said with a cheerful smile. "I'm not going to get confused and think the sex, or the almost-sex, or the kissing for no reason, means anything more than it does. We're still friends, and these lessons aren't changing that," she said, so damn matter-of-factly that she could be teaching a course on nonchalance.

His chest tightened, and he tried to ignore the way those words gnawed at him. They shouldn't annoy him, because this was what he wanted. To stay friends with her, *and* to be the one to help her in her quest.

The friendship mattered too much to him to let this momentary irritation win.

That was why he stayed. That was why he ate sesame chicken and moo shu pancakes and broke fortune cookies with her, handing her his—*now is the time to try something new*—and saying, "I believe this one was meant for you." She gave him hers, as she said, "Then, this must be yours then. *Your fondest dreams will come true this year.*"

"I am going to open a hotel on the moon," he said in an awed voice, and she laughed, then danced her fingers across his chest.

"Here. Right here," she said, tapping his left pec. "I'm going to write that on your chest like a tattoo."

He raised an eyebrow. "That I'm opening a hotel on the moon?"

She shook her head. "No. That you're a good teacher of tricks."

"Trick teacher," he said, with a laugh. "Yeah, that'll be my first tattoo."

"I've always wanted to brand you," she said.

They were back to being friends. They were back to the zone where he'd always have her in his life. Because there, she could never break his heart. She could never hurt him. He could always be happy with what they had.

Besides, he was getting every man's dream. Sex, and no expectations of more.

Or *sex soon,* he should say.

As she gathered up their empty cartons, she tossed out a question. "Do you think Jack would care? If he knew what we're doing?"

"Eating Chinese?" he asked, raising an eyebrow.

"You know what I mean."

"I do know. And I don't know how it could matter to him, because we already agreed that nothing has changed, and that nothing is *going* to change."

She nodded several times, as if reassuring herself. "Right. Absolutely. Everything remains the same."

After he put on his shirt, tie and shoes, she walked him to the door.

"Thank you. For the lesson. I really enjoyed it."

"So did I," he said. "As you saw the evidence of on your chest."

She laughed, but then looked nervous as she fiddled with the neck on her shirt. "So," she began, clearing her throat. "When will I see you again? You know, for my next lesson."

"Such an eager little student."

"We're going to the Yankees this weekend, right? After you get back from Miami?"

He nodded. He was taking off tomorrow to visit his property on South Beach. "I got the good seats and Kat and Bryan arranged for a sitter so all four of us can go."

She pumped her fist in the air. "Yes! But we're not doing a seduction lesson at the ballpark with your sister and her husband."

"Obviously. So after that. The next day. Which territory should we conquer then?" He stroked his chin as if in deep thought. "I feel like that would be a good time to spank you."

Her eyes sparkled with desire. "I like spanking."

He lifted his hand and swatted her ass, and instantly he was erect. Then he grabbed her waist, pulling her close, and whispering in that rough, commanding tone she seemed to love, "If I stay here, I'm going to have to fuck you now."

She grabbed his collar. "*Stay.*"

A tremor of lust slammed into him, threatening to obliterate his self-restraint from earlier. But he remained steadfast. Instead, he left her with something he hoped she could take to bed and feed her fantasies.

Of him. Fantasies of only him.

He threaded his fingers through her hair, and said, "The next time I'm alone with you, I will be fucking you. That's a promise."

CHAPTER TEN

Cyberspace

from: commandonate@gmail.com
to: learnsnewtricksgirl@gmail.com
date: June 10, 8:07 PM
subject: Three Days in Miami

I might have melted. Remind me not to schedule a trip to South Beach in June.

from: learnsnewtricksgirl@gmail.com
to: commandonate@gmail.com
date: June 10, 8:14 PM
subject: Here's your reminder

Don't schedule a trip to South Beach in June. So, how are you beating the heat? Walking around town in your Speedo?

from: commandonate@gmail.com
to: learnsnewtricksgirl@gmail.com
date: June 10, 8:20 PM
subject: A Red One

Do you think that's why everyone in the lobby is giving me funny looks right now?

from: learnsnewtricksgirl@gmail.com
to: commandonate@gmail.com
date: June 10, 8:23 PM
subject: Try pink next time

Absolutely.

from: commandonate@gmail.com
to: learnsnewtricksgirl@gmail.com
date: June 10, 8:27 PM
subject: Benefits to Broiling

On the plus side, I can personally vouch that the air conditioning in The Luxe properties is top-notch. Chilled to arctic perfection.

from: learnsnewtricksgirl@gmail.com
to: commandonate@gmail.com
date: June 10, 8:31 PM
subject: Island Heat?

How are you going to survive Jack's wedding? Pretty sure it's hot in the Maldives in June, isn't it?

from: commandonate@gmail.com
to: learnsnewtricksgirl@gmail.com
date: June 10, 8:33 PM
subject: My classy clothing plans

You don't think he'll mind if I wear a Hawaiian shirt and cargo shorts during the ceremony?

from: learnsnewtricksgirl@gmail.com
to: learnsnewtricksgirl@gmail.com
date: June 10, 8:39 PM
subject: Another sartorial choice . . .

Go shirtless. I won't mind that.

from: commandonate@gmail.com
to: learnsnewtricksgirl@gmail.com
date: June 10, 8:42 PM
subject: Back 'atcha

I would say the same thing about you, but I can't stand the thought of anyone else seeing you naked. Save the naked for me, will ya?

from: learnsnewtricksgirl@gmail.com
to: commandonate@gmail.com
date: June 10, 8:49 PM
subject: Island Attire

I believe I can do that. By the way, want to see the dress I'll be wearing? I was sending Michelle a picture so I have it on.

from: commandonate@gmail.com
to: learnsnewtricksgirl@gmail.com
date: June 10, 8:50 PM
subject: Send Now

Yes.

from: learnsnewtricksgirl@gmail.com
to: commandonate@gmail.com
date: June 10, 8:52 PM
subject: Attachment

Here's me.

Nate slid his finger across the message, clicked on the attachment and waited as it downloaded. The image opened, revealing her legs first, then the rest of her filled the screen. His heart tripped when he saw the picture. She was standing by the open window of her apartment wearing a simple yellow dress. A gorgeous, summery dress that did amazing things for her breasts, and her legs, and her waist, and her hair, and her face. Hell, the whole image was female perfection. Her body was lush and inviting, her hair was soft and falling loosely around her shoulders, and she smiled that fresh, bright smile that lit up her beautiful face. He wished he were looking at her right now. Kissing her. Touching her. Telling her to turn around for him, then dropping to his knees, sliding his hands underneath the skirt and worshipping her body with his mouth.

from: commandonate@gmail.com
to: learnsnewtricksgirl@gmail.com
date: June 10, 8:56 PM
subject: Wow

In case you heard a clanging sound from the south, that was my jaw hitting the floor. You look spectacular.

from: learnsnewtricksgirl@gmail.com
to: commandonate@gmail.com
date: June 10, 8:59 PM
subject: Equal Opportunity

Send me a picture of you.

from: commandonate@gmail.com
to: learnsnewtricksgirl@gmail.com
date: June 10, 9:03 PM
subject: Now?

I'm just wearing a shirt and a tie. Nothing special. But I'm about to have a meeting with my COO about New Zealand. It would look weird for me to send a selfie.

from: learnsnewtricksgirl@gmail.com
to: commandonate@gmail.com
date: June 10, 9:04 PM
subject: Later then.

I'd hate for you to look . . . *weird* . . . *shudders.*

So send one before you go to bed.

from: commandonate@gmail.com
to: learnsnewtricksgirl@gmail.com
date: June 10, 9:07 PM
subject: Later it is.

I promise.

* * *

She waited an hour. Then another one. Sure, she had emails to answer, and product details to approve, and plans from Nelle to review. Through that all, she kept checking her phone as she worked in bed on a hot Friday night with the windows open. She twisted her hair on top of her head and stabbed a pen through it to get it off her neck. Why did she even want Nate to send her a picture? Hell, she knew what he looked like. She didn't need a photo before she fell asleep.

But he'd said he'd send one, and he was a man of his word. Now it was eleven. Okay fine, a meeting could last long. Very long. So long in fact that when she finally fell asleep after midnight he must still have been with his COO, and maybe even at two a.m. too when she woke up in the middle of the night to pee. Because there was no picture.

When she returned to bed, she checked once more. Still nothing.

Maybe he wasn't meeting with his COO. Or maybe he had met with him, and they'd gone to a club, and danced with some women, and one of those women was all over Nate, her long nails trailing along his strong arms, her hair falling against his chest, and her breasts in his hands.

She burned inside at the pictures that flashed before her eyes, but the reel wouldn't stop. It ran faster, and un-spooled more scenes as she saw him pushing the elevator button, stepping into it with a beautiful brunette, pressing her up against the wall, and kissing the stranger the way he'd kissed her. Squeezing her eyes shut, she tried to block out the foul images, but they didn't end until she was see-ing him in a dark and sexy room, stripping off his belt, un-doing his shirt, and fucking this nameless, faceless woman who was surely with him tonight.

Finally, she fell back asleep, the pit in her stomach eat-ing away at her.

When she woke up to the sun streaming through her window, she found a new message. From Grant Abbott.

It was a beautiful day in Hong Kong. It was made even lovelier by the executed copies of our partnership. Little pleases me more than a well-done deal. (Well, perhaps a FEW things do please me more.) In any case, I've said it before, I'll say it again—I am delighted to be in business with you. This partnership will be fantastic for both our companies.

My best,
Grant

She breathed deeply as she pulled on workout clothes. It was a good thing that Grant had written to her. It was the necessary reminder of why she was spending more time than usual with Nate. So she could have a better chance of becoming the woman that the Grant Abbotts and Scott Nixons of the world would want. A woman who'd learned to rein in her *controlling* tendencies, her *alpha* female-ness.

Fine, even if Grant wasn't writing to her about *her*, who cared? Either way, she was a woman on a mission. She was in hot pursuit of the big love, and the only way to get there would be to excise the parts of herself that had held her back from truly having it all. That was what Nate was helping her with.

Only that.

She contemplated heading to her gym for a swim. She'd been on the swim team in high school and still loved the water. But right now, she craved speed. Riding a bike in

New York City required a determined sort of focus that would help clear her head. Heading to the basement of her building, she retrieved her wheels from the bike storage area, strapped on a helmet, and attacked the West Side Highway Bike Path, burning off the final remains of the waste of energy she'd let consume her last night. Jealousy was such a stupid, worthless emotion and there was no need for her to be envious whatsoever of Nate's after-hours activities. She had no claim to him, and besides, he knew the score. He was merely training her to hand her off to someone else.

For a new start.

And a new start called for a new dress. Whether for Grant, or the next man who was suited for her.

After her workout, she'd go shopping. That would pass the time until the baseball game. She'd see Nate tonight, and she'd smile, having forgotten completely about the fact that he'd promised a photo. What photo? Who cared? Not her.

* * *

The emerald-green dress hugged her in all the right places, and her friend Jane agreed.

"That is a rocking dress," Jane said, nodding appreciatively as Casey stepped out of the dressing room of the boutique on Christopher Street. "It's sexy, but it's not over the top."

"So I should get it? Is it first date material? Would you wear it if you were on a first date again with Matthew?"

Jane laughed, practically doubling over, then shook her head, her wild curly brown hair framing her face.

"Then why are you telling me to get it?" Casey asked, parking her hands on her hips.

"That's not what I'm laughing at. I'm laughing because it's been more than three years since I had a first date with Matthew, and we didn't even technically date. We went from him interviewing me for a story about my music to sleeping together," her friend said. Jane was a rock star. Literally. She'd won a Grammy three years ago for a hit album, and had continued churning out top-notch, and top-selling tunes.

"You're no help then," Casey said, teasing, as she checked out her reflection in the store's mirror. The dress hit her above the knees, and had a soft flare to the skirt. It was suggestive, but not inappropriate, and that's what she liked about it.

"Just ask your BGF," Jane offered.

Casey shot her a curious look. "Gay Best Friend?"

"No. That would be GBF. I mean BGF." Jane snapped a few times, like she was trying to recall something. "You know, that guy Nate. Your *Best Guy Friend*."

Casey felt a flush spread through her cheeks when Jane said his name. She didn't know if it was due to the heat, or the secret almost-sex, or the fact that she still hadn't heard from him. Odd, since they were supposed to be going to the ballpark in eight hours.

"Send him a pic and ask his opinion if you don't believe me."

She waved her hand to shut down that idea. "No. I don't want to send him a picture," she said.

"Why not? Isn't that the point of a best guy friend?"

Jane was right. It was the point, or one of the points, but it was also what Casey *should* be doing instead of wondering why he hadn't called or sent a picture. *Normal.* She had to keep things normal with Nate.

Casey handed her phone to Jane. "Take a picture of me."

She struck a pose—a simple, friendly pose—and texted it to Nate.

Should I wear this on a date with Grant? Yes or no?

Then, because this is what she would have done if she weren't sleeping with him, she called him.

He sounded pissed when he answered.

CHAPTER ELEVEN

Washington D.C, Morning…

from: Joannasimone@gmail.com
to: nHarper@theluxe.com
date: June 11, 6:04 AM
subject: Trying to reach you

Dear Nate,

I hope this note finds you well. I'm thrilled that everything seems to be going swimmingly at The Luxe. It makes me so happy to see you thriving in your career, but then I always knew that you would do great things. I tried to call you earlier this week but I haven't heard back, so I'm emailing you at your work address. I hope you don't mind. But there is something important that I need to discuss with you. I would greatly appreciate it if you could give me a ring. I'll try you again soon.

All my best,
Joanna

CHAPTER TWELVE

Washington D.C, afternoon . . .

Nothing had gone as planned for Nate. Not a damn thing. The meeting with his COO in Miami had been quickly derailed when Tom came bearing bad news about the New Zealand hotel manager they'd hired to open the new property in a few months. The guy had flown the coop already, after a competitor in Auckland had wooed him.

Nate and Tom quickly devised a new plan, and jetted to the nation's capital in the middle of the night. The D.C. property manager was their top guy, but his second-in-command was sharp as nails too, so could step in immediately. Nate and Tom had spent Saturday morning convincing the property manager to move halfway across the world to open up the New Zealand hotel. The man was a D.C. native, had only worked at properties in the nation's capital, and he loved his hometown. He drove a hard bargain too, and was asking for a hefty raise for the new international post. But by midday, he was leaning towards yes.

It was a yes Nate desperately sought, since he needed the New Zealand opening to go smoothly.

Nate planned to take him to dinner and then crash in D.C. for the night. Hell, he needed some shut-eye. He hadn't slept last night. Add in Joanna's note to the mix, and it was one of those days where everything was piling on. He had no clue what Joanna could possibly want to talk to him about, and very little interest in knowing either. What sucked the most about this upended Saturday was that he was missing the game tonight. He'd texted Casey earlier that he wouldn't be able to join her, but he hadn't heard back from her yet.

When he checked his phone once more for a reply, he cursed. He must have sent her the text when he was in a dead spot in the lobby. It hadn't gone through. Fucking D.C. hotel had far too many dead zones. This was one more thing he needed to add to the ever-spiraling to-do list. Improve the cell phone service at his hotel that served the nation's political elite. He shoved his hand roughly through his hair, and blew out a long stream of air as he leaned back in the leather chair in the office he was using at The Luxe.

He started to dial Casey's number to tell her he had to cancel, when his phone rang.

He was tempted to ignore Ethan, but decided to err on the side of being a good friend. He slipped his Bluetooth over his ear and answered.

"Hey, what's up?"

"Oh, not too much," Ethan said with a hearty and deliberately drawn-out yawn. "Just tired still from another late night with a pretty bartender."

Nate smiled. This was the first bit of good news he'd had all day. "Excellent. Now I can say I told you so."

"I owe you, man. Thanks for giving me the push to talk to her."

"Couldn't be happier for you."

"I'm seeing her again tonight," he added as a new text message flashed across Nate's screen. He sat up straight. His pulse raced when he saw the text had a paperclip icon on it. Casey had sent him a photo. He tapped quickly on the paperclip to open it.

"I'm going to have to advertise my matchmaking services soon."

"Or your kick-a-man-in-the-ass-to-get-him-moving services," Ethan said as the picture filled Nate's screen.

"Yeah, that too," he said, and that quickening pulse went into overdrive when he saw the image. The gorgeous, stunning image of the woman he wanted desperately to see tonight.

But there was one big problem.

One *huge* problem, as a matter of fact.

The note that came with the picture.

His fists clenched as he read it. His jaw tightened. No way was she wearing that dress for Grant. No way was she wearing that dress for any other man.

Seconds later, her name popped up on the screen—incoming call.

"Hey, Ethan. I gotta go. I have Casey on the other line."

"Joy Delivered Casey?" Ethan asked.

"Yeah, that's her," he said, eager to end the call.

"You doing business with her? I emailed her a few days ago."

Business. Yes, he had business with her. He absolutely had business with her. "You could say that," he said, and then hung up.

He clicked over to Casey.

"I don't like that dress," he said through gritted teeth. Those were his first words.

"You don't?" she asked, surprise in her voice.

"No. I don't like it at all."

"Oh. I thought it was pretty." Now she sounded crestfallen. Shit. He hated upsetting her, but not as much as he loathed the idea of her looking that edible with another man. He grabbed a sheet of paper on his desk, crumpled it up and threw it across the room.

"Sorry. But I don't think it's a first date dress."

"Okay," she said, measured and cautious, like she was distancing herself from him. "Why do you sound so angry?"

"I'm not angry," he said, but he could hear the lie in the bitterness of his tone.

"But you sound angry," she said softly. Traffic hummed behind her. She was probably out shopping in the Village, having fun, and he was ruining it for her. But that dress . . . *fuck*. He couldn't take it. He dropped his forehead into his hand. "And you didn't send me a picture last night either," she added.

He sighed heavily. Everything had gone to hell, and on top of it all, Joanna had reared her head. "I'm sorry. I had a ton of fires to put out. I had to fly to D.C. in the middle of the night," he said, but he stopped there. He didn't feel like breathing his ex's name. "And I tried to send you a text to tell you I can't make the game tonight. I have to take my property manager out to dinner to make sure he can take over the New Zealand hotel."

"Oh," she said, but she didn't sound so distant now. Just disappointed. Hell, he was disappointed too. Then she seemed to pull out of her frustrations, because her next words were sweet. "Well, I totally understand. I'm sorry you have to deal with all of that, but I know that's just how it goes."

"It's been crazy. I've barely come up for air. I'm going to call my sister and let her know I can't make the game."

"Well, I better go. I think I'm just going to get the dress anyway. I like it," she said. "But I do appreciate your input."

* * *

Five hours later, he couldn't get Casey out of his mind. As he and Tom finished up a round of celebratory drinks with the manager, who'd agreed to the last-minute transfer since they'd agreed to his terms, he couldn't stop thinking about how Casey had sounded annoyed, then sad, then let down, then deliberately upbeat again. He tried his best to focus on the men at the table with him in the corner booth at one of the nation's capital's finest watering holes.

But that dress was taunting him. It was an image he couldn't shake. It was his sole focus.

And as they polished off a second round, he couldn't take it anymore. He scrubbed a hand across his unshaven jaw. Hell, this was why he was the CEO. He oversaw the whole company. He hired the right people, trusted the right people, and gave them authority to do their jobs.

He'd done his part in convincing his guy to head to the southern hemisphere. Tom could handle the rest.

He had to see Casey. He had a lesson to teach her.

CHAPTER THIRTEEN

New York, evening . . .

As 50,000 fans erupted in cheers, Bryan's phone rang. The shortstop had just whacked a three-run home run to put the Yankees ahead in the bottom of the eighth. Bryan was ecstatic; he hadn't been to Yankee Stadium in nearly a year. He couldn't complain about his prolonged absence as a spectator—he had his two beautiful daughters to thank for keeping him from sporting events, and he wouldn't trade them for the world. But being here tonight with his wife while his team was winning was an absolute high.

"Man, you don't even want to know what you're missing," he said to Nate as he answered the call.

"I know. Just got an update on my ESPN app."

"It was a thing of beauty," Bryan said and then recounted every detail of the home run as if he were a play-by-play sports announcer.

"That's awesome," Nate said, but hardly seemed interested in the game. He cleared his throat. "Hey, Bryan. Remember that time nine or ten years ago when you stayed at my house for two weeks the summer after business school, and fell in love with my sister and didn't tell me about it?"

Bryan furrowed his brow. Of course he remembered falling in love with Kat. But he couldn't fathom why Nate would bring it up now. "Yeah. Of course I do."

"Good. I hate to dig up the past, but I hope the fact that I was never an ass about you dating my sister behind my back will make this hurt less."

"Okay," Bryan said, nervously looking around the luxury suite. Both Casey and Kat glanced up from their seats by the window. His wife's curious expression seemed to say *who are you talking to and why on earth are you taking a phone call in the middle of us celebrating a home run*? He moved away from them, walking up the three steps to the back of the enclosed suite. "What's going on, man?"

"I need you to leave," Nate said bluntly.

"Shit." Bryan's shoulders sagged. "You can't be serious?"

"'Fraid so. I'm sorry, but I'm also not sorry. I hope you understand. Tell my sister I'll make it up to her and I'll babysit next time. I'll be there in five minutes. You and Kat will need to go then."

Bryan ended the call and shook his head. Damn. His wife was going to be pissed. She'd been looking forward to this night out for some time.

True to his promise, five minutes later Nate opened the door to the private suite. Three pairs of eyes landed on him but he only looked at one person.

* * *

Casey stood, her heartbeat speeding to NASCAR levels, her skin heating up.

He was the last person she'd expected to see. He was supposed to be in D.C. for the night.

His eyes raked over her. He had that hungry look in them—the look that melted her in seconds. She wore a blue tank top with the Yankees logo on the front, a short jean skirt, and blue Converse sneakers. She never wore sandals to Yankee Stadium; too many people, too many pairs of feet that could step on her toes.

Bryan was whispering to Kat, whose eyes widened as she glanced from Nate to Casey. Then she quickly gathered her purse, hugged Casey and simply said, "See you later."

If Casey had been processing what was happening she probably would've asked "Why? Where are you going? What's going on?"

But she wasn't processing anything except the way she felt. For the last several hours, she'd swallowed the disappointment from the night before. Because when he'd told her about his day turned upside down she'd felt so bad that she'd doubted him.

She simply hoped that he wasn't still mad at her.

As soon as Bryan and Kat left, Nate shut the door, then locked it. She glanced quickly behind her at the window that provided a view of the sea of rabid fans. The stadium shook with excitement. Cheers from the crowd vibrated throughout the house of Ruth. Nate stalked down the three steps separating them. When he reached her, a vein twitched in his neck. His mouth was a ruler-straight line. His jaw was set hard. His stare undressed her.

"I was wrong," he said. Each word possessed a hard edge.

"Wrong about what?" Was he talking about the dress? Or about wanting to be her teacher? God, she prayed he wasn't backing out.

"I was wrong about tonight's lesson. It's not spanking."

"What is it?"

"It's role-playing." His voice was hot and rough. His dark eyes prowled over her body.

"What kind of role playing?" She didn't even bother to hide her nerves, but the nerves also excited her. Or maybe he was simply the one who excited her. It seemed whatever he did turned her on. The fact that he was standing here, a solid mass of muscle and strength, of extreme and utter sexiness, sent shivers across her skin. She drank him in: the wavy mess of his golden brown hair, the stubble lining his jaw, the exposed patch of skin on his chest where the top two buttons of his white shirt were undone. All of it, all of him, made her tremble with want.

He took one step closer, and reflexively she backed up so her spine hit the wall behind her. She was caged in, and against her better judgment, she liked it. She liked the fact that it was starkly quiet inside the suite, and that it was intensely noisy outside, a white noise that masked all that she was feeling.

"I'm going to be playing the role of the jealous lover," he said, his voice still laced with the same frustration she'd picked up on earlier. Was he annoyed with her?

"What do you mean?"

"I'm the jealous lover who can't stand the thought of his woman wearing a gorgeous, stunning, absolutely fucking breathtaking dress on a date with another man."

A wild thrill rushed through her veins from his words and what they meant. "But I thought you didn't like the dress?" she asked, coyly, playing along.

He lifted his hand and brushed the tips of his fingers against her wrist. She shuddered from that one subtle touch. Her body begged for more, and she was almost ashamed at how much desire flowed through her bloodstream right now. She hadn't been completely aware of how very much she had wanted to see him tonight, of how truly disappointed she had been for the first eight innings that he wasn't here by her side. Now that he was here, she wasn't sure how she'd survived the game without him.

He brushed his fingers along her arm, across the crook of her elbow, and up to her shoulder. Goosebumps rose in his wake.

"I don't like the dress if you wear it for another man," he said, keeping his eyes locked on hers the whole time. "And sometimes that means I'm going to act like a dick and tell you I don't like the dress at all." He brought his hands to her hair and she wanted to cry out because it felt so fucking good to be touched by him like this, with hands that were both tender and completely possessive. He speared his fingers into her hair. "But what I really don't like is the idea that another man might look at you in it, and want to touch you the way I touch you."

He leaned into her neck, and pressed his lips against her skin. There was nothing gentle in the kiss. His lips were hot and angry, and she felt his teeth nip her skin. A sting of pain raced through her, but it was a good pain, a pain that made her long for more.

"I didn't mean to make you so jealous," she said, playing along, sounding contrite, sliding into the roles they'd assumed. She raised her hand to his chest, and trailed it up to the top buttons that were undone. His breath caught in his throat as she spread her fingers over his warm skin.

He looked her in the eyes. His seemed to be on fire. "It made me crazy. Absolutely fucking insane. Sometimes a man is wildly jealous when he thinks other men are looking at his woman." He dropped his hand to her waist, gripping her hip, and digging his fingers into her bones. "*His* woman," he repeated.

She nodded. "His," she said, like she was in a trance.

"And sometimes a man has to touch her, and mark her," he said, returning to her neck to trace the faint imprint of his teeth, "to make it clear she belongs to him, and to remind her that he's the only one allowed to touch her."

His words were heady. They hypnotized her. She was so used to handling everything, to devising the plans, giving the sign-off, managing and making all the final decisions. Here, with him, she didn't have to think. She only *had to feel.*

He cupped her face, grasping her. "I can't stand the thought of anyone else touching you," he said, his gaze pinned on hers, his warm breath painting her skin.

She swallowed dryly, tried to speak, but could only manage a few words. "I can't either."

She wasn't sure if they were playing roles. If he was talking as himself, as the jealous lover, or as someone else. And honestly, she didn't care.

She ached.

All over.

She ached for him everywhere. Her lips longed to be kissed. Her hair craved to have his fingers threaded through it. Her skin begged for contact. Her body needed to be filled. The desire for him was profound. It dug trenches all throughout her mind and heart.

"And I want to remind you that you're mine. That's why I came back for you," he said, his hands tighter now on her face. He could have squeezed her, could have hurt her, but he didn't. She was safe with him. Always.

"I wanted you to come back," she whispered, her chin tipped up as she kept her eyes on him. She couldn't look away. The spell he'd woven was too strong.

"I couldn't take it. I can't have you send me pictures of clothes you're going to wear for someone else."

She shook her head. "I won't. I won't wear it for anyone else. I'll wear it for you."

"Wear it for me," he said, and inched his face closer. God, he needed to kiss her soon. He needed to touch her. She was about to go up in flames.

"Do you remember what I told you I'd do the next time I saw you?"

She nodded as a rush of sparks tore through her body, making her hot and damp between her legs. Her underwear was fast becoming useless.

"Yes."

He dragged a finger along her jawline, and she hitched in a breath. "You said," she began, but words were so hard right now, especially as his fingers reached the hollow of her throat and he lowered his head, kissing her there next.

Her eyes floated closed. She was comprised of nothing but raw feelings; she was reduced to only red-hot want and pulsing need for him. For this man.

"What did I say?"

"You said you'd be fucking me," she whispered on a moan, vaguely aware that the inning was ending, that the noise in the stadium signaled a fresh round of cheers.

He brought his hand to her chin, lifted it up, forcing her to open her eyes and look at him. "Do you think I'm a man of my word?"

She nodded, breathless.

"I am," he said, staring at her with hunger and unabashed lust. "Now, do you want me to keep my promise?"

"I do," she said instantly, her voice breathy. "I swear I do. I swear I need you right now."

"I need you so much, and I'm completely sorry I didn't send you a picture last night. I hope you can let me show you how sorry I am," he said, taking her hand and guiding her to one of the leather chairs that overlooked the glass windows in the skybox. It was the top of the ninth now. The other team was at bat. Nate sank down into the chair, unzipped his pants, and slid them down to his knees. His beautifully erect cock greeted her, snapping to attention against his flat stomach. Her mouth watered as she stared at him. She couldn't stop looking. He was so fucking beautiful.

"Come here," he whispered, as he held out his hands for her. She was about to straddle him, when he stopped her to dip his thumbs into her panties and skim them down her legs. She helped him when she reached her sneakers, tugging them over her Converses and tucking them into the back pocket of her jean skirt. She was thinking ahead to when she'd need them again as they walked out of here. She stopped thinking ahead when he dipped a hand into his pocket and produced a condom.

Perhaps the condom was the line in the sand. Perhaps it was the symbol of the before and after. Or perhaps it was simply the means to the end. That end was something she desperately wanted. She straddled him, her legs on either side of his strong thighs as he rolled it on his hard, steely length. He brought a hand through her hair, lacing his fingers into her blond strands, then whispering, "Come closer, Casey."

She reached for him, rubbing the head of his dick against her slick flesh. The feel of him was astonishing. The wild thrill that charged through her body from the very first touch of him, of his hardness against her heat, was a mere sign of what was to come.

"All the way now."

She moaned as she lowered herself onto him. Her natural reaction was to close her eyes because the pleasure was so intense. But she fought the instinct, because she wanted to watch him and witness the look in his eyes change from hunger to passion.

She swore she saw something else there too. Something deeper, a longing for more. Something she was afraid to name. But something that touched her heart, and made her want to be closer. Even closer.

She settled on to him, savoring the feel of him all the way inside her. With his hands on her hips, he began moving. Slowly, taking his time, he guided her up and down his shaft. She shuddered all over as pleasure ignited in her, like the start of bright fireworks that only grow more brilliant until they lit up the sky. Hot tingles raced across her skin. She roped her hands around his neck, then up into his hair. He leaned his head back against her hands, groaning deeply as if he savored her every touch. His fingers dug into her hips as he thrust into her, penetrating her to her very depths. Here at Yankee Stadium, in front of 50,000 people, who didn't have a clue what was happening in one of the luxury suites, she took him and he took her.

They took each other. Because nothing about their connection felt like role-playing, or a game, or submission.

Control was not given or taken. There were no power plays. There was only him holding tightly to her hips, drawing her up on his long, hard cock, then lowering her back down and filling her completely, touching her so far inside that she knew it wouldn't take her long.

There was only her, loving every second of the way he felt.

Right now, the only roles they were "playing" were of lovers, coming together for the first time. The only thing that existed between them was a deep and dark desire to be consumed by each other.

As he grasped her harder, moving faster, he dipped his head to her neck, kissing her. He was always kissing her. He mapped a path to her ear and whispered, "Tell me, Casey. Tell me who your jealous lover is."

"You are, Nate," she said in between breaths, as the ripples of pleasure slammed into her and she cried out, squeezing her eyes shut because the feelings were too intense to take.

"Tell me who's about to make you come," he growled into her ear.

"You are," she said as he drove into her, his cock filling her to the hilt.

"Do you have any idea how much I wanted to be with you today?" he said, and his voice was stripped bare. She looked into his eyes, and he was gazing at her as if she was a marvel to him.

She shook her head. "How much?"

"You were all I thought of," he said, his breathing wildly erratic. He was narrowing in on the apex of pleasure too. Watching him near the edge flipped a switch in her body. She went from grasping for the sweet release there in the distance to feeling the start of it, deep inside her, in her belly, in her bones, in all the distant corners of her body and far into her mind. He was taking her there and there was no turning back from this intensity. She dropped her mouth to his lips and kissed him relentlessly as she rode him to the edge of pleasure.

"Say my name," he commanded, breaking the kiss, his voice rough and needy and so damn hungry for her.

"*Nate*," she moaned, as he gripped her hips.

"Say it again. Say my name as you come. Tell me who's fucking you."

"You are, Nate. You are. You're fucking me. You're touching me. You're making me feel this way. *You*," she said, grasping his shoulders to hold onto as she rocked wildly against his cock, as wave after endless wave rocketed through her, electric desire sweeping across every cell in her body and bathing her brain in endless bliss. He chased her there, thrusting powerfully once more into her, his hands digging into her hair, gripping her head as he groaned and grunted, and then called out her name as he came.

Minutes later she was still wrapped around him, not wanting to let go, when she became aware of the white noise of cheers and claps from behind the glass. She tensed for a moment, thinking, even though it was crazy, that everyone at the ballpark was aware of what they had done. But when she craned her neck and looked out the window she simply saw that the game had ended and the Yankees had won. She turned back to Nate and the look in his eyes was one she hadn't seen before.

She couldn't pinpoint what that emotion was exactly. But it matched the way he'd looked at her earlier, when she'd first sunk down on him. She feathered her hand against his chest, wishing she could capture that emotion, study it, and know what to do with it.

"Hi," she whispered.

"Hi."

"I'm glad you came back."

"Me too. How was it?" he asked, gesturing from him to her.

"Are you really asking me?" She tilted her head to the side. "Wasn't it obvious?"

He nodded and smiled broadly, a big satisfied grin on his gorgeous face. "It was obvious. I still want to hear it from you."

She dropped a quick kiss on his lips. "It was amazing. You're going to ruin me for anyone else."

"Good."

"No! It's terrible," she said jokingly. But she wasn't entirely joking when she added, softly, "No one will compare to you."

"Again, that is good."

She laced her fingers through his hair, watching him as relaxed into the softness of her touch, and the sweet unwinding from the intensity of their coming together. "You were really good with the whole jealous lover act," she said.

He raised an eyebrow. "I was?"

She nodded. "Yeah, I believed it."

"You did?" He furrowed his brow at first, then understanding dawned and he slowly nodded.

"You seemed so jealous," she said, trying her best to make it self-evident in her tone that they were talking around the truth without having to fully admit anything. She hoped he understood all that she meant.

"What if I really was that jealous?"

"I like that too. I liked that you felt that way."

"You do?"

"Yeah. I felt that way too. Last night I was convinced you were in a club in Miami and some beautiful woman was all over you."

He laughed and threw his head back. "Nope. Nope. And nope. But I love that you hated the image."

"I hated it so much," she said like a hiss.

"Maybe then," he said slowly, and seemed to be taking his time forming an idea.

"Maybe what?"

"Maybe it can be just us for now?"

"It better be just us," she said pointedly and swatted his arm.

He pretended it hurt. "Ouch."

"I mean it. I don't want you with anyone else while we're doing this. I suppose we should have set the ground rules already, but this is all new to me. There's no way I'd sleep with anyone else. And you better not either."

"I'm not. I wouldn't. I swear."

She held up her hand, her palm facing him. "Swear."

He clasped her hand, threading his fingers through hers. "I swear, Casey, you're the only one."

CHAPTER FOURTEEN

New York, night . . .

As they rode home from the ballpark in his town car, she softly ran her fingers through his hair over and over, as if she regularly stroked his hair as they talked in the back of the cushy car. He loved every second of the contact from her, and especially loved that she felt comfortable enough to do it without thinking twice.

Whether she was touching him as friends or as lovers didn't matter. He didn't have the brain cells working at full-speed to decipher it. They'd all been put to pasture for the night in the wake of finally coming together with her.

As they rolled through Manhattan, the neon lights of Broadway guiding them on their way downtown, he said, "So, um, how was the game?"

She laughed. "The good guys won. And the crowd went wild."

"Too bad I missed it," he joked.

"I'd say you made it just in time for an epic finale. You're like a closer."

He laughed. "I'll happily play that position."

"Hey," she said, as she now trailed her fingertip along his neck. He raised his eyes to look at her. "I told you I'm going to London soon, right? To meet with Sofia's, one of our retailer partners. "

"You mentioned it. You're going to an auction too."

Her eyes lit up, sparkling like a starry sky. "Good memory," she said.

"To buy a kiss. From Miller Valentina," he added, hoping to impress her with the real estate he'd reserved in his brain for remembering details of her.

"Now, you're just showing off," she said playfully. "So I was wondering—is there any chance you have a hotel in London?" There was a look of mischief now in her eyes.

He laughed. "You know I do. You angling for a free room, Miss Casey?"

"Maybe," she said, taking her time with that word, lingering on it suggestively. "But I was also thinking a roommate might be nice. Do you happen to have any business in London you need to do?"

His heart sped up. "Are you inviting yourself to my hotel?"

She nodded. "I am inviting myself. I told you I was known for being direct. It bothers some men. But right now, I don't care. I'm going to be direct and say what I want."

He held up a hand like a stop sign. "I told you I'm not most men. I like your direct side and I like your . . . how shall we say, newly submissive one too."

She flashed him a sweet, innocent smile that nailed him in the heart. He ran his finger across her lips, watching her draw a quick breath.

"What would you think about going with me? Because now that I've had you, I want more of you, and we still have a lot of ground to cover. You haven't tied me up yet or spanked me for that matter," she said, counting off his omissions on her fingers. "Or used handcuffs."

"Damn," he said, with a low whistle. "I'm falling down on the job."

"I'll let you make it up to me across the pond."

"Though, let the record reflect, I have not engaged in any orgasm denial either. Per your request."

"And I thank you very much for that."

"Do you want me to have a spreader bar specially installed in one of the rooms for your trip?" he asked in as matter-of-fact a tone as he could muster.

Her eyes widened in shock and she shook her head vigorously. "No," she said, forming an *O* with her lips to emphasize her complete lack of interest in that particular BDSM activity. Then she raised her fingers to his face, tracing a line down his jaw. "You're very sexy when you don't shave," she whispered, and heat pulsed in his veins from the out-of-the-blue, unexpected compliment. It gave him hope that this thing between them was more than simply a means to an end for her.

But then, he shouldn't feel any sort of hope. Hope was risky, and led to things he didn't believe in. He didn't possess any hope himself, so it made no sense why he'd want her to think in bigger terms that went beyond the here and now.

"Thank you," he said, trying to ignore the way his heart beat more furiously as she continued to trace soft lines along his jaw.

"And Nate?"

"Yes?"

"Because you don't mind it when I speak my mind, I want you to know that I'm really enjoying our lessons. In and of themselves. Sometimes, I don't think about where they might lead. Actually, most of the time I don't think about where they'll lead. I just think about how amazing it all feels with you," she said, finishing her sweet ode with an even sweeter kiss on his lips that sent his heart racing and his mind galloping. This was supposed to be neat and clean, a tidy little deal that was mutually beneficial below the belt for the both of them.

But now, it had become something that turned those clear-cut lines into a wild chaos of zigs and zags. He couldn't sort any of this out. All he knew with any kind of certainty was that he was going to London with her in a week, and somehow his goal had changed. When she'd first proposed their unconventional arrangement, he gave a yes borne from years of lust and desire for her.

Now he was saying yes for other reasons. Reasons that weren't entirely clear in his head—reasons that came from a different place inside him.

A place he tried hard to deny even existed.

* * *

Nate had once thought that his job was pretty damn exhausting, but running a multinational hotel conglomerate was nothing compared to entertaining two newly walking, hardly talking, very busy one-year-old twin girls. Thank the Lord, Casey had handled the diaper changes. The woman needed a medal for that. The rest of the time though, they had been a team, and hell, did his nieces require a team.

After their evening bath, which resulted in his T-shirt becoming completely soaked when they splashed virtually the entire contents of the tub onto him, Casey and Nate dressed the girls in their pajamas.

"So let me get this straight. You yanked Bryan out of the luxury suite and that's why we're babysitting your nieces a few hours on a Sunday night before we fly to London?" Casey asked him for probably the twentieth time as she nudged him with an elbow.

"Hey, I had very important business to attend to at Yankee Stadium and I don't regret it whatsoever."

"Nor do I," she said with a wink as she tugged a short-sleeved shirt on Cara. "And I certainly don't regret spending time with these adorable little chunks of love," she said, cooing at the baby.

He froze momentarily. Her eyes nearly popped out when she saw his expression.

"Oh my God, did you just prematurely freak out about the prospect of a woman wanting children?" she said calling him out on the deer-in-headlights stare he must have been sporting.

He held Chloe tighter. "I love my nieces. That's all I'm going to say. And thank you again for helping me out here."

"There's no way I would let you do this on your own. I'm just as responsible as you are, and I also feel horribly guilty that you took them out of the stadium. Though, not *too* guilty," she said with a laugh, as they made their way to the girls' bedroom and tucked them into their cribs for the night.

But twenty minutes later, Chloe and Cara were crying up a storm, and neither Nate nor Casey had a very good idea of how to handle them. They had fed, bathed, and played with them, so the only recourse was to hold them. They retreated to the living room, each with a baby in their arms.

Nate made a pit stop in the kitchen, grabbing a carton of salted caramel gelato from the freezer and two small spoons. He joined Casey on the couch.

She held a finger to her lips. "Shhh . . ." She gestured with her eyes to Chloe, who was sound asleep already on her chest. Casey whispered, "Looks like she just wanted to be snuggled."

"Let's hope I can work the same magic on Cara," Nate said, gently patting her on the back. After a minute, Cara settled in, letting out a soft exhale as she rested her head against his wet T-shirt.

"Do you want me to get one of Bryan's T-shirts for you?" Casey asked him.

He shook his head. "Guys don't borrow other guys' T-shirts. Especially not guys who are married to their sisters. The only guy who I would ever borrow a shirt from would be my brother. And I don't have a brother, so as you can see, I'm never going to borrow another man's T-shirt."

"On the other hand, I do not have this issue whatsoever. I would happily go take one of Kat's T-shirts right now if I needed it, no questions asked, and I guarantee she wouldn't have a problem with it."

"Another beautiful difference between men and women. Anyway, I'll grab a new one at home before we head to the airport. I need to swing by my house anyway. I forgot to bring my suitcase." Nate popped open the top of the ice cream container and dug in. He brought the spoon to his mouth and was about to take a bite when he stopped and handed a utensil to Casey. "Ladies first."

She took a spoonful of the ice cream then she froze, holding the spoon in midair. "I just had an idea," she said, unfreezing as she snapped her head to look at him, her eyes practically glittering with excitement.

"No, Casey," he chided. "We are not going to do it on my sister's kitchen counter. You're insatiable, woman."

Admittedly there was a bit of truth to that. They'd been together a few times since the ballpark, but then they'd had to take a break mid-week when he travelled to Vegas where he met with Brent Nichols, a wildly successful late-night comedian who was also prepping to open a new nightclub in the city of sin. The club was on the outskirts of town, and Nate had been talking to him about the prospect of relocating it inside The Luxe on the Strip. That trip had cut into his time with Casey, but in the few nights he'd seen her before, they'd made the most of the shortened hours, and she'd passed his spanking course with flying colors. She'd also discovered that she was particularly fond of having her hair pulled when he took her from behind, with her bent over the bathroom sink. He'd told her to look in the mirror as he gripped her hair tight in his fist. My God, the sight of her wild abandon reflected back at him was branded on his brain forever. In fact, the image had proven quite useful one late night alone in Las Vegas when he'd taken matters into his own hands.

"No. That's not what I mean," she said, talking quickly. He recognized the tone instantly—she had entered the idea zone. "I was just thinking back to the night in New Orleans, when we shared the cake."

"The night it all began," he said, wiggling his eyebrows as she finally ate the ice cream on the spoon she was holding, then set the spoon on the table.

"No, seriously. What was I doing beforehand?"

"Do we really need to go there?" he muttered, as he took a bite. "Grant, obviously." He didn't want to admit that there was a Grant. In his world, Grant had ceased to exist. It seemed that way for her too. She hadn't brought him up once in the last week. She hadn't brought up anyone else, come to think of it. She had barely breathed the word *lessons*.

"I meant, why I was even meeting with Grant in the first place? A partnership," she said, answering her own question.

"The deal for the LolaRing. You practiced the pitch in the car, and that toy sounded pretty fucking awesome if you ask me," he said, covering Cara's ears, even though the baby was sound asleep.

"Yeah, it *is* pretty awesome," she said. "And why should Joy Delivered limit itself to only striking partnerships with lingerie companies and retail boutiques?"

He arched an eyebrow. "Go on."

She sat up straighter, her arms still wrapped around the baby as he took another spoonful of gelato. "What if the

LolaRing was carried in a classy, unmarked black box with our silvery J on the top? Or perhaps a silvery L for The Luxe?"

"And why would it say The Luxe?" He knew what she was getting at. His business instincts had kicked in too, but he wanted to hear the proposal from her.

"Let's be honest here. Your hotel is very high-end. And while you serve a lot of business clients, you also serve lovers. The top floor has fully-stocked bars, the walls have mirrors, and there's mood lighting in each room because your hotels are absolutely designed for making love," she said, locking eyes with him as she spoke.

He shifted the baby higher on his chest, away from his lap. He couldn't help it—hearing those words fall from her lips turned him on. "I'll admit that many hotels, especially mine, are known for being a great backdrop for great sex."

"They are," she said enthusiastically. "That's why I could see The Luxe offering a very discreet pleasure box in some rooms. Imagine walking into the room you reserve for your lover and finding an inviting box on the bed. A velvet lined box, perhaps. If you use it, you pay for it. If you don't open it, you don't pay. It's no different than a bottle of champagne chilling in the mini bar. Think of this as the minibar for sexual pleasure. Inside, you would find the classier toys. A blindfold, a red feather tickler, perhaps even a small silver bullet vibrator. But maybe in certain locations, perhaps the hotel that catered to the newly married in Vegas or in the Maldives, you would carry The LolaRing."

"Tell me, why would we want to carry the LolaRing?"

"Because it is the ultimate couple's pleasure device. Nothing even comes close to it. I even have the perfect slogan for it. *You've given her a diamond ring, now give her the LolaRing,*" Casey said, layering suggestiveness into her tone. My God, this woman couldn't be anything but the CEO of a sex toy company.

He had to be careful, though. He had to think with his brain, not with his dick. Because his dick had a very specific agenda when it came to Casey: *get inside her.* He put on his business brain and ignored all that he was feeling below the belt. Because the reality was, her idea rocked. "I have one question for you, Casey."

She raised an eyebrow. "Yes?"

"Actually, I have a couple of questions. One. How long have we been friends?"

"A few years. Why?"

"Two, then why on earth have we never done a partnership before? Because this is an awesome idea."

She clapped, and smiled so broadly, he swore he'd never seen her that happy before. He always wanted to see her this happy.

"You really like it?"

He nodded several times. "I really do love it. I think it needs to be done well, like everything. We run a luxury hotel; you run a high-end premium sex toy company. There are natural alignments. The key is pulling it off in a way that is classy and sexy. But that's exactly what Joy Delivered is known for. You are the classy and sexy toy company."

"It can be great for both of us," she said, beaming.

"I have to agree. *However,*" he said, taking his time on that last word. *However.* It was the kind of word that was known for derailing business ideas. It was the kind of word that set off alarms in the person you were negotiating with. He had chosen it purposefully. He wanted to throw her off, or perhaps just to surprise her. "I would personally feel better if I were able to vouch for this product. We're going to need to use it."

The look in her eyes was priceless. They blazed with sexuality and desire. He was willing to bet she was turned on something fierce. "Do you have one packed and ready to take to London on our flight tonight?"

She shook her head. "But can we swing by my office? I'll grab one there," she said, the most eager tone to her voice. He loved her willingness to go the extra mile for pleasure, and for business.

"Absolutely. By the way, how would you feel about babysitting again, because you seem to come up with really amazing sex ideas when you're surrounded by my wet T-shirt and two small children."

As she laughed, he heard the sound of a key in the lock. Kat and Bryan were home and they took in the scene— Nate and Casey lounging on the couch, a carton of ice cream between them, two babies fast asleep on their chests.

"Looks like you two had a good night," Bryan said, and he was spot on. They'd had a fantastic night. They always did.

* * *

On the way out, Kat hugged Casey. "We had a great time just getting out of the house to see a movie. I can't even tell you how much it means to me that you helped out," Kat said, placing her hand on her heart. "Two little babies are a handful."

"It was truly a pleasure. They are sweet as sweet can be and they love their uncle big time," Casey said.

Nate stood by the town car idling at the curb. He leaned against the gleaming black door, scrolling through his phone as he waited for her. No rushing, no pressure. Her suitcase was already in the car; she'd remembered to bring it along since they were taking off in a few hours.

"One more thing," Kat said in a low voice as she grasped Casey's arm, wrapping her fingers around it. "I always hoped it would be you."

Casey furrowed her brow.

Kat cast her eyes toward Nate, then whispered, "It's not as if I failed to pick up on the sparks between the two of you, or missed the reason why he kicked us out of the game last week."

Casey blushed, and lowered her face.

"Hey, this isn't a bad thing," Kat said, gently squeezing her arm. Casey raised her eyes. "I always thought you'd be the one to break the spell."

She laughed as if Kat were crazy. "What spell?"

"I truly believe he's been in this dark spell after what happened with Joanna. And that eventually somehow the spell would be broken," Kat said. She was clearly even more of a romantic than Casey.

Casey shot her a smile, but shook her head. "I don't know that he's under a spell. I think he's made a deliberate choice."

Kat shrugged happily. "I believe what I believe. And I've always believed it would take a very special woman to break that spell for my brother. Someone he trusts with his whole heart. Who else would that be but you?"

"Oh, Kat. Even if I believed in fairy tales like that," she began, and the funny thing was Casey did believe in fairy tales, and in the kind of love they promised, but as she glanced at the beautiful man leaning against the car, she knew that it couldn't ever be with him. Because he'd made his choice to live on the other side of the dream. "He so clearly doesn't."

Kat pulled her in for another hug. "Spells are made to be broken."

But Casey wasn't so sure. The practitioner of this one had a particularly strong hold on Nate, had molded him, put him in the kiln, and baked him into this kind of stone —impermeable to love. There was no give in this area of Nate's makeup. No room for change.

Besides, whatever dark magic Joanna had wrought was more like a curse, and it showed no signs of being re- versible. She had to remember that. She had to remember what Nate was good for. He was amazingly good at two things—being her friend and sending her into a most fren- zied state. She hoped to achieve many of the latter in Lon- don, and that's why he had the car swing by her office, where she ran upstairs and grabbed her very own LolaR- ing, clutching it tightly to her chest as she raced back down, an electric thrill charging through her from the knowledge that she was finally going to have what The Happiest Ladies in the World were having.

Next, the car made its way to the west side, stopping by the Nate's apartment.

"Be right back," he said as the car pulled up to the curb.

"I need to pee. I'm coming with you."

When they stepped out of the car, they both froze, their eyes landing on a tall, gorgeous, completely captivating black-haired beauty with green eyes that were bewitching. She was dressed all in black—black tank top, black jeans, black lace-up boots, and a thin black scarf, even though it was June. Casey had never met her, and hadn't even seen a photo, but there was no doubt in her mind this woman was the Dark Queen.

CHAPTER FIFTEEN

New York, late night . . .

His gut twisted. He hadn't seen her in years, and perhaps if he had actually returned her calls he wouldn't be seeing her tonight. But he didn't want to return her calls, or respond to her emails, so he hadn't done either. She couldn't possibly have anything to say that he would need or want to hear.

He started walking into his building, like a man on a mission. Maybe he could even ignore her and march straight up to his apartment, grab his suitcase, change his shirt, and act as if he'd never seen her. Hell, maybe she was simply an apparition.

But judging from the tension on Casey's face, the way her lips were parted and her jaw dropped, Joanna was very much real, in the flesh, and waiting for him.

"Nate!" Joanna took a step towards him. He took a step away. She took another step. He closed his eyes briefly, wishing her away, then opened them. She was still here.

"Yes?" He could've said *why are you here, what are you doing, what do you want,* but he didn't want to give her the courtesy of that many words.

"You haven't returned my calls or responded to my messages," she said, sounding oddly apologetic. "So I had no choice but to come here in person."

"Actually, you did have a choice. You had a choice *not* to find me. You always have a choice. You just chose different things. Let's not confuse the issue, Joanna," he said, biting out the words. Perhaps he had more to say to her than he'd thought.

She nodded, seeming to admit that he was right. "In any case, I'm here because I wanted to see if you still have the sculpture of your hands."

The world slowed. Her strange request echoed in his ears, and he was sure he was hearing things. This is what she wanted from him? A work of art?

"That's why you're here?"

"Yes. There's a museum in Chicago that's putting together an exhibition of all my work, and that seems to be the one missing piece. I hope it's not too much to ask, but I really think it could round up the exhibition quite nicely. And, truth be told, I was always rather proud of it."

He scoffed, his derisive huff carrying into the breeze of the warm June night, trailing over the noise of the cars and buses on Columbus Avenue. "Well, in that case, since you're proud of it, let me just go take it off my dining room table where it's the centerpiece," he said staring hard at her. "I like to enjoy it every night. Have dinner with it. Gaze at its beauty. I'm rather proud of it too. But since you want it, I will of course give it to you."

She pursed her lips, lifting her chin up high. He wondered how he'd ever been in love with her. As he looked at her now, he had no clue how he'd intended to share his life with this person who only cared about *taking*—taking what she wanted, when she wanted it, at any time. But that was his big problem—he hadn't seen it coming. He'd had no clue that he couldn't trust her. He might possibly be the worst judge of character when it came to love, and he damn well needed to stay far away from the foolish emotion.

"Touché," she said calmly, then gestured to Casey and extended a hand. "Hi, I'm Joanna Simone. You must be?"

His ex-wife stood there waiting for an answer from Casey, and that made his blood boil. But Casey was classy, always classy, and she took her hand, saying, "Casey. I'm Nate's friend."

Joanna turned her focus back to Nate, tapping her toe. "I'm really sorry to bother you, but might you have it?"

Nate winced. He honestly didn't know, but he was pretty sure he'd packed it up and stuffed it into the back of a closet somewhere. "I'm not sure," he muttered.

"I'm happy to pay you for it. I certainly don't expect you to simply hand it over."

"Thank you. Thank you so much. That's really amazingly generous of you to offer to pay me back for a wedding present, but I don't need your money, and you know what? I don't want those stupid hands," he said, spitting out the insult, hoping it stung. But the presence of Casey, mere inches from him, was the only thing that made him smooth out the next few words so they weren't filled with the vitriol inside him. He didn't want her to know that he still harbored this kind of anger towards his ex-wife. "But I'll check, and I'll get back to you."

"Thank you," Joanna said on a nod. "I'm ever grateful. If you have it, I would really like to get it by next week. If that's doable."

Casey stepped in. "We'll get back to you. Thank you for stopping by. We have a plane to catch," she said, then she wrapped her hand protectively around his arm, and the way she touched him made all his anger dissipate. It was like a pin deflating a balloon, and all he felt now was some kind of calm, some kind of peace.

They walked into his building quietly. Once they stepped into the elevator, he pressed the button for the top floor, leaned his head against the wall and closed his eyes. Her warm body pressed against his. It wasn't sexual, and it wasn't the start of something. It was simply comforting, and he needed it, so he wrapped his arms around her, resting his chin on her head.

"I'm sorry you had to see her," she whispered.

"Me too," he said. "But I'm glad you were here."

"Do you want me to look for that sculpture? So you don't have to? I can be the one to return it to her."

He pulled back momentarily. "You'd do that for me?"

"Of course. Unless you want to drop it from a window and smash it on the sidewalk. I'm completely fine with that too."

He grinned briefly. Only Casey could do this for him. Take him in all these directions. Take him through lust and passion, through business and babies, and then from rage to laughter in mere seconds. He didn't deserve her, but oh, how he wanted to give her what she needed from a man.

CHAPTER SIXTEEN

Over the Atlantic . . .

Maybe Kat was right, because the spell Joanna had worked on Nate still seemed to be going strong. He was quiet most of the flight, chatting only briefly with her and with a few of his employees who were sharing the plane. He also slept across most of the Atlantic, and so did she. But they were both awake now and he was more subdued than usual, bordering on sullen. She certainly didn't expect him to be a barrel of monkeys, or to be flirtatious with her in front of everyone, but she knew that he wasn't himself, and that he hadn't quite yet emerged from his Joanna funk. He'd been nose-down in his laptop for the last hour as the sun rose across the Atlantic.

His frown was like a cut in her skin. It burned, and she wanted the cure. She wanted to seal off the pain, and feel good again. That was wholly selfish, she knew, but there it was. More so, her heart lurched towards him, and she desperately wanted to ease his mind, to be the one to take him away from this sadness his ex-wife had draped over him. She could be that person, right? She knew this man, and she knew him even better now that they'd been spending these nights together. She could be his Sherpa and guide him up and over this mountain of gloom.

There was one surefire way.

She took out her iPad and opened her email. A note popped up. Crap. Ethan at Victoria Hotels had emailed her the other week and she'd meant to respond, but then was sidetracked, so she'd flagged the note as important. With it blaring in her face now, she skimmed the contents: *Idea for partnership . . . would love to discuss . . . proposal attached.* She banged out a quick reply simply so she wouldn't have to keep reminding herself: *Promise to look at this in detail shortly! Thanks for thinking of us. More soon.*

Then, she started a new email. Her fingers hovered over the keypad as she screwed up the corner of her lips, trying to figure out where to start. Something dirty. But something funny too. That was a hard combo for Nate to resist.

from: learnsnewtricksgirl@gmail.com
to: commandonate@gmail.com
date: June 20, 8:12 AM
subject: Dirty Jokes

Knock, knock . . .

Crossing her legs, she peered at him over the top of her iPad, waiting for the moment when he opened his email. He sat across from her, the oak table between them, his COO a few seats over, and a pair of his VPs still sound asleep in their chairs a couple rows near the back. In the meantime, she clicked open a browser window to look up the open hours for a popular London attraction. A minute later, he raised his eyes briefly at her. A new email landed in her inbox.

from: commandonate@gmail.com
to: learnsnewtricksgirl@gmail.com
date: June 20, 8:14 AM
subject: I'll bite.

Who's there?

She reined in a grin as she tapped out a reply. Admittedly, knock-knock jokes were not the pinnacle of sophisticated humor. But Casey had an arsenal of them now, thanks to Nelle, so why not call on the low-hanging fruit of a knock-knock joke to entertain the man she cared so deeply for?

from: learnsnewtricksgirl@gmail.com
to: commandonate@gmail.com
date: June 20, 8:15 AM
subject: I approve of your biting.

Gladiator.

from: commandonate@gmail.com
to: learnsnewtricksgirl@gmail.com
date: June 20, 8:16 AM
subject: Show me the spot where I bit your collarbone
yesterday afternoon.

Gladiator who?

A hint of heat bloomed across her cheeks from his subject line command. She shot him a look that was both
flirty and dirty as she subtly tugged at the scoop neck of
her soft purple shirt, revealing the spot where he'd bitten
down hard during a quickie at her house that involved her
in handcuffs, and him putting her under arrest. He raised
an eyebrow approvingly, then she returned to her screen.

from: learnsnewtricksgirl@gmail.com
to: commandonate@gmail.com
date: June 20, 8:19 AM
subject: You like marking me?

He's gladiator before they screwed.

Nate laughed softly, then looked up. *Good one,* he
mouthed. *There's more where that came from*, she said, letting him read her lips too.

from: commandonate@gmail.com
to: learnsnewtricksgirl@gmail.com
date: June 20, 8:26 AM
subject: Yes, I fucking love marking you.

And more of you coming. There will be more of that
very soon.

from: learnsnewtricksgirl@gmail.com
to: commandonate@gmail.com
date: June 20, 8:29 AM
subject: The other way around

Or maybe more of you coming . . . very soon

from: commandonate@gmail.com
to: learnsnewtricksgirl@gmail.com
date: June 20, 8:31 AM
subject: Tell me more of your plans

It's getting hard to concentrate in here . . .

from: learnsnewtricksgirl@gmail.com
to: commandonate@gmail.com
date: June 20, 8:33 AM
subject: I will tell you and show you

Want to know what I'm thinking of?

from: commandonate@gmail.com
to: learnsnewtricksgirl@gmail.com
date: June 20, 8:36 AM
subject: Let me guess

What I plan on doing to you tonight?

from: learnsnewtricksgirl@gmail.com
to: commandonate@gmail.com
date: June 20, 8:39 AM
subject: Wrong guess

Sooner than that. What I plan to do to you this morning.

from: commandonate@gmail.com
to: learnsnewtricksgirl@gmail.com
date: June 20, 8:42 AM
subject: TELL ME NOW

NEED TO KNOW

from: learnsnewtricksgirl@gmail.com
to: commandonate@gmail.com
date: June 20, 8:49 AM
subject: Picture this

It involves my lips and your cock.

from: commandonate@gmail.com
to: learnsnewtricksgirl@gmail.com
date: June 20, 8:51 AM
subject: Image is burned on my brain

That's a favorite combination of mine. You have been remiss in sucking my dick, incidentally, Miss Casey.

from: learnsnewtricksgirl@gmail.com
to: commandonate@gmail.com
date: June 20, 8:54 AM
subject: Forgive me

I plan to rectify that. Soon.

from: commandonate@gmail.com
to: learnsnewtricksgirl@gmail.com
date: June 20, 8:56 AM
subject: I will forgive if you suck good and hard

Do you?

from: learnsnewtricksgirl@gmail.com
to: commandonate@gmail.com
date: June 20, 8:59 AM
subject: Is there any other way?

Yes. Because you only gave me that one taste our first night together, and I want more. I want to feel you lose control for me. Let go for me. I want to taste you sliding down my throat.

from: commandonate@gmail.com
to: learnsnewtricksgirl@gmail.com
date: June 20, 9:02 AM
subject: No

Can. Not. Think. Straight. Now. All. Blood. Diverted.
South. Of. The. Border.

from: learnsnewtricksgirl@gmail.com
to: commandonate@gmail.com
date: June 20, 9:05 AM
subject: Staring at your hard-on right now, you sexy
man

I want your hands in my hair, and I want you deep in
my mouth.

from: commandonate@gmail.com
to: learnsnewtricksgirl@gmail.com
date: June 20, 9:07 AM
subject: You fucking temptress

You are playing with fire, my sweetness. When I get you
alone in the room, the things I will do to you will drive
you wild with pleasure.

from: learnsnewtricksgirl@gmail.com
to: commandonate@gmail.com
date: June 20, 9:09 AM
subject: Tempting you is what I like

The things I will do to you.

She snapped her iPad shut, and flashed him a satisfied grin. She had plans for him when they landed. Big plans. A rush of excitement tore through her body. It felt foreign at first, then quite familiar. It was a feeling she hadn't embraced in a few weeks, but it was one she had loved—being in control in bed.

Even though what she'd planned for him wasn't going to take place in a bed.

CHAPTER SEVENTEEN

London, mid-morning . . .

As the green awnings came into view, Casey shrieked in excitement and pointed.

At the other end of the block was the signature London department store with its elaborate red brick facade, and flags blowing in the breeze. She grabbed his arm. "Remember I told you about the dress I needed for Jack's rehearsal dinner? They have them in Harrod's. Is there any chance I could pop in for just five minutes? They've been selling out quickly and I heard they got a new shipment in last night."

Ah, hell. Not now. Not when they'd be at the hotel in ten more minutes. Every single second until he was alone with her was agonizing.

Nate was ready to launch into a myriad of questions to poke holes in her proposition, starting with how the hell would she know a store received a new shipment, and why did she need to go now, but he didn't have a chance to ask, because she was already telling the driver to make a pit

stop, then asking his co-workers if they would mind waiting. "I swear it'll just be a quick in and out," she said to the
lot of them, in the sweetest, most eager voice, pressing her
hands together as if in prayer, that led Tom and the other
guys to say *of course*. Damn, the woman was irresistible,
even when asking to go shopping. He was such a goner.

She pushed open the door, and grabbed Nate's arm.

"You need me?"

She shot him a wide-eyed stare. "Yes." Then came a roll
of the eyes. "I need your opinion on the dress, since you're
the best man. I told you about this dress before."

He gritted his teeth. "Best man's duties," he grumbled,
and in seconds, she'd grabbed his hand and was tugging
him through the mid-morning crowds, bustling along the
street, and then through the door the green-uniformed
doorman held for them.

"I swear I don't remember discussing a dress at Harrod's," he said on the escalator, because he could have done
without the detour. He was dying to get to the hotel and
take her. Just fucking take her. Throw her on the bed, rip
off her panties, and slide into her heat. Anything for some
relief for his aching balls. The relentless pressure in his dick
from her emails and the images they'd stirred up was nearing painful levels, and he'd kept his computer bag on his
lap for the entire ride into the city from the airport. The
only thing that had kept him from pouncing on her in the
car was the presence of those co-workers.

His brain functions had been reduced to a one-track
level. He didn't give a shit about lessons, or seduction, or
submission. All he wanted was to have her. To own her
body. To finish what she'd started.

"Yes. I told you," she said insistently, waving her hand in the air as if she were trying to get him to recall a long-forgotten conversation. "The Herve Leger. You forgot?"

She parked her hands on her hips and stared at him pointedly. He stared at her hips. At her jeans. At her long legs. Her heels. He plotted the fastest course to stripping off the denim when they finally reached the hotel.

Yank the jeans down to the knees, and bend her over the bed. Ass in the air, her elbows on the bed, her back bowed.

He jammed a hand in his hair. He needed to find a way to be near her without operating like a walking hard-on. Because that's all he was right now. A man led by his balls. She could have asked him to jump, and he'd be twenty feet in the air.

He shrugged and held up his hands in defeat. "Don't remember the dress at all," he said as they reached the next floor. She stepped off the elevator and he followed her, figuring the least he could do was enjoy the view of her ass as she walked. Maybe he was stooping to the basest levels today and objectifying her, but he didn't care. She had the most fantastic ass he'd ever seen, touched, felt, held or . . .

Dammit. There he was again, speeding on the express train to Lust Ville.

He tried to redirect his mind to the meetings he and his team were having here in London this afternoon, and the trick worked briefly as they weaved through displays of designer dresses. Casey made a beeline for a light-blue dress, grabbed it and marched straight up to the saleswoman to let her know she needed to try it on.

Nate lagged behind as she headed for the dressing rooms, figuring he'd use the time to answer a few emails from business partners. That would help him in his quest too.

Then the neck of his shirt grew tighter, and he turned to find Casey jerking on it. "I need your opinion, goofball. That's why I brought you here," she said and practically dragged him to the dressing rooms, where classical music piped in overhead and the voices of other shoppers were hushed. It was like being in a church. She pressed her hands to his shoulders and pushed him down in a beige upholstered chair.

"Stay here. I'll be right out to show you."

She disappeared into the dressing room, and clicked the door shut behind her.

All his business thoughts fled his brain once more as he imagined her skimming down her jeans, tugging off her top, sliding those curves he loved into that dress.

He heard the door open and Casey popped her head out.

"That was fast," he said, because she'd been in there for about five seconds.

She crooked her finger. He followed her lead, entering the dressing room. She was still wearing her jeans, her shirt and her shoes. The dress she brought into the room hung on a hanger on a hook. He pointed to the blue fabric and parted his lips, but the words he was about to say died quickly when she grabbed his collar, and pushed him against the wall. In an instant, her lips were on his, devouring him. All his questions and all his irritation leaked away in the wild hunger of her mouth. She kissed him relentlessly, sucking on his tongue and his lips so hard that he felt the kiss deep in his bones. It vibrated through his bloodstream. His brain went haywire. His body launched into maximum overdrive from the ferocity of her kiss. Her hands threaded through his hair as she rubbed her lush, delicious body along his, grinding her crotch against him, sending him spinning.

She broke apart, whispering, "You really had no idea?"

"No idea what?" His brain was still foggy and probably would be for days.

With lightning speed, she dipped a hand below the waistband of his jeans, stroking him. "Why I brought you here."

He nearly growled from the temporary relief. "I really haven't been able to think straight since the plane."

She unzipped his jeans, freeing his erection. He was ready to get down on his knees and thank the heavens for her touch. Her soft nimble hands stroked him, and he began rocking into her fist, seeking friction, seeking heat. He didn't care what she was going to do to him right now. As long as she didn't stop touching him anything would be okay.

A groan rumbled through him.

She pressed a finger to his lips. "Shh . . . you need to be quiet. Harrod's is a very classy place," she said softly in his ear, her breath tickling his skin. "I need you to do that for me. Can you promise me you won't make a sound?"

There was something so sexy about her voice right now, in the way she owned every single second of his pleasure. She'd taken charge, and she seemed to relish mapping out all the details of whatever it was she planned to do to him.

"I promise," he said. He would agree to anything right now.

"Then," she said, lingering on every word as she breathed hotly in his ear, "fuck my mouth."

She dropped to her knees, pushed his jeans down a few more inches, and dived in. There was no teasing, no licking, no flick of her tongue against the swollen head of his cock, and he was damn grateful. He didn't want finesse or foreplay. He wanted to be touched.

"Just like that," he said on a groan. "All the way."

She stopped, and shook her head. The message was clear. She was in charge, and he had to listen. He mimed zipping his mouth shut, and she returned to lavishing attention on his cock.

This blow job was straightforward. She took him all the way in and went to town on his shaft. It didn't matter that he'd been told to be quiet. Even if he could talk, he had nothing to say. The only sounds he'd have made would have been animalistic. Besides, she didn't need any direction from him.

She swirled her tongue along his dick and sucked so hard she was blowing his mind too. The friction was astonishing. She was fast, and she was furious, and her lips were locked so tightly around him that she looked exactly as she had when he'd dreamed of her doing this.

Unspeakable pleasure slammed into his body, twisting, rising, coiling through his veins. He was close, so close. She stopped once and he was ready to grab her head and drag her back to him, when he looked down to see her licking his balls. The sight of that made him nearly explode.

She worked her tongue over on him until he could no longer take it. He speared his hands into her hair, whispering harshly, "Get back on me now."

She raised her eyebrows, the hottest look of satisfaction in her gaze as she wrapped her lips around his dick once more, then grabbed his ass in her hands and rocked him into her mouth.

This was it. This was the motherfucking blow job of his life. He gave it to her good and she took it, obliterating his hold on any thread of sanity with the way her wicked tongue licked him and her lips sucked hard, so hard that the pressure built and built and built, then it simply crashed into him, ripping all the breath from his lungs. White-hot light erupted behind his eyelids.

He gripped her head, curling his fingers around her skull as she dug her sharp nails into his ass. He came hard in her mouth. It was an explosion of pleasure in his body, a sheer blast of intoxication rocketing through his cells.

Blow jobs were certainly known to sink a man's hold on logic, to lead a man to say things that he wouldn't ordinarily say. But he'd retained some awareness of his surroundings, and the proximity to other people beyond the dressing room doors. Otherwise, he probably would've blurted out something he wasn't ready to reveal. Not just something sexual or dirty, but something deeper, about how much he had wanted that from her. For years.

As she stood up, he was damn near ready to tell her then he had dreamed of that, and not merely because he wanted her physically, but because he simply wanted *her*. More than he'd ever expected to.

But her finger was back on his lips again, keeping him quiet. She had no idea he'd been about to tell her how long she'd been the star of his fantasies, and how he hated the idea of ever letting go of their new reality.

* * *

Turned out Harrod's really did have the dress she wanted. Casey didn't even need to try it on. She told him she knew Herve Leger fit her like a glove, so she'd grabbed the dress from the dressing room, slapped down her credit card, and snapped it up for the rehearsal dinner.

When they slid back into the car a few minutes later, zipped back up, hair straightened, she spoke first, brandishing her shopping bag. "Look! It was so worth the stop. Thank you for waiting for me."

Nate put the brakes on a naughty grin, turning his head to stare out the window so his colleagues wouldn't know that their boss had just gotten blown in Harrod's.

CHAPTER EIGHTEEN

London, noon . . .

The top floor of The Luxe in Kensington was stunning, with gold-trimmed walls and a royal blue carpet leading them down the hallway to a penthouse suite. He slid the card through the slot, then held the door open for her. She had stayed at his hotels many times, so she knew better than to let her jaw drop when taking in the richness and sensuality of the rooms, but she had never stayed in the penthouse suite in London before. The suite was palatial, and impeccably appointed with a British flair to the furniture, but still outfitted in the sleek and sexy style The Luxe was known for.

She was about to make a quip about how *it's good to know the CEO*, when he dropped their two suitcases on the floor, grabbed her wrists, and backed her up against the wall.

"Look at the room later," he said in warning, his eyes blazing at her. He had that hot and hungry look that made her feel as if he wanted to eat her up.

"I have my meeting soon with Sofia's," she said in protest, but he didn't seem to care, because he'd nudged her legs apart with a strong thigh, and she was spread-eagle, standing up, pinned to the wall.

"This doesn't need to take long," he said, grasping her wrists so tightly his fingers dug into her flesh, delivering a sharp bite of pressure. Of ownership. Of possession.

"But it's at one p.m. I don't know how long it will take to get to Hyde Park," she said breathily, fighting the battle her body was waging, because her body wanted to take him up on his quickie offer, thank you very much.

He dropped one hand from her wrists to run his thumb along her cheek. "Don't think you can wriggle away from me. After what you did to me at Harrod's, I'm going to need to bend you over the bed, and show you what happens when you try to take control like that."

She made a purring sound, momentarily feeding his appetite and their game. "What will you do?"

"Fuck you into submission. Fuck you until you come again and again. Fuck you until you beg for me to do it again."

"Is this supposed to be a punishment for me taking charge? Because it sounds pretty good," she said, arching an eyebrow in some sort of challenge.

"Don't test me, Casey," he said, and surely, he was playing a role again. He was her lover, calling all the shots, keeping her under his command. Dropping his hold on her wrists, he crushed his lips to hers, kissing her so hard that she was nearly ready to throw in the towel and say screw the meeting.

Especially when he turned on his tender side, and whispered, "Let me take care of you now."

But she had an appointment and she intended to keep it. Tardiness for the sake of an *O* might be momentarily rewarding, but it was foolish long-term.

She gently, but firmly pushed him away. "I want to. I truly do. But I need to shower after the flight and change and freshen up. I don't want to be late," she said, then ran a finger along his jawline. He hitched in his breath, closing his eyes softly. When he opened them, there was something different in his expression. A vulnerability she hadn't seen in him often.

"Besides, I need you to know that I didn't do that to you in the dressing room to get something back," she added, looking him square in the eyes. "This thing between us doesn't just have to be about you teaching me. Sometimes I want to lead, and sometimes I want to give. I hope you didn't mind that I took the lead on that and just kind of pushed you up against the wall at Harrod's."

He shook his head vigorously. "God, I loved it. Casey. When is it going to get through to you that I love everything you do to me?"

Warmth bloomed inside her chest, like a big daisy flower in the summer. This man made her feel so sexy, and so passionate, and no one had done that for her in years. When she'd been with Scott, she'd spent her days engineering pleasure for others, and her nights trying to figure out where she'd gone wrong in the bedroom. With Nate, she felt both beautiful and desired. She wanted to clutch this feeling close to her chest, and hold onto it for all time. She wanted to share it with him too. "I'm happy you liked it. I wanted you to feel better," she said, running her hand along his arm. "I hated that Joanna put you in a funk, so I wanted to do something to get you out of it."

He wrenched back, narrowing his eyes, staring at her in surprise. "Please tell me you didn't give me a blow job because you felt sorry for me because of my ex-wife."

Cold needles of worry pricked into her. She shook her head quickly. "Of course not," she said, her voice rising.

He backed away, shoving a hand through his hair. "*Casey,*" he said, in a frustrated tone as he reached the doorway to the bathroom, leaning against it.

"Nate, it wasn't a pity blow job," she said, closing the distance between them again, refusing to let him shut down.

"You just said you did it because you felt bad about Joanna."

"I did feel bad about Joanna. I also wanted your dick in my mouth," she said, choosing to be particularly blunt.

He laughed once, then stopped. "I like the second part of that better than the first. Can you say that second part again?"

She tap-danced her hands up the front of his shirt. "I *loved* doing that to you. But I'm not going to shy away from saying the hard things. And that's this—I wish Joanna didn't have such a hold on you," she said with a sigh.

"She doesn't have a hold on me," he said quickly, perhaps too quickly, too insistently.

The memory of last night outside his apartment flashed before her, and she pressed on. "I think she does, though.

She hurt you and seeing her reminds you of how deep that hurt is. Right?"

He sighed, then held up his hands in admission. "Fine. She hurt me. And, fine. I don't like seeing her. You got me on both accounts. Can we just talk about anything else?"

"We don't *have* to talk about her," she said. "But sometimes I want to talk about the past. I want to understand it. I want to move beyond it, and I want you to be able to as well. And maybe sometimes I want to do something physical to bring you back to the present, okay?" she said, staring hard in his eyes, refusing to let go of this issue. It was important to her. She didn't intend to let Joanna stand in the middle of them, whether they were friends or part-time lovers. "I hate that she hurt you. I don't want anyone to hurt you ever. But don't let the hurt define you. Don't let *her* define you. You have so much to give a woman, and I don't want you to lose out because of what she did, Nate."

He nodded slowly, then swallowed. "You're right," he said, as if the admission cost him something. "Seeing her just reminds of how stupid I was to ever trust her, and how I had no clue what she was up to. I had no idea that it was happening right under my nose. I was such a fool, Casey," he said, shame thick in his voice. "I went out to dinner with the two of them. They were at our apartment for a New Year's party once. He even thanked me for supporting my wife and putting her through the MFA program. The whole time they were having an affair. It probably would have gone on for another year if she hadn't left an email open on her computer when she asked me to check the movie times for a film we going to see that night," he said,

192 · LAUREN BLAKELY

cringing, and she rubbed a hand gently down his arm, as if that would somehow take the pain away. It wouldn't, but it was all she could do. "What if it happened again? How would I even know?"

"She's the exception. She's not the rule. Most people don't do that. I've never done that. I never would."

"I know you wouldn't," he said softly. "And yeah, I'd really like to keep moving past her too. So if you want me to be totally honest, this thing with you," he said, gesturing from her to him and back, then wiggling his eyebrows in a suggestive fashion, "has done more for me than anything has to put her farther in the rear-view mirror."

Her lips curved into a smile. "Aha! So this isn't totally one-sided!" She pumped a fist.

He dropped his hands to her shoulder, clasping her firmly. "It was never one-sided. Get that through your head once and for all. It's *all-sided*. It's me-sided. It's two-sided. It's fifty-million sided," he said. "But if you want to start bringing up exes and talking about the past, I could say the same for you. Because Scott made you think you can't be true to yourself with a man. That you can't be forward. But some men love when you talk back and say what you want," he said, flashing her a naughty grin that was like a shot of sunlight in her chest when he pointed at himself. "Yet he somehow convinced you that you're not as beautiful or sensual or passionate as I've known you to be in just a few short weeks of playing your lover," he said, and she bristled at the word *playing*. Right now, she didn't want him to be playing. She wished they could stop playing, and he could simply be her lover. Not forever, not for all time, but for now.

For real, here in London.

But she focused instead on what he'd said about Scott. If she expected him to be honest with her, she had to do the same. "Yeah, he did a number on me. I felt like a failure in bed after him, and you've made me feel anything but," she said, and there it was again. That flash of vulnerability in his eyes. She'd seen playfulness in them, she'd seen laughter, she'd seen passion, and she'd seen anger. But now, there was something that seemed to go deeper; something that was usually reserved for someone who was much more than a friend.

He raised a hand to her face, softly brushing the backs of his fingers against her cheek. "You didn't need to learn to let go. You didn't need to figure out how to give up control. You're perfect the way you are, and I love what you did to me in the dressing room. Giving up control isn't what makes for great sex. At least, that's not what does it for me."

Casey swallowed dryly. A swarm of butterflies flew in her chest. Things were changing with Nate, and she hardly understood what was happening, only how it felt inside her heart. Wild and free. "What does it for you?"

He locked eyes with her, and her insides flipped, a spark of desire swooping from head to toe. "What turns me on are two people who have to have each other. That's what makes for great sex—when you need to be as close to a person as you possibly can. It's about wild, sweat–slicked, hot desire and your pulse pounding in your ear. It's about heat and need and want, and fucking in stairwells, and screwing standing up, and clawing off clothes to get at each other. It's about kissing her while you make love to her, and fucking her senseless at the same damn time."

Her skin sizzled. Her heart tried to fight its way out of her rib cage. Her fingers ached to touch him. The way he gazed at her made her feel as if all those words were meant for her. Maybe he was talking in general terms, or maybe he was talking about her. Her throat was dry, but she pushed past it. "Tonight? I have a request for tonight."

"Anything." His voice was raw.

"I want you to make me crazy. Drive me wild. I want to feel that abandon I've only felt with you. I want to be so wound up with desire that I practically beg for it," she said, and his eyes nearly popped out of his head. He licked his lips, and blew out a long stream of air. "Would you do that for me?"

"Don't you know by now? I'd do anything for you."

"Then on that note, I need you to let me slip away from you to shower," she said playfully, and he lifted his hands and she slid away. She grabbed her clothes for her meeting along with her makeup, then she rooted around in her bag for her toiletries, hunting for her Alba Botanica shampoo, but the search was fruitless. She cursed. "Crap. I did it again. I forgot my favorite shampoo."

She headed into the bathroom and reached for the hotel shampoo on the vanity. It was a good brand. She really couldn't complain about Aveda, even though it wasn't her favorite. His hand wrapped around her wrist, and he gently removed the Aveda bottles, and turned her around. Her eyes widened and she grinned like a fool to see him brandishing two small bottles of Alba Botanica. They were in a

Ziploc bag and he dangled them from his fingers high above her head.

"Oh my God! Did I put them in your bag?"

He shook his head, looking as pleased as a cat that had captured a mouse.

"How do you have them then? Don't tell me it was in my bag and I didn't even notice."

He continued to shake his head. "Wrong again."

"Well?"

"I brought it for you."

"You did?" she said, her jaw going slack.

He nodded. "It's your Achilles' heel when you travel. You sometimes forget to bring your shampoo. And you're kind of obsessed with your hair."

"That's putting it mildly."

"So I brought some along just in case you forgot," he said, handing her the bag.

It was *only* shampoo. But it was so much more than shampoo. Her heart started a stampede again, galloping closer to him. To this man she was having some kind of strange, friendly, temporary affair with. A man who knew so much about her, and who seemed to embrace all her quirks, her habits, her needs, and in the last few weeks, her desires.

Her lips parted, and she was about to say all these things, but the clock was ticking. She tipped her forehead to the shower. "Thank you," she said, and then stripped to her birthday clothes, and stepped under the spray.

When she finished her shower, he handed her a towel, and as she started to dry off she knocked playfully on the shower door.

"Knock, knock."

"Who's there?" he asked.

"Dewey."

"Dewey who?"

"Do we really have to use a condom?"

He blinked once, like she'd caught him off guard. "I'm clean. I was tested before you," he said.

"Me too. And I'm on the pill," she said, trying to keep the conversation casual as she toweled off water droplets on her legs. But standing naked before him, having just showered, discussing the sex they planned to have, and sharing a room with him? It hardly seemed that what had started as casual could be classified that way anymore.

CHAPTER NINETEEN

London, afternoon . . .

Sofia showed Casey the new display at the signature retail location in Hyde Park, gesturing proudly to the shelf of white boxes emblazoned with the silver *J* for Joy Delivered.

"Look at all my babies," Casey said, pretending to grab at the boxes.

The tall and statuesque British woman flashed a bright smile. "And they've probably helped make a lot of babies too," she said with a wink.

"Good one."

"In any case, I wanted you to see our gorgeous new display. It's increased our foot traffic too, and boosted word of mouth. We're so excited to carry your products at the locations we're opening soon. Can you just imagine how smashing it will be to have the LolaRing join all her friends here?" Sofia said, clasping her hand over her heart, as if she truly was enthralled about the addition of a new vibrator to the crew of high-end pleasure devices the fancy pharmacy sold.

"I'm sure Lola will be delighted to keep such good company," Casey said, continuing the banter now that they'd finished the business details. The I's had been dotted and the T's had been crossed upstairs in Sofia's office, and the boutique was on board as another one of the exclusive launch partners for Joy Delivered's newest toy.

Sofia exuded class and sophistication from her understated black pumps, to her sleek navy dress, to her brown hair, twisted in a chignon. She was the head of the company named after her, and Casey wondered briefly if Sofia was a so-called *alpha female* too, and if she'd ever struggled in her social life because of it. Her gaze drifted briefly to Sofia's left hand—no ring. But then, the presence or absence of rings proved nothing. Sofia could still be in a committed relationship. Perhaps someday, the two women would chat about love and the challenges of its pursuit as women in business. For now, the focus remained on the products they peddled.

Sofia's voice turned more earnest. "I'm truly delighted to add the LolaRing to the lineup. I know you're choosy with your retail partners when rolling out new products, and I'm glad to be on the short list."

Casey bowed her head slightly. "I assure you, the honor is all mine. I couldn't be more thrilled to continue our partnership. It also looks like," she said, crossing her fingers, "we'll have a hotel chain on board too. I'll share names when it's finalized."

Sofia gave an approving nod. "Excellent. I'm sure I'll be wowed, since already it's an impressive short list," she said, lowering her voice as if they were discussing state secrets. "I hear Grant Abbot is on it. I only wish I had a reason to be in business with him." Sofia pretended to fan herself. "My, he's a handsome devil, isn't he?"

Casey laughed politely. "Yes. He is."

"I love Entice lingerie, of course, too. I had drinks with him at a conference once. He's such a flirt, and I even told him as much," Sofia said, as they walked away from the display.

Flirt. Yeah, that kind of described Grant. Flirty, and charming, and incredibly savvy, he was also a good business partner. The man had been fantastic so far to work with, delivering contracts on time, lining up the right people, and planning the details for marketing. Soon, she'd be seeing him so they could put the finishing touches on the rollout at his boutiques, and perhaps too exploring the possibilities of other partnerships. Her shoulders tensed at the thought. She wasn't quite sure how to behave with him. It had been a while, and so much had changed, hadn't it? She furrowed her brow, momentarily trying to recall her last meeting with Grant. But it had grown fuzzier, and much more muted, and she was going to have to do something about that very soon.

* * *

Casey tapped her foot and peered down the street. The early evening crowds weaved past her—men in suits and ties, women in smart dresses and business slacks. The workday had ended and Londoners were moving onto their nights, walking briskly along the chic New Bond Street in the heart of the West End. She stood under the black awning of the famed auction house with its elegant white facade, searching for Nate in the crowd, seeking out his familiar frame, his broad shoulders, his golden brown hair, his amber eyes. He'd texted her that he was running late, then texted her again to let her know his car had dropped him off several blocks away. The roads were so clogged with traffic that he'd get there faster on foot. The auction started in ten minutes, and if he didn't make it soon she'd have to go in solo. Which was fine by her because she didn't want to miss a chance to vie for the painting she'd been coveting.

She flipped open the catalogue to look at the image again.

Unfinished Love—a simple, but sumptuous image, the painting's story was told in broad brushstrokes and bright colors, depicting a man in a white shirt and a woman in a black dress kissing under a red umbrella. The best part was the woman's reaction. The leg pop. Ah, that got to Casey every time. The heel in the air, the one-legged kiss—the flamingo, she liked to call it. Such a symbol of the power of a certain kind of kiss, of the way it could undo a woman. To be kissed like that had always been her dream, and so this image was her quest, and she wanted it badly.

Like a gambler ready to lay down bets, she was poised to bid. She'd already registered and picked up her paddle. The clock drew nearer to the start of the auction. Another glance at her phone, another scan down the street, but still no Nate.

She reread the details, and the expected starting price for the painting: £3000. She could manage that. Extravagant, yes. But not wildly insane. Besides, art was her indulgence. Art like this made her happy; it made her heart sing. It was an uncomplicated love, one that fed her soul, and her hope for that kind of love someday. She sighed wistfully, wishing that that someday would come soon.

Until then, there was art, and that kept her going.

She thumbed through a few more pages to pass the time, then she gasped out loud. There was a new painting in the catalogue, and it called to her, with outstretched arms. Casey ran her index finger longingly over the photo. A late addition to the lot, the image was of that same man and woman, but this time without an umbrella, staring up at the sky, caught in the rain—big, buoyant raindrops that shone like stars.

She read the description.

Miller Valentina hadn't told anyone he was working on this new painting and had simply delivered it, along with his other works, to Sotheby's as part of this auction of modern art. Titled *Big Love, Sans Umbrella*, the catalogue entry contained a note from the artist: "This work took me by surprise. I hadn't planned to paint it, but perhaps *Unfinished Love* truly was unfinished because I had the insistent feeling that the sky had broken open and that there was more of their story to tell. So I told it."

She didn't entirely connect with the kind of metaphors and art-y language that painters told their tales in, but even so, something about this work touched her. Maybe it was the unexpectedness of it—for the couple, the painter and the sky.

She read the price. It was more than *Unfinished Love*, but not by too much. Did she want both? Would that be too greedy? She craved the pair, but she talked herself down. They were just paintings. She didn't *have* to buy both. She'd do just fine with the one she'd come for. Even though they fit together, like a perfect match.

But where the hell was her date?

Then her spine straightened, and goosebumps rose on the back of her neck. She spun around, or maybe he spun her. It all happened so quickly, she couldn't tell where one moment ended and another began, only that *this*—her waiting—had blended into her being kissed, one second sliding seamlessly into the start of something ever more wonderful.

The kiss told her so much—that he was sorry for being late, that he'd missed her for the last several hours he'd been without her, and that this was the best part of his day.

Hers too.

This kiss was air, it was breath, and it was her heart on her sleeve. In the soft, slow sweep of his lips, in the hungry sighs they both made, in an instant, the kiss was everything.

Her heel popped up.

There it was. The final proof that no one had ever kissed her like he did, and no one probably ever would.

CHAPTER TWENTY

London, evening . . .

Green.

All he saw was emerald green hugging every luscious curve.

Clinging enticingly to her body, a lure for him, and him alone. Like she'd clothed herself in the secret of their affair —the dress that drew him back to New York, and into the first night he'd made love to her. It was a private message in a language only he could understand.

"You wore it," he said, and something dangerously close to hope dared to surface inside him.

She nodded. "I told you I'd wear it for you. I keep my promises. Let's go," she said, pointing inside Sotheby's. She walked quickly, guiding him up the stairs, down the hall, and into one of the sales rooms that was abuzz with activity. The hum of hushed voices filled the air, and the auctioneer presided over the podium at the front of the room.

She pointed to a row in the middle and he slid in next to her. As she sat down and adjusted her skirt, he dipped his head to her neck, and whispered, "All day long, Casey. All day long."

She turned to him. "All day long what?"

The auctioneer spoke. "Good evening, ladies and gentleman, and welcome to tonight's sale of modern art."

"All day long I thought of driving you wild," Nate said, finishing the thought.

She shivered against him, pressing her shoulder closer to him. My God, touching her was such a high. She was like a cat, arching her back to be pet. Every move of her body in response to even the slightest touch drove him mad with lust. He dropped his hand on her knee, tracing lazy lines across her bare flesh as the first item went up for bids. It was a lithograph by a Belgian artist, and nothing she was keen on. She showed him her paddle, and said in a hushed tone, "Would you like to use this on me later?"

He raised an eyebrow. "You'd like that, wouldn't you?"

"I guess you'll have to see," she said, that taunting look in her eyes. It threw him off for a second; he wasn't sure if she'd returned to their games of seduction. Was she playing a part again, that of the tease, the temptress? He had no interest in those roles anymore. He'd need to rid her of all interest in them too. One more night of driving her wild might do the trick.

"Sold for four thousand pounds," the man said, and his assistants promptly brought a new work to the stage. "And now we have a sculpture from Franz Dubliner."

Casey shot him a concerned look at the word *sculpture*.

He leaned in. "I'm fine. Don't even think about it," he said. To keep proving his point, he brushed his finger along the inside of her knee, heading in the direction he craved. The woman next to Casey had her gaze locked on the item on display at the front of the room, but he honestly didn't care if anyone noticed that his hands were all over the woman in the emerald-green dress.

Casey's eyes fluttered closed as his finger drifted north. He continued his travels, a grin working its way across his face at her reactions. The subtle hitch in her breath. The sweet, sexy sigh she tried to hide. The press of her thigh against his as she moved her leg closer, seeking any kind of contact as art buyers surrounding them bid on a sculpture.

"I can spend all night doing this," he whispered.

"And the opening bid is five thousand pounds," the loud voice boomed through the room.

The woman next to Casey raised her paddle, as Nate fingered the hem of her skirt. "Do you know what I thought when I first saw the picture of you in this dress? The one you texted me when I was in D.C."

"What did you think?" she asked as their neighbor continued to raise the stakes.

"That you looked edible in it." He traced the outside of her dress, skimming her thigh where she was pressed to his leg. "That the dress was like a goddamn temptation. When I saw you in it, my only thought was how much I wanted to push it up to your waist and slide my tongue over all the tight places in your body."

Her hand shot out and grasped his, her fingers digging into the bones of his hand. A bolt of lust rocketed through him from her reaction.

"What would you do if I were against the wall right now?" she whispered, and he loved that she craved more dirty words. He had a whole arsenal of them to feed to her, to send heat between her legs, to turn her damp and hot and needy for him.

"If you were up against the wall, I'd fully expect you to hike up your skirt for me. Jut out your hips. Run your fingers along the outside of your panties and give me that naughty, wild look that tells me how much you love touching yourself. Then you'd need to dip your fingers between your legs. And once you do that, you'd better let me suck all that sweetness off them."

She drew a quick breath, clamping her lips shut. He suspected she was trying to hold in a moan. Excellent.

"You're good and wet already, aren't you Casey?"

She nodded, breathing hard.

"So wet I could get down on my knees, spread those legs wide open and worship your perfect body with my mouth?"

A small pant emanated from her lips—those lips that had sent him straight into oblivion earlier today. "Yes," she murmured.

"So wet that you'd be calling my name in less than sixty seconds, right?"

"Yes." Her chest rose and fell with each breath. "I want that so much."

He licked a quick path along the shell of her ear. "You fucking love everything I do to you."

"Everything, Nate" she said, her voice all hot and wanton. She turned to him, firing up every synapse in his nervous system with the look in her sapphire eyes—they were hazy with desire, and she gazed at him like a woman in heat. Lust rolled through his body, chased by pride. He loved turning her on. He loved being the one who could get her in this state. She was so patently aroused.

"And now, we have a new painting from a rising star in the European art world. Miller Valentina. I start the bidding at three thousand pounds. Do we have three thousand pounds?"

She swiveled around, snapped to attention and thrust the paddle in the air. Damn, she was even hotter with her focus on the prize.

"We have three thousand in the room," the man at the podium intoned, pointing at Casey, as he scanned the crowd, then quickly nodded to the other side of the crowd. "3,250 in the room," he said from his post.

Nate followed the auctioneer's gesture. A man in a pinstriped suit near the back raised a paddle too. His shoulders tensed. Casey had a competitor. Nate tried to size up the guy from a distance. Slick gelled hair, a too-tight suit, and a goatee.

Casey raised her arm again. "That's 3,500 in the room," the man called out, as the price rose in increments.

She turned to Nate, speaking in a voice laced with pure determination. "I'm not letting this slip away. I want a Valentina," she said, having shifted from lust-struck to single-minded in seconds.

"3,750," the man at the front said.

Cheetah fast, Casey raised her paddle once more. Damn, she was hot going after something she wanted.

But the goateed-man wanted the painting too and signaled his intent.

"We have four thousand in the room."

Casey's arm went up again. Nate glanced at the guy in pinstripes. He matched her bid.

The pair of them went on like that for another few rounds, neither Casey nor her new nemesis backing down. Nate was tempted to jump in and offer some ridiculous price to guarantee the painting would be hers, but he knew that wasn't what she wanted. She didn't come here to have a man swoop in and save the day with his wallet. She came here for the thrill of the chase, and for the prospect of winning the prize. She wanted to win it on her own terms. But there was no way he'd let this guy take what his woman wanted, so he figured he could help her along in another way.

She raised her paddle again at five thousand pounds, her jaw set, her lips pursed.

"You are so fucking hot when you bid on art," he said to her, and she flashed a quick smile.

"Does it make you want me more?" she whispered as the goateed man hesitated briefly, but stayed in the game.

"He's wavering," Nate whispered. "Go for it. Go big, and then I can take care of that sweet ache between your legs like you want."

She trembled and her eyes flashed a hot and hungry look at him. "We can't leave. I want the other Valentina too," she said. "I just decided it. I need both."

"And you'll get both. And as soon as you get this one, we'll find an office or another sales room or a coat closet, I don't care. But I'm going to have my hands up your dress in about fifteen seconds," he said roughly, and his tone seemed to spur her on.

"Do we have 5,250 pounds?"

Casey raised her arm high, and then spoke in a loud, but measured tone. "6,500 pounds."

The auctioneer raised his eyebrows in appreciation, then scanned the room, his gaze settling on Casey's opponent. Nate watched the pin-striped man start to lift his paddle, but it was half-hearted at best. The man shook his head.

The auctioneer beamed. "I shall sell it then. It's the woman in the green dress' bid at 6500 pounds." He slammed the hammer down. "Sold."

The expression on her face was one of pure victory, then she wrapped her fingers around his wrist and stood. She tipped her head to the exit. When they walked out, he heard the man who'd lost out utter a curse of frustration. Nate didn't take it personally; not getting what you wanted was a bitch.

Thirty seconds later, they were inside a bathroom at Sotheby's, locking the door behind them.

"By my calculations we've got less than eight minutes 'til the next Valentina goes up for bidding," she said, and locked her arms around his neck. "Give me something."

A tremor of desire shook him to his bones. He wanted nothing more than to take her hard and fast, and send her back into the sales room, ready to bid again, looking like a woman who'd been fucked thoroughly. But her pleasure always came first for him, and what turned him on most was sending her flying into bliss. He'd wait for the hotel to get his own needs met.

"Turn around," he told her, and she slinked around in his arms. "Look in the mirror," he said, gesturing at the gold-framed glass along the wall, reflecting her back at him. "See how sexy you are? You're all fired up from winning, and you're heated up from wanting me. This is who I've been looking at all night—the most beautiful, stunning, sexy and powerful woman I've ever seen. A woman who goes after what she wants. Who pursues what she wants. And no one has ever aroused me like you do," he said, savoring her reaction to his words as she trembled in his arms. He clasped his hand around her throat, not too tight to hurt her, but firm enough to hold her as his. To let her know she belonged to him. Her lips fell open, and she breathed out sharply as he stared at her captivating reflection.

He dipped his mouth to her ear. "Watching you bid on that painting made me so fucking hard," he whispered in a ragged voice as he yanked her backside against his hard-on.

A sexy whimper escaped her throat. "I'll bid on more then. I love turning you on," she said, sliding her hand between them to rub her palm against his straining erection. The feel of her was extraordinary, but he hadn't taken her to the private bathroom to let her play with his boner. He gripped her hand and tugged it away, then took her other hand and raised both her arms over her head.

"And you do it exceedingly well. But the answer is no. You took care of me earlier today, and now it's my turn to have my way with you. You keep your hands to yourself right now, and let mine do the work," he said, sharply. "Put your arms around my neck."

She reached behind, threading her hands around his neck, her body molded to his. She was so damn vulnerable in this pose. She was his like this, restrained simply by the position.

"I need you to keep your arms around me the whole time, Casey," he said, as he lowered his hands to the hem of her dress and yanked it up. "Can you do that?"

"I can," she said, her voice feathery.

One hand traveled up the soft, smooth skin of her belly, while the other made its way due south, sliding into her lacy panties and meeting her slick heat instantly. He groaned appreciatively. She matched him with a needy, desperate sound. God, this woman loved being touched.

"That's how I want you to feel with me," he said, sliding his fingers across that delicious wetness. "This aroused. This hot. This wild."

"I do. I swear I do," she said on a sexy pant, leaning her head on his shoulder, her cheek hitting his face. She was a fucking sight—her lush body all curved along his, her neck long and inviting, her hands bound of their own volition behind his head. She was giving him control yet again, turning her pleasure over to him.

Her sensuality was like a gift given freely. No, it was a goddamn treasure, and he intended to treat it that way. He slid his fingers across her slick folds, his lungs burning with desire for her as her body took off under his touch. Instantly, she rocked into him, her hips arching into the source of her pleasure. When he brushed over her swollen clit, she practically shoved herself into his hand.

"Oh, sweetness, you want it badly, don't you?" he whispered in her ear, yanking her even closer.

"So badly," she moaned.

"As much as I want it? Can you feel how much I want it?" he said, making absolutely certain she could feel every damn inch of his erection jammed against her back.

"I can feel it. I want it too, Nate," she said, arching into his hand, hunting for more friction, more speed. He couldn't resist. He wanted to tease her, but her pussy was too ready, too perfect. The feel of her heat in his hands was some kind of drug. It scrambled his brain.

"You wanted me to make you beg for it," he said, trying to hold onto her wishes from earlier. "You wanted me to send you to the brink, but not over, right?"

"Oh God, no, please," she cried out, her voice pitching. "Don't tease me, Nate. I'm close. I'm so close."

He met her eyes in the mirror. They were wild and hungry. She thrust her hips against his hand, riding his finger as she held tight to the back of his neck, offering herself to him so completely.

"Don't you want me to drive you wild with desire?"

"You have," she cried out, riding his hand as far and as hard as she could, writhing against him, a wriggly, wild creature in his arms. "You are. I'm going crazy. Please don't make me wait," she said, then repeated it, like a desperate chant, a plea for relief. "Please don't make me wait. Please don't make me wait."

He held on tight to her belly, slamming her as close to him as the laws of physics made it possible for two clothed people to be. He stroked her faster, thrusting a finger inside her beautiful cunt, as he said, "Never. I could never deny you. Come, sweetness. Come in my arms. I've got you," he said, and she cried out, rocking harder, faster and more beautifully than ever as she rode his hand, coming undone for him at Sotheby's.

Minutes later, after hands were washed and clothes were straightened, they returned to the sales room. Casey stopped in her tracks, and pointed, then clasped her hand over her mouth. The man with the slick hair and pin-striped suit grinned as if he'd caught a huge marlin.

"And *The Big Love* is sold for six thousand pounds."

The auctioneer pounded the podium with his hammer.

She cringed. All her features tightened, and she clenched her fists in utter frustration. "I wanted it," she said on a heavy sigh. "I wanted it so badly."

He wished he could steal it away for her. But the painting was no longer on the market.

She turned to him, grabbed the lapels of his jacket, and said, "Win some, lose some. Take me back to our room and do that to me again and again all night long."

CHAPTER TWENTY-ONE

London, night . . .

There was no more time for waiting. There would be no more teasing. Her dress pooled at her feet less than five seconds after entering their suite.

"I'm not anywhere near done with you," he said, unknotting his tie, yanking it off, and tossing it on the floor. That answered one question that had hovered in her mind —he wouldn't be tying her up with his tie tonight.

She stepped out of her shoes. She wore only her lingerie.

"I want you on the floor," he said, unbuttoning his shirt, revealing his strong, hard chest. Her mouth watered as she stepped backward.

"Is this another lesson?" she asked, her voice wobbly as she flashed back to the first night in New Orleans when he'd told her to get down on her knees.

He shook his head. "I'm done with teaching you. There are no more lessons. Did you want more?"

"No. I only want you," she said in a small voice, somehow managing to admit that she was ready to move on.

Where they were headed next she had no idea. This might be their last night together, until he cut her loose, adrift in the world as a newly-trained woman who'd learned how to let go of all her tightly held need for control. She shuddered inside at the thought of this ending, but then pushed all the worries out of her mind as he reached the final button on his shirt.

"Good. Because I'm about to do something you've wanted. Something you asked me to do. But I'm not doing it as your teacher. I'm doing it tonight as your lover."

"That's who I want you to be now," she said, and the words were easier than she'd expected, so much easier, because they were so damn true.

He swallowed. She watched his Adam's apple bob up and down. Such a vulnerable point on an otherwise hard body. So much of him was hard and fierce, but so much was vulnerable too. He'd begun to show more of those sides to her, and she thrived on knowing all of him—all his passion, all his pain, all his hurt, all his hope.

All of him.

"Take everything off," he said.

She stepped out of her black lace panties, grateful to be rid of the damp scrap of fabric, then her bra, leaving them in a soft heap on the plush carpet. He groaned at the sight of her, and a ribbon of heat unfurled in her chest—to this desired was such a rush, such a pure, unmitigated high. She had never felt so sensual as she did under Nate's heady gaze. The low neon lighting in the room set the mood, though the mood had technically been set long ago. Back in New Orleans one hot steamy night when she'd propositioned her best friend, and he'd said yes. They'd hurdled down this sensual road through the Big Easy, to their hometown of New York, and now, here in London.

Only this time, they were shedding the seduction. They were stripped free of games, and relying solely on themselves.

She didn't want it any other way.

She didn't want *him* any other way.

He grabbed a chair and dragged it over to her, swiveling it around so the slats faced her. "Hands on the chair. Grip it hard."

She kneeled before him, knotting her fingers through the wooden slats, like she was in church at a pew, praying —praying for release. A quiver sped through her body, chased with a dash of fear. But it was the good fear; the kind that twisted and curled hotly through her blood as he led her down this path. She didn't know what he planned, but she loved exploring the unknown with him.

Only with him.

He walked behind her, gently covering her hair with his big, strong hand palming her head. She craned her neck, peering up at him. He dragged his hand down her hair, threading his fingers through the blond strands.

"When you first asked me to teach you to let go, I agreed, even though it meant you were learning things to use with someone else. Right now, there's no teaching. I'm only taking. I'm taking something I want for me," he said, and the roughness in his voice sent shivers on a thrill ride down her spine as he shrugged out of his white shirt. He widened his stance, a foot on each side of her naked legs. She felt overpowered, thoroughly under his control as electric sparks shot across her skin.

"Take whatever you want," she said, as he bent over her, his shirt in both hands. Then he twisted it, round and round, turning the item of clothing into a taut, makeshift rope. She offered her wrists, and he wrapped the shirt around them, then threaded the material through the slats, tying her to the top of the chair.

He tested the knots in the shirt. "Nice and tight," he said, then he trailed his fingers through her hair once more, gripping it in a ponytail, twisting it around his fist once and yanking her head back. "What do you think I'm going to take right now?"

"I have no idea," she said, nerves lacing her voice. Her knees dug into the carpet.

"Then let me show you what I want from you. You can start by spreading your knees."

She did as he asked. Completely exposed to him, she was wide open and waiting. Heat pooled between her legs as she grew wetter with anticipation.

The next thing she knew he was on the floor, sliding under her. His hands were on her thighs and his face was between her legs. "You're going down on me like this?"

He shook his head, his thumbs digging into her thighs. "I'm not going down on you. You're going to fuck my face."

A white-hot bolt of lightning streaked through her body. Desire burned in her veins as she positioned herself over him, straddling his face, watching the dark and hungry look in his eyes.

"It's all you now, Casey. Hump my face. Go to town. Have a field day on me," he said, and her nipples pebbled as sensations that she'd never felt before raced through her bones. He hadn't even touched her yet, but his words and his breath so close to the center of her world had her skin sizzling.

He grasped her legs tightly, and even though she was on top of him, he had all the control, with her hands bound, and her knees spread. There was nothing left to do but ride his face into blissful oblivion.

"Go fucking wild and let go. Come on my face," he told her.

She lowered herself the final few inches and his tongue darted out, so eager to taste her. He moaned loudly when they made contact, her sounds and his murmurs sending jolts through her body. She rocked against him, pleasure igniting in her core as his tongue and lips worked their magic across her wet folds. Moving her hips, picking up the pace, she gave in to all that she felt with them, to the pleasure that pounded through her blood, to the electric desire that thrummed in her core. To the wildness of this kind of contact.

That word flashed through her brain.

Wild.

She felt wild with him. Wild and free and reckless as she rocked into his face, grinding, pushing, thrusting. Having a field day. Humping him. Fucking him. Riding him for dear life, holding on with her thighs until her belly tightened, and she felt the first tremor of possibility.

Her orgasm wasn't far off. She was so worked up already from what he'd done to her at the auction, from the way he'd talked to her in the room, and simply from the way he treasured her, even when he was a filthy, commanding, controlling fucker.

Maybe even especially then. She loved that dirty side of him as much as she loved the tender side.

"It feels soooo good," she cried out as she rocked harder and faster into him. She might have had all her weight on him. She was sitting on his face, after all. But that was what he wanted, and she wanted it too. To ride him to bliss; to come undone as he lay on the floor, prone beneath her.

The sound of a zipper being worked open landed in her ears. She turned her head as she kept up her frantic pace. Her breath caught in her chest. He'd undone his pants with one hand and was stroking his cock. "That's so fucking sexy," she said, the pressure in her center skyrocketing as she witnessed how utterly turned on he was. He was so goddamn aroused he *had* to touch himself. "Have you done that before while thinking of me?"

Somehow, he managed a nod. And that information launched her off the cliff.

The vision of him fucking his own fist while she rode his face was as hot as anything ever was. Screw submission. Screw control. Nate was right. Great sex was two people who clawed at each other, who tore off clothes, who had to have each other. He licked and kissed her with such passion and desire that she had no choice but to do as he'd told her—to go wild and let go.

"Everything is so good with you. *Everything,*" she shouted, as she gripped the wood tighter, her fingers curling around the slats, holding on hard as she thrust into his face, riding into a kaleidoscope of neon and color and chaotic bliss, chanting his name over and over.

Her legs shook, her heart beat at a million miles, and she shuddered from the aftershocks that rippled through her.

She wanted to sink onto him, to fall to the floor, to simply bask in the glow of this epic orgasm he had wrought from her as the world slowly slipped back into focus, only better, brighter, more beautiful.

But he had other plans, because he'd slid out from under her to stand up and skim down his pants. Turning her gaze over her shoulder, she drew a sharp breath at the sight of his hard cock, ready and throbbing. He brought his hand back down to his dick, stroking it.

"I need you," he gritted out. "I fucking need you so much."

Then his hands were on her backside, and he yanked her up on her feet. Her hands remained bound on the chair, so she was bent at the waist. He positioned himself between her legs, and dragged the head of his cock through her wetness, drawing another cry from deep inside her chest. She flattened her back, lifting up her ass, giving him all the access he'd need.

But then his palm came down hard on her rear, sending a sting through her from the surprise.

"Ow," she cried out.

"You know you loved it," he said, as he bent over the chair and untied her from the slats. He kept her wrists bound together, and picked her up, carrying her to the bed a few feet away. He gently laid her down on her back, then lifted her arms above her head, rearranging her on the bed into the pose she'd been in at the auction house.

She didn't wait for directions from him. She knew what she wanted. Him inside her. She spread her legs.

"Oh fuck, Casey. You can't do that to me," he said as he stared at her hot center.

"Why not?"

"Because I'm not taking you like that yet. I'm saving that," he said, then promptly flipped her over onto her stomach in one swift move. She started to prop herself up on elbows and knees, figuring he wanted her on all fours.

But instead, he gently pressed his hand on her lower back pushing her down. "This is how I want you," he murmured.

He climbed over her, pressing his thumbs on the inside of her thighs, opening her up again. Bound, flat on her belly, legs spread, she was his for the taking. He covered her with his strong body. His skin was hot, and the soft hair on his chest tickled her spine. His erection was nestled between her cheeks, and for a second, maybe more, she wondered if he might go there, and claim her ass. She wasn't sure if she wanted that. Maybe someday, but not yet. She was about to voice her protest when she felt him guiding his cock lower, away from her ass, teasing her heat with the tip.

"Please," she said, so eager to have him fill her. She longed desperately for penetration, for that glorious moment when he buried himself all the way in her.

"Please what?"

"Please, Nate. I need you inside me. I'm dying to feel you."

He wrapped an arm around her chest, one hand cupping her breast, rubbing her hard nipple. "God, Casey. You are my weakness. I can't deny you a fucking thing. You say one word and I give it to you."

He sank into her, and she soared. She flew. She rocketed into a whole new dimension of bliss and sensual joy as he stroked into her.

Their sounds mingled—their sighs, and moans and pants collided in some kind of sinfully sexy melody of coming togetherness. He moved inside her, taking long, luxurious strokes as his fingertips grazed her nipples, and he held her tight, imprisoning her with his body.

She arched into him, matching his thrusts. He angled his mouth against her neck, kissing her there, working his way up to her ear as he swiveled his hips, then paused, making her want him even more before he answered her body's prayer and drove into her.

His hand came down hard on her chin, gripping her. He turned her face, so she was even closer to him. Her body sang out in response, wetness coating him. "Do you feel that? How wet you get with me?"

"Yes."

"I can feel you all over my cock. I can feel you when you get more aroused. Your pussy gets so hot, and you grip my dick, and then I slide in even more," he said, in a harsh whisper in her ear. As if on command, she felt that rush of heat swoop from her belly straight between her legs. "Like that," he groaned. "Just like that. God, I love it, Casey. I fucking love everything about this." He picked up speed, fucking her harder and faster, his hand on her chin, his other hand still gripping her breast. She could barely move, and she didn't want to. All she wanted was this pos- session, this complete and utter possession.

"Me too. No one has ever made me feel this way," she managed to say in between her pants and moans.

"How do I make you feel?" he asked, raising up, and then slamming back into her.

She searched for the words; she felt them on the tip of her tongue. She knew what she was hunting for, but she was afraid to say it, so she managed something close enough. "Like you can't get enough of me," she answered, looking up at him, even from this position. His eyes blazed at her; they were full of such passion. She was caught in a tractor beam of intensity.

"I can't get enough of you," he said, so raw and hoarse as he ran his finger over her mouth, brushing it along the inside of her bottom lip. She nibbled on his finger then opened her mouth to lead him in. He slid his finger between her lips. She eagerly took it, sucking, swirling, loving on his finger as if she were sucking him off while he pushed deeper into her pussy. "Do you have any idea how long I've wanted to be with you?"

"How long?" she asked as he simulated fucking her mouth.

He moved his mouth to her ear. "I've wanted you so fucking much. For so fucking long," he whispered, and it was a confession. A complete and utter confession that shocked her to the bone then sent a glorious burst of pleasure down her spine and straight to her core.

"Nate," she moaned. "I need you to untie me. Flip me over, and make love to me like that."

In seconds, he'd freed her hands from his shirt, and turned her over, missionary style. He slipped out of her in the process, and she sat up, reaching for his erection, sliding him home again as she lay back on the mattress, raising her knees to clamp them on his hips.

She was free now. Free to touch him. To hold him. To run her fingers across his skin. "Sometimes, I need to have my hands on you too," she said softly as he returned to that lingering pace, that slow and sensual rhythm that drove her just to the brink, but not quite over.

"Touch me," he said, in the most tender voice that nailed her straight in the heart. His vulnerability took center stage right now, even as his strong body topped hers. She brought her hands to his face, cupping his cheeks, tracing lines along his jaw. He gasped and closed his eyes, a barely-there moan of her name escaping his lips.

"Nate," she whispered. "Look at me."

He opened his eyes, and she melted. She absolutely melted under his gaze. She was in heaven with him. She was in complete and utter bliss. "I love the way you feel in me," she told him as she wrapped her legs around his back. "You make me feel so good."

"You should feel good."

"I love the way you move in me. I love having you inside me," she said, hooking her ankles behind his ass, drawing him deeper.

"Oh God," he groaned. "You're killing me."

"Do you know why I love it so much?"

"Why?" he asked, and his voice sounded nearly broken, like she'd stripped him of all his defenses, and he was bare before her.

"Because," she said, her fingers tracing his beautiful face. "Because it's you."

Then her back bowed, and she grabbed his neck, an orgasm sneaking up out of nowhere, pulling her under, crashing over her, consuming her in a tidal wave of bliss. "Oh God, I'm coming again," she said, crying out as she grabbed at him, pulling him closer.

"Fuck, I can feel you coming on me," he groaned.

She clutched at him, holding on tight to his shoulders as the pleasure rolled through her.

When the waves subsided, he was still right there above her, and hard as a rock inside her.

"There's a problem," she said playfully, in between breaths. "I'm three tonight to your none."

"Don't worry, sweetness. We've going to make it four to one soon. Where's that LolaRing we were going to try?"

Somehow, she managed to scramble out from under him to grab the toy from her suitcase. When she returned to the bed he was on his back, his hands behind his head, his dick at full attention.

"I believe you like to be on top, Miss Casey," he said, with a wink, and her heart tripped on itself. In that moment she knew for certain everything had changed. He was still her Nate, making her laugh in the middle of the most intense night of lovemaking in her life. Through it all, he'd possessed her, he'd revered her, and he'd revealed himself to her. And now, he was giving her back the thing he'd taught her to give up.

Control.

"My favorite position," she said, as she straddled him, sliding her hand over his cock, slick with her wetness. She leaned closer, her hair hitting his chest, as she purred in his ear. "You're all hot and wet from me."

He thrust up into her hand on a groan. "Yes, I am. Now finish us both off."

She rolled the toy onto his shaft, pushing the ring all the way to the base, and angling the Lola vibration exactly where it would hit her most sensitive spot. "Not that we would ever say this in our marketing, but for your ears only . . . I hear this is like being licked and fucked at the same time," she said, as she flicked it on and sank onto him and . . .

The earth stopped rotating. Time stood still. She nearly wept from the pleasure that burst in her body. Her bones rattled, her brain hummed, and she rode him, rising up and sinking back down on the toy as it buzzed merrily on her clit.

His hands found their way to her hair. "Kiss me while you fuck me," he whispered, and she obeyed.

Her lips crashed down on his, and she devoured him. His mouth was the sweetest thing she'd ever had, and she hungrily sought more of him. But she could barely sustain the kiss because her body was taking off again. "Oh God," she moaned into his mouth. He slid his hands along her spine, gripping her ass, taking over the work. She couldn't focus. She couldn't concentrate. The pleasure was too intense. Her brain short-circuited, and he thrust deep, moving her up and down on his fantastic cock that was made even more perfect by the insistent pressure from the toy. She felt so greedy, so ravenous as she sought out another orgasm. She couldn't help herself; Nate had turned her into this wild woman.

"Come with me," she moaned. "Please, Nate. Please come with me. I have to have you."

"You have me, Casey. You have me, I promise," he said, hoarsely, as he rocked hard into her, unleashing another round of ecstasy in her body. She shattered, bright white lights exploding behind her eyes as she convulsed around him, and he joined her, slamming up into her, driving deeper and harder and farther as he gripped her hips, and released himself inside her, groaning her name like she was his everything.

"This can't stop," he said as he shuddered, and pulled her close to him, his arms encircling her. Bliss radiated through her entire being. Sheer joy was all she consisted of. And happiness, so much unexpected happiness from his words.

"It can't end. I can't let this go. I can't let *you* go," she said, lifting her face to look him in the eyes.

"Don't let me go," he whispered.

"I won't," she said, running her fingers through his hair. She should have felt nervous. She should have been scared with what they were saying, knowing his track record, knowing his lines in the sand. Perhaps, if she were smarter about men and sex and love, perhaps if she truly did play games, she'd have held back. But her heart was so damn full it was about to burst with all these feelings. There was no way to contain all she felt. There was no way to keep it to herself. "When we were first together, I wanted you to teach me how to be submissive, and show me how to be seductive. But now I've been seduced by you."

His lips quirked up in a smile, and he shook his head. "No, it's the other way around. You've seduced me."

CHAPTER TWENTY-TWO

Las Vegas, later that week . . .

"Do you ever miss the stage?"

Brent Nichols tilted his head to the side and considered the question that Nate Harper posed to him. He leaned back in his chair, crossed his legs and nodded. "Yeah, I definitely miss the stage. But not as much as I thought I would," he said. "I still moonlight, doing a show once a month, and that seems to be enough to feed me. The late-night TV circuit kept me pretty satisfied for a few years. Better to go out on a high note."

Brent had just finished a wildly successful run on a late-night TV show that his brother, Clay, had arranged for him. The show had generated record ratings, legions of fans, and more success than he had imagined. He'd made a purposeful decision to walk away when it was still a hit. One of the things he couldn't abide by was wearing out his welcome. Brent had always prided himself on never staying in one place, one gig, or at one job for longer than he was wanted. So he'd "retired" from the nightly work as a comedian. He'd also hungered for a change, eager to be more than the so-called "bad boy of comedy," with his tats, motorcycle boots, and edgy style. He craved the new challenge of building a business.

That was where Nate came in. They'd been talking about moving his first nightclub inside The Luxe, one of the most coveted properties on The Strip, and they were about ready to close the deal. Brent was in Nate's office at the Vegas property, laptop in hand, ready to share plans.

"Man, I already miss your show. Your bit about first date waxing always killed me," Nate said, and Brent chuckled. That had indeed been a popular routine, and had cracked him up a few times too when he'd practiced it. "But I'm glad to see the next phase of your career is working out. You want to show me your plans?"

Brent flipped open his laptop. "Here's what I've got in mind for the club." He rolled his chair closer to the computer screen, and clicked open the file, but he'd misfired, and a browser window popped open.

Fuck. He half wished it had been porn on screen, but no such luck. He'd left open the Facebook profile of Shannon Paige.

Curvy. Gorgeous. Brilliant. And probably hated him.

Nate tipped his forehead to the screen. "Doing a little Facebook stalking?" he asked him dryly.

If it were anyone else, Brent probably would've tossed out a quip, tried to make a joke. But he knew Nate well enough by now, because the man was friends with his brother and his brother's wife, Julia, courtesy of the mutual friends they all shared in New York. "Ex-girlfriend," he admitted.

"Ah. Recent breakup?"

"About ten years ago," Brent said with a self-deprecating laugh.

"Not so recent then," Nate said in a deadpan voice. "Sounds like she's still got a hold on you."

Brent shrugged, his way of saying *yes*. "College girl-friend. Haven't seen her in years."

"Well, I hope that changes—that is, if you want it to change."

Hell, did he ever want that to change. But he had no clue what Shannon was up to these days beyond a few posts she made on her Facebook profile, and chances were he wouldn't run into her again. He hadn't heard much from her since he'd walked away that night ten years ago.

He closed out the window, shifting gears, and showing Nate his vision for the nightclub.

After they discussed the logistics, Brent gestured to the door, and the world of the casino beyond it. "You up for a round of blackjack?"

"Hell yeah. I'm a gambler these days," Nate said. They left his office and headed to the casino floor at The Luxe.

"What is it that's making you a gambling man?"

"This and that," he said, as they parked themselves on stools at a nearby blackjack table, the hustle and bustle of the casino surrounding them, the slap of cards on tables, the cha-ching of money from slots, and the scent in the air of desire for bets to turn into bigger bets.

Brent didn't press it. Whatever Nate was betting on these days was clearly private.

* * *

Nate was betting on change. He was betting on possibilities. He was betting on hopefully someday soon having the guts to tell Casey how he was really feeling.

That prospect scared the hell out of him. He had no clue how to find the courage to even begin to verbalize all that he felt for her, and how much she was changing his ideas of everything he'd ever wanted in his post-Joanna life. In a few short weeks she'd upended his priorities, and had him considering everything he'd sworn off since he'd stumbled across the emails from Joanna and her professor.

But then, that wasn't entirely true. He hadn't *only* started thinking of Casey that way in recent weeks. Those notions had been forming since he had first started to get to know her. They'd simply elbowed their way to the front of the pack after he'd touched her, kissed her, held her, and experienced the magic of her coming apart in his arms. He supposed that was the power of such intimacy—it could shake a man to the core. It could change a man.

If he let it.

That was the big *if.*

That night in London had rocked his world, and had ended their roles as teacher and student. They'd become lovers for real. They'd been together like that again and again in New York when they returned, spending nights tangled up in each other, unable to resist touching, exploring, discovering the depths of their connection. The answer? It was endless.

Which was both wonderful and terrifying.

It was the dark unknown.

Maybe that was why neither one had said more about what the night in London meant. All he'd managed was to let her know that he didn't want this time with her to end. Which was terribly unfair because he knew deep down that he could never be enough for her long-term, and he'd have to figure out what the hell to do with this crazy mass of emotions that was rattling around in his head and in his heart.

For now, he had a soft seventeen, so he asked the dealer to hit. He was willing to take a chance on twenty-one. He overshot though, and lost a handful of chips to the house.

"Win some, lose some," he said to Brent, and the two men played a few more rounds.

Later that afternoon, he settled into his seat on the Gulfstream, along with a pack of Chihuahua-Mini Pin mixes from a local shelter that was overrun with dogs. They were sharing the flight with him from Vegas to Manhattan, en route to their new homes. The tiniest of the crew had insisted on curling up in his lap, a small brown and tan creature who liked to snuggle.

The flight attendant stopped by and stroked the little dog's head, then rested her hand on the armrest. A brunette with a gorgeous figure, she was exactly the type of pretty that would have lured him to talk to her had he met her at a bar—his type being sexy and someone he never expected to see more than three times.

But he had no desire for her.

He had no desire for anyone but his good friend who had rocked his body, his head, his heart, and his whole entire world.

"The pilot said we'll be ready to go in five minutes, Mr. Harper. Is there anything I can get for you?"

"I'm all set," he said, and she returned to the front of the cabin.

His phone buzzed, and he checked the new message. It was a text from Jack. He read the note and laughed. Rather than text back, he gave him a ring.

"Lucky me. A phone call from my best man," Jack said when he answered.

Nate laughed. "Yeah, and to answer your question, I'm pretty sure there are no strip clubs at my property in the Maldives."

"Damn. I was really looking forward to a lap dance at my bachelor party."

"Sorry to let you down," Nate said, but it was all in jest. Jack had no plans for a bachelor party, and certainly none at a strip club. He wasn't the strip club type, nor was Nate, for that matter. Besides, there was only one woman he wanted to see stripping—

Shit.

It hit Nate like a flying ton of bricks. It wasn't as if he'd forgotten Casey was Jack's sister, but it simply hadn't mattered much when they were merely messing around. Now it mattered, and Nate was going to have to man up and say something to Jack. Something like, "I'm falling for your sister." Or maybe something closer to the truth. "I've been crazy about her for years, and I'm pretty sure the feeling is mutual, and I have no clue what to do about it, and if I hurt her I will hate myself forever and ever, and I don't know how to *not* hurt her, but I don't know how to not be with her either. Got any advice?"

But his flight had begun to taxi, so now was not the time for that conversation. Perhaps next week, when Nate

234 · LAUREN BLAKELY

saw his buddy in person. Actually, that would have to be item number one on his agenda since there was no way Jack, or Michelle especially, would miss the vibes between him and Casey.

They chatted for another minute, then Nate told him the plane was about to take off. He said goodbye, then quickly fired off a text to the woman who was front and center for him: *Looking forward to seeing you later tonight. Your place?*

They'd been at his home a few times, and at her apartment the other nights. Her next-door-neighbor had even started saying hello to him when they ran into each other in the hall. There was something that felt right about being a part of her life like that.

Then he added one more line to the text before he sent it off.

Thanks again for helping with the sculpture.

As promised, Casey had helped him find the one-time wedding gift on a back shelf of his closet, then boxed it up for him. He'd told Joanna he'd deliver it to the gallery where she was showing some of her work. Casey had offered to take it, but he couldn't let her do all his dirty work. Besides, if he was going to move forward with her, he had to be man enough to face his ex-wife, even if it was simply to hand over a sculpture.

Once the jet was airborne, he reviewed the formal proposal that Casey had sent him for The Luxe's rollout of the pleasure packs in some of their resorts, with the LolaRing as the centerpiece. He sent a few minor notes back, suggesting they announce the pending deal soon. All in all, it looked good, and they were on the same page when it came to marketing—no need to say it felt like *being licked and fucked at the same time*. For the business deal, they'd decided to go with her classier suggestion for their honeymoon suite wording: *You've given her a diamond ring, now give her the LolaRing.* An exclusive partnership, it made The Luxe the only hotel chain in the world to partner with Joy Delivered on the new product's launch.

Funny how all the details of their business deal were laid out in black and white, and all the specifics of their lessons had been determined in advance. But now, he was flying blindly with Casey, operating without a guidebook, and completely unsure how to navigate this new stretch they'd encountered.

He only hoped he didn't crash.

CHAPTER TWENTY-THREE

New York, same day . . .

As Casey finished a sip of her cinnamon dolce latte, she tossed out a question that had been nagging at her.

"I have no clue how to do this, Jane. When I see him tonight, do I just say *I'm absolutely crazy for you and I want to have a go at this for real?*"

Jane nodded enthusiastically. "That's certainly one way you can do it. Just be completely direct and upfront with him," her friend suggested, as she drank her tea.

"It's not as if I've had the best luck being totally direct with men," Casey said. She'd caught Jane up to speed with the Nate situation, from how it had started, to how it had changed, and to what she wanted now with him. The answer to that was starkly clear. She wanted him all to herself for a long, long time. She had never expected this to happen, but she'd fallen for him something fierce. He was tender and protective, funny and smart, and so damn passionate. Her intensity for him knew no bounds, and she was sure he was crazy for her too, even though he hadn't said as much in words. The connection between them, though, was so strong that neither one could stay away from each other. The last few nights had been nothing short of amazing.

They hadn't tried to put a label on what was happening, but Casey knew herself, and she couldn't do casual. She needed to define what they were and where they were going. She needed to know if there was a real future, like she longed for. The best way to do that was to be straightforward and put it all on the table, even though the thought of that terrified her, given her track record of speaking her mind with men.

"From what you told me, Nate doesn't seem to be like those other guys you dated. Those assholes who had a problem with you saying what you wanted."

"He's definitely in a class by himself," she said.

Jane slapped the table with her palm. "Then go for it. Tell him how you feel."

"How is it that you've never had this problem with men? You're a rock star. I can't imagine anybody more intimidating than you," Casey asked.

Jane laughed. "Oh, maybe it had a little something to do with the fact that my first husband turned out to be gay and I fell madly in love with the next guy I was involved with," Jane said with a laugh. At least she was able to joke about that heartbreak now.

Casey laughed. "Good point. Fine, you win."

Jane raised her arms in victory, then turned serious. "But for what it's worth, I do think you should just be up front with him. At the least the two of you can know what you're dealing with."

238 · LAUREN BLAKELY

"What if I lose him as a friend though? I hate the thought of that happening."

"I think the more direct you are now, the better off you'll be at staying in each other's lives in whatever capacity that is," Jane said.

Casey nodded several times as if this conversation was giving her the courage to show her cards to the man she was falling for. He was on his way back from Vegas and she was looking forward to seeing him tonight after he returned Joanna's sculpture. He'd insisted on doing it himself, and she had to admit she was proud of him for facing up to what scared him the most—Joanna and all the pain she'd caused him.

As they cleared their mugs and left the coffee shop, the name Grant Abbot flashed across her phone. Her blood froze. He was supposed to be overseas still, and she'd planned on telling him when he returned that things had changed, and her heart was elsewhere. She took a deep, fueling breath, steeling herself, then answered with a breezy and business-like *hello*.

"Any chance you would be free for a drink this evening? I find myself in New York City sooner than expected and I'll be in the mood for a cocktail tonight."

Casey gulped. A flock of nerves swept through her body. She could hardly believe that three weeks ago she wanted to seduce him, and now the prospect held no interest for her. But she also didn't want to leave the man hanging. Being upfront with Nate would need to start with Grant. She'd have to let him know they were only in business together, and nothing more. Perhaps, the timing was serendipitous. She'd end things before they started with Grant, then she'd start something more with Nate.

She gave Grant the address for Speakeasy and said she'd see him there this evening. She returned to the office, plowed through work, and finally remembered to respond to Ethan Holmes.

She clicked on his note from nearly two weeks ago, then opened the attachment and read his proposal. He was a smart guy, and it was ironic because he'd suggested something a bit similar to the deal she and Nate were finalizing. Ethan didn't know about the LolaRing. Joy Delivered was keeping the new toy under wraps until the official launch later this summer. Ethan had, however, suggested the Victoria Hotels start offering The Wild One, a popular toy in the Joy Delivered catalogue, as part of a "Late-Night Sex Toy Menu to satisfy the red-hot appetites!"

He hadn't quite hit the mark with the brand positioning she'd established at Joy Delivered—discreet, sexy and sensual being the watchwords. Nonetheless, she admired his gumption, so she fired off a quick reply: *Love the concept! Really appreciate you thinking of us. There's so much I like about this proposal, but we are in the process of finalizing a deal with another hotel, so we'll have to pass at the moment.*

Then, because it was always best to leave future partnerships open, she added a final line.

Looking forward to exploring possibilities with you! Drinks soon?

The idea did have some merit though. Maybe not for Joy Delivered, but perhaps for another company. Casey was friendly with one of Joy Delivered's competitors, Good Vibes, and could envision Ethan's concept working better for that firm. So she typed once more: *I actually have a great idea for this. Let me make some calls and I'll get back to you.*

When she gathered up her purse a bit later to head out for her meeting with Grant, she clicked on her text messages. Laying it on the table with Nate could start with this level of honesty—the one hundred percent kind, so she hit reply on the note he'd sent her before he left.

Hi. Grant Abbot is in town. I'm meeting him for drinks to discuss our deal. I plan to let him know as well that I'm taken these days. Speaking of taken, perhaps you can take me tonight.

She hit send. There. It wasn't so hard taking that first step.

When she reached Speakeasy, she said hello to Julia behind the bar, then gave a quick hug to her husband, Clay, who was enjoying a scotch and chatting with his wife as she mixed drinks.

"Didn't think we'd see you until the flight next week," he said, since he and Julia, along with Michelle's brother and his wife, would be sharing Nate's plane to the Maldives.

"You know I can't resist Speakeasy," Casey told him, then gestured to a booth. "I'm meeting a business associate. I better go grab a spot."

"See you soon."

A few minutes later Grant strolled in, scanning for her, then grinning widely when he spotted her. She waved, and soon he was wrapping his arms around her in a warm embrace. He was, as always, a handsome devil. And though she'd been keen on him for a year, whatever had been there was gone. She felt nothing—no spark, no zing, not even a frisson of attraction. That was good. After all, she was downright crazy for another man, and she didn't want to feel anything for anyone but Nate.

Even so, she felt a bit like a first-class jerk knowing she was about to *break up* with the guy before they'd even started.

"Such a delight to see you again," he said, and then slid into the booth. He signaled a waiter, ordered a vodka, then shot her a smile once more. He'd always been an outgoing guy, but oddly enough he seemed less flirty this time, and more . . . *friendly.* As they chatted about their deal, she noticed his innuendo was gone, and he was simply being straightforward.

Which was exactly what she needed to be with him.

"Grant, I'm so glad you're here and that everything is all set for our rollout. I do need to be upfront though about the other matters we talked about in New Orleans—the possibility of us getting together," she began, keeping her voice as business-like and cordial as she could.

He held up a hand to stop her, shaking his head, and grinning.

"Actually, I need to be direct with you too. And I need to say I'm sorry if I led you on," he said, his Southern charm shining through in his tone. But the words surprised her.

She furrowed her brow. "What do you mean, Grant?"

He took a deep breath. "You see, I have a natural tendency to be flirty, and I should truly curb that habit. I've been told, in fact, that I'm too much of a flirt. I would never cross the line with a business partner, so I hope you'll forgive me if I made you think otherwise in New Orleans. I remain, as ever, completely committed to our business deal. But I wanted to make it abundantly clear that I should not have been trafficking in so much innuendo that evening. Do forgive me."

Casey was in the twilight zone. Up was down, down was up, and inside was out. While she came here to be up front with him and tell him that her heart was elsewhere, it turned out that he hadn't even thought of her that way. And though she never regretted any of her nights with Nate and where those lessons had taken them, she couldn't help but feel like a stupid idiot for having misread Grant so badly.

However, she had no intention of revealing that her man radar was this faulty. Better that they have a good laugh about it than he take her for the fool that she was.

She forced out a laugh, hoping it sounded legitimate. "Grant, you have nothing to apologize for. I've looked at you as a solid and dependable business partner and I couldn't be more thrilled that everything is all set for launch. As for being a flirt, who isn't every now and then?" she said, in the best flirty voice that she could muster in that moment, hoping it covered up all the embarrassment she felt inside at having been so far off the mark with him.

He mimed wiping his brow. "Whew. I'm just glad we're all good."

"We are all good," she said, flashing the biggest, brightest smile she could. "Now, let's talk about how things are going to work as we rollout in a month," she said and they focused on business for the rest of the time until she said goodbye and walked away from Speakeasy, weaving through the evening crowds in midtown, keeping her chin held high, until she finally let a few stupid tears fall. She should be happy. This was what she wanted. A clean break from any complications, and the chance to move forward with Nate, having taken care of the Grant Abbot problem.

But Grant Abbot had never truly been a problem, and once again Casey was left feeling like she had no clue what a man wanted from her.

What if she had it all wrong with Nate too?

She stopped in her tracks, grabbing onto the doorframe of an apartment building to steady herself as her heart plummeted. If she had misread the situation with Grant that badly, was she misreading things with Nate? He hadn't said how he felt about her.

Just like Grant had never said it either.

Sure, she knew Nate enjoyed the sex, but had he ever remotely suggested he wanted more with her? The same kind of more that she wanted? The sidewalk swayed beneath her, and her stomach roiled with the answer—*no*.

He hadn't breathed a word about more.

She was about to put her heart on the line, but she'd learned that she had a bad habit of reading men completely wrong. As she resumed her pace, walking through a sea of New Yorkers, she had no faith in her own instincts anymore.

The trouble was the one person she wanted to turn to for comfort was her best friend. The same person she had fallen for.

CHAPTER TWENTY-FOUR

New York, evening . . .

As Nate neared the art gallery in SoHo, he tried his best to keep his mind blank and his emotions in check. The steel bars around his heart were solid, and there was nothing Joanna could do to hurt him. She'd inflicted all the pain she could already, and the past was the past. As Casey had told him in London, he needed to stop letting that hurt define him. The simple act of handing this wedding gift over was a step in that direction.

As a throng of hipsters in slouchy shirts and tight pants clicked past him on Grand Street, the gallery came into view. A party appeared to be underway as the crowds spilled from the brightly lit art fete to the sidewalk.

With the box tucked under his arm, and the warm June air rushing by, he walked through the open doorway. He scanned the crew quickly in the overstuffed gallery—packs upon packs of skinny women in black with long, dangly earrings, and men with goatees and sideburns, nibbled on cheese and crackers and drank wine and champagne, probably discussing the fleet of paintings on the white walls—images of surreal still-lifes. Not his favorite style. He liked Casey's taste in art so much better. Hers came from her heart. A heart he wanted to protect, to care for, and to cherish.

The momentary thought of her brought a flicker of a smile to his face, and he hoped that image would feed him as he sought out the too familiar figure of his ex-wife. She hadn't mentioned a party was on the agenda tonight, but who cared? It was probably a send-off before her Chicago exhibition. No big deal. Nothing he couldn't handle.

He felt a clap on his back out of nowhere. He startled, but turned quickly, and ice crystallized in his veins at the sight of Claude—the tall, lanky, bearded and mustached much older man she'd been fucking while she had his last name. Memories snapped cruelly in front of him, slamming him back in time to the day he'd discovered their affair. Her hands had been dirty with clay from the sculpture she'd been crafting in the small studio they'd fashioned for her in one corner of the apartment. He'd parked himself on the living room couch, clicked on the touchpad on her laptop to look up movie times, and was greeted with an email exchange from a few hours before, when he'd been at work on a Saturday. The note started with Claude reminiscing about their last time together: *So glad you could stay late with me. But my bed is lonely without you spending the entire night in it, wrapped in my arms where you belong. When can you manage another night that lasts into the morning?* She replied: *Soon. He heads out of town again on Tuesday. Can't wait to see you all day and night then. I will be counting down. I promise.*

Nate had blinked, rubbed his eyes, and read it again, shock vibrating in his system. He walked into the studio, grasped the doorframe, and said in a dead voice, "So you're looking forward to me leaving town?"

Her jaw dropped, and her cheeks flamed red. But that marked the end of any shame on her part. That night she moved out, and shortly after she married the guy.

Claude held out his hand, brandishing a huge smile. "Nate. Haven't seen you in ages. You look good," the man said, and Nate was sure his auditory processing had malfunctioned because the man couldn't possibly be making casual chitchat with him.

He shrugged off the hand on his back, ignoring the one Claude had extended.

"Where's Joanna?" he managed to ask as the ice inside him turned to fire. Red flames licked his veins. His fists clenched. It was an affront to the universe that he had to be in the same fifty-foot radius as this asshole. The very same asshole that he'd had dinner with many, many times during his marriage. *Let's have dinner with my professor and some of the others in the department*, Joanna would say.

"She had to step out to talk to one of the organizers of her exhibit in Chicago. Isn't it amazing that she's going to have all her work shown at the museum?"

Nate grumbled something unintelligible.

"I'm so proud of her. What an honor," Claude continued, and Nate was ready to deliver his clenched fist into Claude's gut. The man brought his glass of champagne to his mouth and took a sip. A fucking sip. *Drink like a man; knock it back.*

"Yeah. Great honor," Nate muttered and thrust the box at him, suppressing his desire to drop it on Claude's foot. Or his face. Or down a sidewalk grate, for that matter. "Here."

Claude's eyes widened and a thin smile spread on his thin lips as he opened the box. "Ah, at last! It's come home. She's going to be so happy to see this back," he said as he dipped a hand inside the cardboard and stroked the art lovingly. Nate's stomach roiled. His gut twisted, and he curbed every impulse to slug this scum. His mind tried desperately to grip onto pictures of happier times, of being far on the other side of this deceit. He fought hard to cling to images of the good things in life—his nieces, Kat's new dog, his work, and Casey. Most of all, Casey. Her heart, her laughter, her strength. But the images felt slippery, and slid through his fingers as Claude spoke once more, "Thank you for all you've done for Joanna. You are truly a prince among men."

Nate bit his tongue, sucking down the invectives he wanted to spew. Instead, he fixated on one simple fact, letting it echo in his brain, and fuel him with bravado. *I am better off without her. I am better off without her. I am better off without her.*

Nate shook his head and raised his chin, glad to be taller than this man. "No, Claude. I'm the one who must thank you," he began and Claude cocked his head and raised a curious eyebrow. "You did me a great service by taking Joanna off my hands. So from the bottom of my heart, thank you for fucking my wife and having her at your place all night long and into the morning. It was the best thing anyone ever did for me. Because you gave me my freedom from that woman. You, sir, are truly the prince."

The color drained from Claude's face. It was a priceless moment, and Nate flashed back on something Brent had said. *Go out on a high note.* Nate turned on his heels and walked out of the gallery and into the New York night. He wanted to pump his fist in victory. To savor the vindictive joy at having reeled off the right zinger at the right time.

Instead, the latent anger inside of him raged on, higher and faster. Gritting his teeth and breathing out hard through his nostrils, he desperately wished to feel nothing. Not a single thing. But every time he entered her orbit he was sucked under by his own anger and the residual shame. Those were nothing though compared to the utter self-loathing that welled up at having chosen the wrong fucking person to love. He was such a fool for having loved this woman. He was an idiot for marrying her. His radar had malfunctioned, and he hated that it was simply out of the question for him to ever trust again, to feel again, to love again.

There was a woman he desperately wanted to let into his heart, but he didn't know how. Joanna had made it impossible for him to love.

And he hated her for it.

When he reached the red light at the crosswalk, all that anger coiled in his chest, rising up inside him. Tightening, like a hard metal spring with no give. He wanted to eradicate the side effects of Joanna, but he'd had no luck doing that. He didn't know if he ever would.

He cocked his arm and slammed the streetlamp with his fist. It hurt like a son-of-a-bitch, reverberating into his bones. He cursed loudly.

"Are you okay?"

He swiveled around to see a young woman in running shorts and a T-shirt, her hair in a ponytail, a look of concern on her face as she bounced on her sneakered feet.

"Fine. Sorry," he muttered.

"Hope your night gets better," she said, and picked up the pace, running across the street, returning to her evening jog.

"Me too," he mumbled to himself as he shook out his hand, the pain still echoing in his knuckles.

* * *

He sounded empty when she'd called, his voice terribly hollow. The Joanna effect, she reasoned. Surely, it would dissipate soon. It had to. She waited outside his building, fidgeting with the silvery pendant she wore as she stood under the navy-blue awning. She ran her thumb over the smooth, stone surface. Worry flooded her nervous system —worry over him, over her, over them. Soon, she spotted him turning the corner onto his block. Her heart rose as the tiniest sliver of a smile formed on his face when he saw her, then it fell when he was close enough for her to see the scrapes on his hand.

"What happened?" she asked as she reached gently for his right hand. The knuckles on his index and middle fingers were cut open, the skin snarly and scratched up.

"My fist met a streetlamp. They did not agree," he said, chuffing out a humorless laugh.

"Let's get you cleaned up," she said, immediately segueing into Nurse Casey mode, as her brother had called it when they were kids. Though Jack was older, she was usually the one who'd tended to his scrapes and bruises from the baseball games he'd played in. Grasping Nate's other hand, she led him past the doorman, through the lobby, up the lift and to his apartment with its view of Central Park. She parked her hands on his shoulders, pushing him down on his couch.

"Stay here."

She headed for the bathroom, opened the medicine cabinet, and rooted around for Band-Aids. She tried to shield her eyes from the big box of condoms. True, he'd used them with her. But he had the large stash because he didn't like being tied down. He operated free and easy. Played the field. He probably hadn't said a word about wanting more with her because he preferred what they had—hot sex, good friendship, and no commitment.

A weed took root in her belly, twisting insidiously around her organs. She forced herself to focus on the task at hand. She found peroxide in the vanity, grabbed a washcloth, wetted it, snagged some Band-Aids, and returned to him on the couch. He was sunk down in the plush gray cushion, his eyes closed.

"Give me your hand," she said softly, and he held out his bruised fingers. But he didn't open his eyes. As she cleaned up the cuts, him wincing a few times, she asked what had happened.

"I really don't want to talk about it," he muttered.

That statement lodged like a brick in her chest. How were they ever going to be together if he couldn't talk about the simplest things? She'd never been one to shy away from tough topics. Hell, she'd pushed her big, broody brother to open up. She could certainly do the same with Nate. "Hmm. Let me play a guessing game. I'm guessing it happened when you went to Joanna's gallery?"

He tapped his finger to his nose in answer. At least they were getting somewhere with that small admission.

"And I take it that it didn't go well?"

"It went fine. I gave the sculpture to her husband," Nate bit out in a snarl, his eyes snapping open.

"Ugh. That must have sucked to see him," Casey said, squeezing his wrist gently. But even as she sympathized with him, the weed twisted tighter in her gut with the reminder—the reminder that came in the tortured look on his face, and the acid in his tone—that he was still so easily affected by the past. How could he move forward with her when he hadn't yet moved on?

"*Sucked* is putting it mildly. That guy made a chump out of me for a year. A whole fucking year. Hell, it's not like Joanna and I have kids. Or joint custody of a dog. There's no reason I should have to see her, let alone him. But there he was. In the fucking middle of it all, making small talk about how *awesome*—" he stopped to sketch air quotes, "—she is."

"And that pissed you off so much that you hit the streetlamp?" she asked as she pressed the Band-Aid softly over his knuckles.

He nodded, a heaviness to his voice. "Yep. That's the whole story. I should have taken you up on your offer to smash the sculpture. I swear, I should have."

She brought his hand to her lips and brushed a soft kiss to his skin. "It's better not to expend that type of negative energy on her. You did the right thing. It may not feel that way now, but it's part of the healing."

He scoffed. "You sound like a shrink now."

"Maybe Michelle is rubbing off on me."

"Maybe. I still think I should have dropped it from ten flights," he said with a sigh, then ran his fingers through her hair. His touch felt good; it probably always would. But the gesture didn't reach all the way inside her soul. The emptiness in him was evident even in how he touched her —it wasn't the way he'd touched her all their other nights together. It was hollow. He was not her Nate right now. He was the Nate defeated once again by his ex-wife. Her heart cried, leaking crimson tears inside her chest as the evidence mounted, so clearly pointing to one conclusion: he wasn't over that woman. He wasn't ready. She had no idea if he was ever going to be ready.

"Enough about my fine night. Tell me all about Mr. Abbott," Nate said, that bitter edge still present in his voice.

She chose to ignore it, focusing on answering as she would have one month ago, one year ago. He was her friend, and she craved his comfort as a friend now. "Turns out Grant never thought of me romantically. I went to the meeting ready to tell him I was happy to be business partners, but there was nothing happening between the two of us. But he served first, making it pretty damn clear that he had no attraction for me whatsoever," she said, holding out her hands wide.

"That's a damn good thing," Nate said with a smirk.

"Maybe it's technically a good thing, but it kind of made me feel shitty about myself."

"Did you want him to be interested in you?"

"No. But I felt completely stupid. Don't you get that? I went there to tell him that I had feelings for somebody else, but before I could even say that he told me he never even saw me romantically and that he was sorry for leading me on. My God, I was so sure he was interested in me, Nate. I asked you to teach me how to be seductive for him because I was damn certain he was attracted to me. And it turns out I was completely off the mark with that," she said, shaking her head in frustration. She'd felt like such an ass at Speakeasy with Grant.

"Do you wish you'd never asked me?" he asked in a measured voice.

"No," she said, her voice rising. "Of course I'm glad I asked you because everything that happened was amazing, but don't you see how his comments would make me feel?"

He shook his head, looking thoroughly perplexed. "No. Enlighten me."

"It just made me feel that Scott was right—I'm good at business and bad at relationships. And all I wanted afterwards was to see you and tell you and commiserate with you as a friend. But can we even do that anymore?"

"You tell me," he said softly. "Can we?"

A lump formed in her throat. "That's the question, isn't it? Can I be your lover and your friend? Because the one thing I wanted when it was over was to see you, and then have you tell me he's a douche, and that I deserve better, and that he and all the other guys in the world can go fuck

254 · LAUREN BLAKELY

off," she said, dropping her voice an octave or two to imitate him.

"He's an ass, and you deserve better, and all the other guys in the world can go fuck off," he said, flashing her a brief smile. Then the corner of his lips dropped, and he furrowed his brow. "Wait. Can we back it up a bit? Did you actually say you had feelings for someone else?"

She straightened her spine and lifted her chin. *Just do it.* "You, obviously, Nate. *You,*" she said and his eyes seemed to light up for a moment. To sparkle. "But what is this? What are we doing? Are we friends? Are we lovers? Can we even be both?"

He ran his fingers through her hair. The gesture threatened to melt her heart once more for him, because now it felt like how he'd touched her that night in London. It felt like the start of something. She tamped down her desire to climb up on him, straddle him and smother him in kisses that led them back into another reckless night. She had to stop reading so much into the way he touched her. Words mattered more.

"Yes. We can be both," he said, his voice trailing off. She watched him, waiting as he swallowed. He seemed to struggle with words. "But I don't want to hurt you," he added in the softest, most tender voice, as if he was terribly frightened by the possibility.

She squeezed her eyes shut, trying to hold back the sting. A lump rose in her throat. He clearly didn't want her in the same way. Telling him she had feelings for him was as close as she could come to taking a chance with him, and once again her radar had failed her. They weren't on the same page. He didn't want more. He wasn't ready for all she wanted with him. If he felt the same, if he felt *any* thing for her he wouldn't say he was afraid of hurting her.

You're only afraid of hurting people when there's an uneven distribution of love.

"I understand," she said, trying to stay strong.

"I care about you too much to hurt you," he said, each word falling from his lips awkwardly, as if he were trying to explain. But he didn't have to. His explanation was evident in his eyes—they were so sad. The broken look in them reinforced that she needed to protect her heart. If she were to reveal more about all she felt it would only push him away. If she gave voice to the true depth of her feelings, she might risk losing him as a friend. She had to retreat before she fell any further.

"I don't want either of us to get hurt," he said, quickly backpedaling as he sighed heavily. "And I don't want to lose you as a friend. Our friendship means too much."

"It means everything," she said, her voice breaking now, and he reached for her, wrapped her in an embrace and held her as silent sobs fell down his shirt. His arms around her were so comforting, and she would miss terribly the feel of what would have come next—slow, sensual kisses that spread into hot, passionate ones, that turned into moans and sighs and deep desire that ran wild through the night. She longed for that physical connection so deeply, but she would miss even more having him in her life. And if they kept venturing down this rocky, dangerous road, she'd fall further for him, and that would make it impossible to be friends.

She steeled herself for what she knew she had to say. "We can't lose this," she began. She had to be the strong

one. To make the cut so they could preserve what they'd
had.

* * *

He agreed. He completely agreed. He was terrified of
losing her from his life, but he wasn't ready to let her go.
He didn't intend to let Joanna win. He had to tell Casey
how he felt. That she was the one for him. That as much
as the past had steered all his choices for the last four years,
he wanted to move forward into the great unknown with
her. He wanted to explore all that they could be. He'd been
misfiring with words so far tonight; he had to right this
ship. He shoved the past hurts, the past anger, and all that
nagging fear under the carpet, took a deep breath, and pre-
pared to tell her he was falling for her. "We can't lose this,"
he said, agreeing with her simply to start this most challenging of conversations. "But we also can't—"

She pressed her finger to his lips, shushing him. "I know
what you're going to say. We can't risk losing our friendship. And that's why I think we should take a break from
the sex. Focus on the friendship so we don't lose sight of
what matters."

The air was ripped from his lungs. He parted his lips to
speak, but no words came. The protests were lodged in his
throat, and he tried to push them past his lips, but they
wouldn't budge. Shock took root yet again. He hadn't expected her to say that. But the message had made landfall,
and she clearly meant it, so he had to respect it. He nodded and said, "Yes, you're right."

She closed her eyes, a pained look on her features. But
when she opened them again, she seemed to be forcing a

smile to her face. "Friends," she said, holding out a hand to shake.

"Always."

As she rose, smoothing a hand over her skirt, it was like watching the scene unfold in slow motion. He was here, but he was somehow floating above it all, watching it happen to someone else as she slung her purse on her shoulder, gave him a hug, and walked to the door, waving goodbye.

The sound of the door shutting stabbed him in the heart. This was the real hurt. This was the big wound. He headed for his kitchen and rooted around for a bottle of whiskey. He found one and took a long swallow, letting it burn.

Then another that scorched a path down his throat.

The night hadn't gotten better at all. It had turned far worse.

* * *

Keep it together.

She repeated that mantra over and over as the elevator chugged to the ground level, then as she stepped out onto the marble floor of his lobby. With her chin up, she marched purposefully to the door, clenching her teeth so the doorman wouldn't see her cry. She didn't want to be that woman. The woman who leaves a man's apartment in tears.

That night in New Orleans when she'd asked Nate to be her temporary lover, she'd never expected it would come to this. That a few weeks later, she'd leave his home heartbroken.

"Do you need a taxi, ma'am?"

The first tear slid down her cheek. Because this random stranger knew what she needed more than her best friend did.

"Yes, please" she said, and he scurried to the curb, thrust his hand in the air, brought a silver whistle to his lips and ten seconds later, was holding open the yellow door for her. He handed her a tissue, and gave her a sympathetic smile.

As the cab shot her downtown, the neon lights of Manhattan blaring by, she let all those bottled-up tears fall. She'd have to get them out of her system now, since they had a wedding to go to in four days.

CHAPTER TWENTY-FIVE

New York, afternoon . . .

Indiana Jones jammed his snout under a bush along the path in Central Park, and after a few seconds of nose-to-ground recon, Nate tugged on the leash. The dog backed up and continued on the trot-like pace that his little Dachshund legs necessitated as Kat chattered on about something.

It had been three days. Seventy-two entire hours of not talking, not calling, not seeing her, and not touching her. Every single one of those hours was killing him. As if he'd been cruelly excised from her life. Or maybe he'd been the one who'd done the slicing. He didn't know. He couldn't figure out a damn thing. He'd gone for long runs in the heat of the late June mornings, he'd logged endless hours at the office, he'd finalized all the arrangements for the travel to Jack's wedding. Every second he'd been aware of her absence.

She'd texted him twice. Simple, friendly messages. One was a photo of a guy roller-skating in jeggings, and she'd captioned it: *Saw this guy on Seventh Avenue. New fashion trend?* Then, she'd snapped a shot of a woman in the Times Square subway station who'd painted herself gold and moved robotically for tips. Only, she was snoozing on a bench. *Sleeping on the job*, Casey had written.

Innocuous messages. Harmless notes. The kind of texts she'd occasionally sent him before they'd started sleeping together. He hadn't received a text like this since they were truly *just friends*. She had switched gears so efficiently, from the sweet, sexy, romantic, open, vulnerable and utterly passionate woman to his witty, funny, firecracker of a friend. He'd responded to both notes in kind, replying with *Who knew jeggings were all the rage?* And *It must be tiring to move in slow motion.*

He scratched his head as Indiana Jones found a new patch of grass to sniff. This was Nate's one moment of relaxation in the last few days—taking his sister's dog for a walk as she pushed her girls in a stroller. Cara had conked out for a late afternoon nap, and Chloe was clapping and shouting *doggie* at every pooch they passed. Girl after his own canine-loving heart.

"So then Chloe wound up spilling all of it on the floor for Indiana Jones," Kat said with a laugh, then left a pregnant pause.

He raised his chin and stared quizzically at his sister. Shit. She'd just delivered a punch-line to a story and he hadn't a clue what she'd been talking about. "That's funny," he said, trying to recover from his fumble.

She slugged him on the arm, then brought her hands back to the stroller. "You weren't listening."

"I was too listening," he said quickly, reeling off a white lie.

She shook her head at him. "Oh yeah? What did Chloe spill?"

He had no idea. "Milk?" he asked, taking a stab in the dark.

"Busted. It was spaghetti. She thought it was hilarious that the dog was trying to get her food from the high chair."

He held up his hands in surrender. "Fine. You caught me. I was drifting off."

"If I didn't know better, I'd be worried that I'm boring," she said as she wheeled past a pack of teenage boys tossing a Frisbee across the lawn. "But yet, I do know you, and I'm pretty sure I also know what's causing your astronomical levels of distraction."

"What's causing it?"

"Casey," Kat said in a matter-of-fact tone, shooting him a pointed look, one that said *I'm right and you know it.*

"Yeah?"

She nodded. "You're in that guy state. That moody, irritable guy state that only comes from trouble with a woman. Which tells me you messed up with her."

His eyebrows shot into his hairline. "Not true. Not true in the least, and why would you say that?"

She nudged him with her elbow as they walked around a curve in the path, heading towards the 5th Avenue side of the park. "I made an educated guess."

"Hate to break it to you, but you guessed wrong. I didn't mess up. She decided she only wanted to be friends. So there you go," he said.

Kat shot him a doubtful look. "She just wants to be friends? I have a hard time believing that," she said, bending over the front of the stroller to point out to Chloe a Beagle running alongside his owner.

"And why do you have a hard time with that?"

Kat turned to look him square in the eyes. "Because that girl is in love with you, Nate."

He stopped in his tracks. His feet were stuck to the concrete. All the sound in the park had been zipped up in her words. Her beautiful, hopeful words. "What?" he said, stumbling on the question.

His sister nodded several times, stopping too. "I saw the two of you at Yankee Stadium. And at my house. I've seen the way you look at her, and the way she looks at you."

"How does she look at me?" he asked, and he couldn't deny that his sister's words felt exhilarating.

"The same way you look at her," she said, and it was as if the sun broke free on a rainy day. But then, something didn't add up.

"Why would she say she only wants to be friends then?"

"Oh, gee. I don't know. Is it maybe because you give off the *I'm-not-over-my-ex* vibe?" Kat asked in a singsong voice.

"That's not true. I'm over her. Completely." He slashed a hand through the air to emphasize his point.

Kat arched an eyebrow. "Are you, Nate?"

He nodded. He was sure of this. Absolutely sure. "Yes," he said confidently. Then he lowered his voice because he didn't like admitting this out loud to anyone but Kat. "Maybe my pride isn't over it. But the rest of me is."

She gripped his arm, squeezing him. "I get it. I understand," she said softly. "Pride sometimes takes even longer to heal than the heart does. But maybe it's time to let that go?"

He shrugged. "Maybe."

"And look, I'm not dismissing what happened to you or the way your marriage ended. I'm simply saying maybe it's time to fully jettison the past."

"It's not that simple."

"Actually, it is that simple," she corrected. "And I know that from experience. Bryan broke my heart when I was younger, though obviously not for the same reasons your marriage ended. His reasons were different, but five years later when we reconnected, I had to make the choice to forgive him. The heavens didn't split open. I didn't wait for a sign. I didn't see an apparition. I made a choice to move into the future. You can do the same."

A choice. It was as simple as putting one foot in front of the other. But could he make that choice? Could he truly choose to shuck off the way he'd lived his life in the last few years? That was the big question.

"So that's it? Just let it go?" he asked skeptically, miming tossing trash into a garbage can.

She nodded. "Yes, especially since if I'm picking up on the ex-vibes, you can bet Casey is too. Maybe that's why she said you should just be friends."

Once more, he nearly froze in place. His sister was turning on the light-bulb in his brain left and right today. "You think Casey assumes I'm not over Joanna?"

"I can't imagine she'd operate under any other assumption, considering how you sometimes act. I know dealing with your ex-wife can hurt, but part of letting go is choosing to let go of all of it. Not just the emotions, which you shed a while ago, but all the residual pain. The anger and the pride too."

Those were his reliable companions. His armor, and his safe harbor too. They'd served him well, and protected him from falling for any woman who might hurt him.

Until now. Those twin emotions hadn't held him back when it came to Casey. They hadn't rescued him from wanting more with her than he'd ever wanted from anyone. But perhaps they had held him back from actually having the guts to go for it.

"You really think she's crazy about me?" Nate asked, returning to a simpler matter.

Kat rolled her eyes, then held up her thumb and index finger to show a sliver of space. "Maybe a little."

He dropped his arm around her shoulders and squeezed. "A little? C'mon. Feed my ego."

"Ha. Never. I will never feed your ego. Besides, I already fed it when I told you she feels the same way you do."

If she felt the same way then he was the luckiest son-of-a-bitch in the world. But now he'd have to figure out the hardest part—how to put his heart on the line. Knowing something in his head, and being able to act on it were two different things.

CHAPTER TWENTY-SIX

In the air . . .

There wasn't a chance of a private conversation on the plane. They were nowhere near alone. Sharing the jet with Michelle's brother, Davis, and his wife, as well as Clay and a pregnant Julia, and also Michelle's best friend, Sutton, and her husband left them with no privacy.

Maybe that was for the best, since Nate hadn't figured out yet what to say, how to say it, or even how to deal with the way his heart raced just from looking at Casey. The noise in his head from being near her and all of these people at the same time didn't make the situation any easier. Never had he been so eager for a flight to end. But this was a humdinger of a plane ride—they flew across the Atlantic Ocean, rode over Europe, and then soared above the Middle East en route to the island paradise. The eight of them passed the long hours sleeping on and off under soft blankets, playing Scrabble, watching *The Italian Job*, and reading.

Somewhere above the Indian Ocean Julia challenged them all to a game of poker.

That might've been the toughest part of the plane ride to get through as they gathered around the table, laughing, telling jokes, and raising the stakes as Julia dealt. During the game, he met Casey's eyes several times—countless times, actually—and she often smiled in those moments. But he couldn't read her. All he knew was that she seemed like the Casey she'd always been—outgoing, upbeat, quick with a joke. She fit in seamlessly. Not that he expected anything else. But he longed for an hour—heck, even thirty minutes would do—to steal her away to the back row of the plane, and talk.

But the rhythms of all the passengers didn't align, so he never found himself with a quiet moment to do anything more than make amiable chit chat.

At least there was that.

When they landed in the city of Malé in the late afternoon, they were shuttled onto a speedboat. Casey slid in next to Nate. Her leg was wedged against his, and the slightest touch tripped his heart rate into overdrive, not to mention sent other parts of his body into an upright position.

Damn, he hoped the ride to the hotel was a fast one.

The boat ferried them twenty-five minutes across the sun-kissed, crystal-blue waters of the Indian Ocean as the sun cast its perfect cloudless rays. The motor slowed as they neared The Luxe's property on a secluded, tranquil outpost among the islands, the dust-white sand of the serene beach coming into view.

Once inside the hotel, they found Michelle and Jack waiting in the open-air lobby, looking windswept and relaxed as overhead fans turned lazily, stirring up the faint scent of coconut through the tropical air. Michelle's hair was pinned up on her head and she wore a sundress, while Jack was in shorts.

"Never seen you in shorts before except on a basketball court," Nate said with a laugh as he shook hands with his friend.

"We're thinking of moving here next. The island lifestyle suits me as a man of leisure," Jack joked.

Jack's gaze snapped away from Nate and went to Casey, who had launched herself into his arms. Jack roped his arms around his sister, and hugged her tight. "So good to see you," he said, and Nate turned away, leaving them to their private sibling moment.

He gave Michelle a kiss on the cheek, then was extraordinarily grateful when his property manager pulled him aside and said she wanted to share some good news about the increase in bookings during the last few weeks. He was grateful to sit down with Nicole, and chat business. It helped him clear his head of Casey.

* * *

Casey let out the longest breath when she reached her villa.

God, that had been hard. That had been the most difficult plane ride of her life. She laughed out loud, alone in her spacious villa, the sound echoing across the walls, because, a flight on a luxury jet should never feel difficult.

But she'd white-knuckled it through, sucking in all her heartache, and keeping her desire for him locked up where he couldn't see. The speedboat might have been the toughest part. With him so near to her like that, and the wind whipping past them over the aqua water, she could smell him. Delicious, alluring, and all man.

At least they were succeeding on the surface, though, in returning to what they were before—friends. Funny how they'd gone from friends-to-lovers together, and now she was reverse engineering that path all on her own, from lovers back to friends.

The tropical breeze beckoned to her, so she strolled onto the gorgeous hardwood deck that led to a private infinity pool, perched at the edge of the ocean. The sun began to dip overhead, the pink fingertips of the pending sunset tugging it to the horizon. This resort was as far away as possible from the sights, sounds and smells of New York— that city cacophony of sensory overload that fed her drive everyday to do, do, do. But here, the lure of relaxation wafted over her in mere minutes. This resort was the opposite of Manhattan in every way—quiet, tranquil, and incredibly calm. Tilting her face to the sun, she let the rays warm her. Maybe this break from the hustle and bustle of work, maybe the bliss of the island breeze, maybe the palm trees gently swaying would cure her of this heartbreak.

As she drank in the intoxicating beauty—the wide, open sea, the endless sky, the succulent air that kissed her bare skin—she made a wish that someday she would have this with someone.

She turned around, the ebb and flow of the ocean flitting past her ears, and flopped face down on the crisp white sheets of the king-sized bed.

A bed for lovers.

She squeezed her eyes shut, trying to eradicate him from her tired brain. The last thing she needed was to dream of him, a task that was infinitely harder here in a hotel outfitted not only for romance, but for the private bliss of those in love.

Soon, she succumbed to sleep, jet-lag doing its trick in erasing Nate momentarily from her mind.

CHAPTER TWENTY-SEVEN

The Maldives, morning . . .

She spent the next morning having breakfast with Jack and Michelle and the two sets of Sullivan parents. Casey hadn't seen her mom or her dad in a year, and she didn't have fond memories of the coldness between the two of them back when she was growing up. But at least her parents were happy now, and happily remarried.

Then the women spent the afternoon at the spa, a gift from Michelle to her wedding guests. Afternoon rolled into evening and it was time for the rehearsal dinner, held in the restaurant on the property that overlooked the turquoise waters. Casey showered, dressed and clipped her hair in a twist on top of her head, loose tendrils falling by her face. She zipped up the light-blue Herve Leger dress that she'd purchased at Harrod's. She shoved away the sexy memories of those fevered moments in the dressing room. A dress was a dress was a dress.

She wandered across the property, strolling along the sandy, palm-tree-lined path to the restaurant. She was early, but figured she'd grab a glass of champagne at the bar to smooth over the evening, and take the prickly edge off being near to Nate.

She almost tripped in her peep-toed sandals when she spotted him already holding court at the bar, a stunning brunette by his side. The woman looked shockingly like Joanna. The resemblance chilled her. This dark-haired beauty had the same mane of luxurious hair, the same emerald-green eyes, and that same long and lean body. She wore a black pencil skirt, a silky tank top and black pumps. As for Nate, he was too gorgeous to be believed in slacks and a button-down shirt, open at the neck. No tie tonight. The tropical weather simply wouldn't allow for it.

He held a scotch, clinked his glass with the woman's, and then took a long swallow. Casey winced at the ease of their interaction, and the way he seemed to slide seamlessly from her to the next woman he wanted in his bed. Some kind of vibe was working between those two. She could tell from the way he laughed at something the slinky brunette said, then the way she dropped her hand onto his forearm, ever so briefly, before letting go. A worm of jealousy slithered in Casey's gut, turning into a full-blown snake when the woman danced her fingertips across the bar and leaned forward, her silky sheet of hair dangerously close to Nate's arms, those strong, sexy arms that had held her, pinned her, tied her up.

Oh, hell no. That was not going to fly.

Casey gripped the doorframe, ready to launch an attack. Visions of a fantastic catfight danced in her head. She'd lunge at the woman, grab that black hair, twist it hard, then scratch the woman's neck. Maybe even her gorgeous face. Anything to keep those claws off her Nate. The battle would rage on, and Casey would yank her off the wooden bar stool and tackle her, landing them both in a heap on the floor of the bar, Casey inflicting punishing blows. All this coiled-up tension would be released in a cathartic, mano-a-mano fight between Casey and the woman she hated for no reason other than that she was laughing and flirting with the man Casey was crazy about.

She lingered on her *Fight Club* fantasies for another minute, then shooed them away. She was not a violent woman, and didn't intend to become one now. She believed in pleasure, in intimacy, and in love. That's why she did what she did for a living. The more she fixated on this jealousy, the further she'd stray from who she truly was.

Besides, she had no plans on ruining her brother's wedding for the sake of fisticuffs.

She relinquished her grip on the doorframe, smoothed a hand over her gauzy blue dress, then fixed her gaze on the large table near the edge of the sand.

As she walked behind Nate, he shot out an arm as if he were signaling to turn left on a bicycle, and physically stopped her. He cocked his head to the side, and flashed his trademark grin. "You don't say hello anymore?"

She smiled, the kind that didn't reach her eyes. "I didn't see you. How are you?" she asked him as diplomatically as possible

"Great. This is my property manager, Nicole," he said, and the woman extended her hand. Casey shook, but didn't let go of the possibility that Nate's property manager had her sights set on him.

"Nice to meet you. I have to go. I'm needed out there," she said, gesturing to the veranda and the empty table reserved for Jack's party, then picked up her pace.

In seconds, she heard the click of his shoes. His hand was on her arm. She turned around and looked down at his fingers wrapped around her wrist. She shook them off.

"What's wrong?"

She gave him a pointed stare, as if he were crazy for even asking the question. "Nothing," she said with a nonchalant shrug. "Why would anything be wrong?"

"You gave me the cold shoulder back there. And now. That's not like you."

"That's because I have a rehearsal dinner to be at," she said in a crisp, businesslike voice.

"So do I. But you're early, and no one is here yet."

She raised her chin. "I wanted to be early. Now, if you'll excuse me."

He furrowed his brow. "Casey, I thought you wanted to be friends."

"Oh, I'm so sorry. Was I not trying hard enough? Would you like me to work even harder? Maybe sit down with you and Nicole and have a drink together? Because that's what we'd do as friends, right?" Her voice heated up angrily with each question she flung at him.

"Casey, this isn't you."

Something dangerous welled up inside her. Something that felt horribly like no-holds-barred anger, like ragged jealousy, like all the pain she didn't want to show him. But she was tired, and she was jet-lagged, and on top of that she was really fucking sad. She let it all loose. "Maybe it's not me. But maybe you don't know me. Maybe you should go spend time with Nicole. She sure looks like she wants to be much more than friends with you. You can get what you want from her," she said, the cruel remark coming out of her mouth before she could stop it.

Nate nodded several times, absorbing her below-the-belt comment. His hand came down on her arm again, and he tugged her into a quiet hallway of the restaurant, leading to the restrooms.

"Do you want to go there? She's one of my goddamn employees, and you better know me well enough to know I would never cross that line. But if it bothers you so much that I'm talking to my property manager about how to keep growing the hotel's revenue, then let's discuss how much it bothered me that you were after Mr. Lingerie," he said, biting out the words.

She held her own against him, standing tall. "It didn't seem to bother you at all. It didn't even seem to affect you one bit when I told you why I was no longer going to pursue anything with him."

"Are you crazy? You think it didn't bother me that you were hot for that asshole? Did you already forget Yankee Stadium?"

She shivered briefly as the memory flashed before her eyes of their first time together, the way he'd talked to her, so rough and jealous, and the way it had turned her on to no end. But that had all been a game, another move in the chess match of their lessons in seduction. Those lessons were over.

"No. I didn't forget it. But sometimes I think you did," she said, crossing her arms.

"I didn't forget a thing. I remember everything about every night with you. Every day with you. Every hour with you. Like when you bought this dress," he said, raking his eyes over her from head to toe. "By the way, nice dress."

"Thanks," she said coldly. "I'm thrilled to learn you can recall details of a blow job. I was worried that was starting to fade from your mind."

He shut his eyes briefly and pursed his lips, fighting to hold back, it seemed. She should do the same. She really should. It wasn't her style to lash out. She was direct, she was upfront, but she was also kind. Only right now, she wasn't. She was playing dirty because the snake inside her was stronger. She wanted to shake Nate, yell at him to get over his ex-wife, shout at him to stop flirting with another woman. And then slap him and tell him he never should have toyed with her heart in London. "I'm sure, though, that all those lovely things you said to me that night in London have completely faded from your mind. But then, I suppose it's not a surprise. We already know I'm not terribly good at reading men and what they really want. Especially when they only say those lovely things in bed."

"What do you mean?" he asked, jamming his hands through his hair, messing it up. "I meant everything I said that night."

"What does it matter now? We're friends. We're fabulous, amazing, wonderful friends."

"Casey," he said softly, reaching out a hand to try to touch her. She shirked away. "You're not really acting like a friend right now. But then, I don't feel that friendly either. When I see you in that dress, I don't feel the least bit buddy-buddy. I feel—"

She cut him off. "I don't care if this dress makes you want to fuck me. All you ever wanted was sex and friendship. I'm sorry that you only have one of those things now, but it's all I can give you, and even then it's really hard to be your friend with the way I feel for you." Her voice broke yet again. She swiped at her face, trying to erase the start of the insubordinate tear. "Excuse me. I need to go to the ladies room," she said, giving him the universal excuse that freed a woman from any situation. She rushed into the bathroom, grabbed some tissues, and sank down in a soft chair in the sitting area, her head in her hands.

A minute later she heard the soft whoosh of the door opening. "Please don't come in," she said in a harsh warning.

"Hey. Are you okay?"

It was Michelle, and Casey couldn't keep her feelings inside her any longer. "I'm not okay at all. I'm a raving bitch," she said, then spilled nearly everything to the woman who was about to become part of her family.

Michelle listened calmly, her warm brown eyes fixed on Casey the entire time. "Now what?" she asked, holding out her hands helplessly.

"You need to apologize for the things you just said to him. And then you need to tell the truth," Michelle said in a firm, but warm voice.

"Oh. It's that simple?"

"No. It's *that* hard. It will be incredibly hard to speak your truth, and to take ownership of the things you said to him. But isn't it better than the alternative? Feeling crappy and keeping it all inside?"

Casey inhaled deeply, then breathed out. She did it again. The big breaths spread through her, cooling her jealousy, calming her angry heart. "Why do you have to be so wise about everything?"

Michelle smiled, and grasped Casey's hand. "I'm not so wise. I'm just trying to help you see your way through. And look, I know it's not easy to open up to someone you love. It can be incredibly scary. There was a time when I thought I had lost Jack from being too open with him. But it turns out being open was exactly what he needed, and what we both needed to have what we have. I wouldn't be where I am today without having gone through that uncertainty. And I couldn't be any happier to be where I am now," she said, squeezing Casey's hand in emphasis.

"But I don't know what's going to happen if I open up. I don't know that I'm going to have the same thing you have."

Michelle laughed. "Of course you don't. And neither does he."

"He might be pissed at me. I was a bit, how shall we say, bitchy to him. Just a teeny bit," Casey said, a tiny smile creeping back on her face as she made fun of herself.

"I don't think you've done anything that you can't recover from."

Another deep breath spread through her chest, fueling her with something other than the anger that had steered her wrong a few minutes ago. "I'm so glad you're marrying my brother," Casey said.

"Me too." Michelle beamed, unable to contain a bright, shining smile.

"And you know," she said, flashing a toothy grin and wiggling her eyebrows, "don't forget I was kind of a matchmaker for the two of you. Hopefully that'll keep you from being too mad at me for behaving terribly before your rehearsal dinner."

"One, you did not behave badly. You behaved like a woman in love. And two, I will happily give you all the credit in the world. Jack is wonderful, and I know a lot of that is because he has you as his sister."

After Michelle left, Casey took a minute to compose herself, touching up her powder and reapplying her lip gloss. Then, she joined her family and friends on the veranda. Torches flickered in the early evening light, casting pretty shadows across the deck and the sandy beach mere feet away. She found her place card, and a waiter pulled out a chair for her. Her stepmother would be sitting next to her.

She scanned the group for Nate, but didn't see him anywhere. Reaching for her glass of water, she took a sip and waited patiently, peering at the other place cards to find where he was seated. Across from her, two chairs down. She'd have to grab a private moment with him as soon as she could. She'd talk to him without tears or agenda, and simply speak the full truth. All this time of saying less than what she felt wasn't helping anyone.

A minute later, her spine straightened and goosebumps rose on her arms as his mouthwatering scent drifted by. He took the chair next to her. "Michelle just told me the seating had changed. I hope you don't mind," he said, moving in next to her.

She didn't wait a second longer. "I'm so sorry," she said softly, because there was no time like the present. She went for the truth, and she hoped those three words could begin to convey how contrite she was. But they were only the beginning. "I shouldn't have said any of those things. When I saw you with that woman, it made me so incredibly jealous."

A flicker of a smile appeared on his lips, those gorgeous, delicious lips she loved to kiss. "Like that night I was in Miami and you thought I went to a club," he said, speaking in a hushed whisper.

"Yes. I was so jealous then. And now I feel that way ten times, fifty times, a thousand times more. I can't stand the thought of anyone else with you. Except me."

He parted his lips, and a sexy sigh escaped. "Casey," he said, breathing her name like she was precious to him. "I feel the same. I completely feel the same."

But there was no more time for any conversation, because Jack and Casey's father stood up, clinked a glass, and thanked everyone for coming to the other side of the world to celebrate the wedding of his son. After that, their father's wife commandeered Nate's attention. Seated on the other side of him, she peppered Nate with all sorts of questions about the resort, asking about the scuba diving, where she might see turtles underwater, and if there was a way to swim with the dolphins.

When the appetizers cleared, Jack rose and cleared his throat. Quickly the noise died down, and the only sound was that of waves gently lapping the shore.

280 · LAUREN BLAKELY

"Thank you so much for joining us here. We hope it wasn't too much of a hardship to come to the Maldives," he said with a smirk.

"It was a piece of cake," someone called out.

"But seriously, we know we asked a lot of you to have you come here, and I'm delighted to see so many friends and family with us. It is an honor to be able to share this moment with all of you." He stopped talking to lock eyes with Michelle, who was watching his every word with a huge smile on her face. "I could not be happier or more ready to make this amazing woman my wife. Nothing has ever felt more right or true to me than loving her. It's the easiest thing in the world to do."

Casey catalogued the reactions at the table to Jack's speech. Davis beamed with pride and love at his sister, Julia brought her hand to her heart then wiped a tear from her eye and Clay dropped a kiss on her cheek. Casey sneaked a peek at Nate, who was intently listening. He must have felt the pull because he turned to meet her gaze, and the look in his eyes melted her. It was the way he'd looked at her in London, in New Orleans, in her apartment. His gaze zeroed in on her collarbone, that spot he loved to kiss, and instinctually she raised her fingers and touched it. She heard a hitch in his breath, then forced herself to focus as Jack continued.

"I've often said I'm the luckiest man in the world to have this woman," Jack continued, and reached for Michelle. She threaded her fingers through his, and the tender and passionate love between them was evident even in how they held hands. "And yes, there's some luck to it, and some chance, but there's also my sister."

Casey sat up straight, jerking her head from left to right, as if to say *Who, me?* She hadn't expected to be part of his speech.

Jack moved away from Michelle and walked closer to Casey. "I wouldn't be at this dinner, ready to take Michelle Milo as my bride tomorrow, if my sister hadn't stuck by me, and believed in me, and encouraged me to move on from the things that had held me back. She's been my anchor and my best friend, and in many ways she is the reason I'm here today. So thank you, Casey, for speaking your mind, never giving up on me, and then administering the kick in the pants I needed to fall in love with Michelle," he said, bending down to give her a hug, then raising a glass to toast.

Her cheeks flamed red, and huge tears of joy streaked down her cheeks. She brought her hand to her mouth to cover her lips that were quivering. She was a mess. She was a total mess, with mascara surely staining her cheeks. All eyes were on her, as everyone at the wedding toasted.

She couldn't speak. She simply raised her glass in response, and then felt a hand on her thigh. It wasn't naughty or suggestive; it was caring, as Nate handed her his napkin. She brought it to her eyes, and dabbed them, and once the focus of the guests returned to the groom, who was now telling a story about adjusting to life in Paris, Nate leaned in to whisper. "Don't give up on me either."

* * *

After the dinner plates were cleared, a hand came down on his shoulder. "Got a minute?"

Nate craned his neck in Jack's direction. "Of course," he said, tossing his napkin on the chair and following Jack, who weaved through the tables, past the torches, and onto the soft, white sand. They walked away from the wedding guests, and towards the water, moonlight bathing the ocean in its soft nighttime glow.

Jack stopped and faced Nate. "Let me ask you a question. Do I look stupid?"

Nate furrowed his brow. "What?"

"Just answer the question. Do I look stupid?"

"No."

"I didn't think so. Because I'm not stupid and that means I know you're in love with my sister."

Nate blinked several times. "What?"

Jack stared hard at him. "Again. Not dumb. Don't you play dumb, either."

He swallowed dryly. This wasn't how he'd intended to tell Jack. But then, nothing had gone as he'd intended the last few days. "I won't play dumb."

"Good," Jack said in a firm voice. "What are you going to do about it?"

"Aren't you going to tell me I'm going to break her heart and that I need to keep my hands off her?"

"It's not for me to tell you what to do or not to do. I simply want to know *when* you're going to deal with it."

"Why?"

Jack rolled his eyes. "Because I'm getting married to-morrow. Because I want everything to be perfect for the woman I love. Because if you're standing next to me with my sister pissed off at you, or some scowl on your face, or waiting to have another fight in the bar—yes, Michelle told me, so don't look so shocked that I know—that will make her unhappy, and that will make me unhappy. And all I want is for her to be happy. So can you deal with this tonight, please?"

"I was planning on dealing with it tonight," Nate replied.

Jack clapped him on the back. "Good. Let's go back, and you're excused for the rest of the night. This is more important."

He laughed. "Yes. It is," he said, and all he wanted now was to take Casey in his arms and make her his.

"Oh, and one more thing," Jack said as they neared the veranda. "I'm not even going to tell you not to hurt her, because I know you know better. But remember this— Casey and Michelle are the two most important people in the world to me. And you're next. So treat her like she's the world to you."

"I promise," Nate said, then an idea flashed before him. A brilliant idea. "Hey. You're doing some work with European companies, right?"

Jack nodded.

"There's something I need," he said, then gave him the details.

"I'll see what I can do after the wedding," Jack said, then gestured to the rehearsal dinner. "Now go take care of business."

But Casey was no longer at the table. His heart beat faster as he searched for her on the veranda, but he didn't see the woman in the light-blue dress. He stopped by Michelle's seat, bent down, and asked her if she knew where Casey had gone.

"She had to take a work call. She stepped out. She'll be right back."

Hopefully, she wouldn't be right back. Hopefully, neither one of them would return tonight. He walked through the restaurant. The chef spotted him and tried to call him over, but Nate shook his head. "Another time."

He made it to the doorway and found her outside, leaning against a palm tree, chatting on the phone. Her face lit up when she saw him, and he walked right up to her as she was saying, "Thanks, Sofia. Glad everything is all set."

She ended the call and tucked her phone in her purse.

"Hi," she said softly.

"Hi," he said, stopping just a few inches from her. His gaze drifted once more to her collarbone, that spot that drove her wild, and him, too. He met her eyes, her gorgeous sapphire eyes that he loved getting lost in.

"Do you forgive me for getting so mad earlier?" she asked.

He smiled as his heart raced just from being near to her. "It's not something that needs forgiveness. We've both gotten mad and jealous, and I love your crazy, jealous side, because it matches mine."

"Good," she said.

"Do you forgive me for being an ass about my ex-wife instead of just admitting to you that it hurts my pride to see her, but that's all? Because I have no feelings for her. None whatsoever. I only have feelings for you. I have so many feelings for you, I barely know what to do with them all."

"It's not something that needs forgiveness," she said, repeating his words. "But thank you for saying it."

She closed the sliver of distance between them, dropping her purse to the ground, and placing her hands on his face. "You taught me how to give up control, and you also taught me that you liked it even when I took charge, so that's what I'm going to do right now. Because I can't go any longer without this," she said, then planted a dizzying kiss on his lips, sending his head spinning and turning his world hazy, filled only with thoughts of her, of ravaging her, of sliding inside her and sending her into ecstasy. He could barely believe he'd gone without touching her for five days now. Those five days were hell and he never wanted to experience that kind of torture again. No, he wanted to be tortured only by his lust for her, by his bottomless desire.

And though he never wanted this kiss to end, he had so much to tell her, so he cupped her shoulders and gently separated from her. "I may have taught you how to give up control, but you showed me something even more important, and that's how to feel again and how to love again," he said, and the words were remarkably easy to say. So much easier than he'd ever expected. "Because I love you, Casey. I am completely in love with you, and I want to be your friend, and your lover, and the man you love. I want to be all those to you. I want to be everything to you because you're everything to me."

She trembled, and ran a thumb along his jawline. "You are everything to me. You're the man I love."

His heart thumped wildly in his chest. He was flooded with happiness, and even though they were heading into the great unknown, he was finally ready for that journey. Because of her. Because she'd stood by him over the years.

Because she made him laugh often, she turned him on relentlessly, and she showed him every day that trust didn't have to be broken—it could be strengthened by the bond of friendship that turned into this beautiful love.

Because she was the *only* one he wanted, heart, body and soul.

She brushed her fingers across the buttons on his shirt. She was practically bouncing on her toes as she brought his mouth back to hers, stopping when he was millimeters away. "Show me how you kiss me now. Show me what it's like to be kissed by the man I love."

"Like this," he said, crushing his lips to hers, and wrapping her so damn close that their bodies were nearly fused together. He kissed her hard, and passionately, and for a long, long time, savoring every second of her shivers, and her sexy sighs, and of the way she wrapped her leg around him.

Like she wanted him to take her right then and there.

He groaned as she brushed her calf against his leg, and that was all he needed to break the kiss, grab her hand, and make their way to his villa.

CHAPTER TWENTY-EIGHT

The Maldives, all through the night . . .

Off.

Her clothes needed to be off. His busy fingers had already lowered the zipper on her dress as they walked along the winding path to his villa, stumbling at times, but holding on, drunk on each other, tipsy on touch, on the kisses he layered on the back of her neck, on her nimble hands undoing the buttons on his shirt. Half-undressed already, they finally made it inside, wrapped up in each other.

His was the most secluded villa on the entire property, the equivalent of the top floor penthouse suite at a high-rise hotel. Perched on stilts over the water, the island hut was framed on one side by the wide, open sea, and on the other by a private little lagoon a mere one hundred-feet away from the long dock at the edge of the villa.

With his hands on her waist, he kicked the door shut. The sound of it closing cordoned them off from everyone else. She was the only one who mattered.

This, them, here, now.

His brain could only process what was happening in one-word bursts. And the word that blared through his frontal lobe now was *naked*.

He yanked off her dress, letting it pool at her feet by the hardwood floor next to his bed. She stepped out of it and her lacy underthings too, then slipped off her shoes. His hands shot out, grasping her waist, then traveling north across the soft flesh of her belly to their final destination for the moment—her beautiful breasts. A guttural moan rumbled from deep within his chest as he cupped those two perfect globes, rubbing his fingertips across her peaked nipples. She gasped, and then that sound turned into a long, sexy moan.

"I can't keep my hands off you," he said, as he reacquainted himself with her tits, her delicious ass, then her hips, his thumbs digging hard into her hipbones. He wanted to claim her body with the intensity of his touch, with the ownership he felt for her.

"Keep them on me then," she said, with a sly little smirk on her gorgeous face.

He grasped her wrist and led her out to his deck. A bird swooped down, landing on the railing of the villa, singing his avian approval of Nate's plan to send Casey into bliss under the moon with the ocean breeze kissing her skin.

"Do you have any idea how hard it is for me to see you in these dresses and skirts that you wear all the time?" he asked as they passed the infinity pool at the edge of the deck, then walked down the steps that led to the long dock. Night had turned the ocean inky blue under the starlit sky.

"How hard is it?" Her voice was flirty and playful. He loved that she was so comfortable in her own skin. She hadn't always been. She'd doubted she could be her true self with a man. But he wanted her to know she could be whomever she wanted with him.

"With you," he said taking her palm and rubbing it across his erection that strained against the fabric of his pants, "it seems I'm always like this. And every single thing about you turns me on. Every thing you do to me. Every way you move. Every naughty word from your lips. Every time you take control, and every time you give control. All of it." Her eyes lit up, and she licked her lips, looking both incredibly happy and tantalizingly sexy at the same time. "I have had dirty thoughts about you for years. I've seen you naked so many times in my mind before I laid eyes on your sinful body in the flesh. I'd stare at you in the short little skirts and imagine licking my way up your legs. I'd picture my tongue on the inside of your thighs, you shivering, moaning, and then opening your legs for me."

Her eyes glittered darkly and her breasts moved with each breath she took as he praised her sensuality. He was turning her on, and he loved it. "Tell me something, Casey," he said, dipping his head to her neck, finding that spot that drove her wild.

"Tell you what?" she asked, her voice breathy as she wrapped her arms around his neck, holding on tight as he brushed his lips lightly against the column of her throat.

"Tell me. If I slid my hands between your legs right now, would you be wet for me?"

"So wet," she said, jutting out her hips, trying to angle her body as near to him as possible. Her fingernails cut into his skull, urging him to move closer. "But why don't you find out for yourself?"

"I intend to. Because I'm about to re-enact one of the dirty dreams I've had of you. And I didn't just have this thought last night. I've had it all the times I've been here. I've pictured you on these stairs before," he said, glancing down at the steps.

"You have?" she said, as goosebumps rose on her arms, revealing more of her want. Telling her he craved her was the ultimate turn-on for this woman.

"You've come on my tongue here before. You've begged for my mouth. I've touched your sweet body all the other times I've been here. You've screamed my name in pleasure." The desire that flashed in her eyes stoked the blaze inside of him. He was consumed with the need to touch his woman. He was obsessed with her pleasure. "Now let my fantasy become reality."

"Oh God," she moaned, threading a hand in her hair as her eyes went glassy with lust.

"Sit down on the steps now," he told her and she did as instructed, perching her sweet, sexy ass on the middle stair.

"Now grip the railings with your hands," he told her and she reached for the slats, grasping them. "And spread your legs for me."

"Only for you. Always for you," she said, as she let one knee fall to the side, hitting the railing gently. Desire swamped his system at the sight of her bare pussy, glistening and wet. He had to have her now. She let her other knee fall open, and there she was, arms and legs spread, body revealed, with nothing to do but hold on to the railing as she gave herself to him.

Lust pounded incessantly in his bloodstream, his pulse speeding up with the full realization that she wanted him in exactly the same way, which was *every* way, and that she needed him with the same kind of wild intensity.

"All I'm thinking about now are the thousands of ways that I intend to have filthy, wild, hot, dirty, beautiful sex with you," he said, his voice raw and hungry as he dropped to his knees, latched his palms on her thighs, and spread her open for him.

Her slick pink flesh beckoned to him, and he desperately needed to bury his face in her heat. To feel the slippery wetness from her on his jaw. To be coated in her desire. "It's been too long," he muttered. "So please forgive me if I'm too loud."

She knit her eyebrows together momentarily. "Too loud?"

"I'm so fucking hungry for you," he said as he dived in, groaning instantly as he licked a delicious line along her slippery, wet opening. She cried out. He kissed her clit, then swept his tongue back down, and was rewarded with a primal moan. A rumble escaped his lips as he flicked his tongue across her engorged clit. Soon, her sounds of pleasure mingled with his groans as he feasted, and she offered all of herself.

"Oh God, your mouth. I want more of it. More of you. *Please*," she said, practically begging, as she delivered on his fantasies.

They were both loud and hungry, a carnal duet of two people deeply in lust and love with each other.

She tasted divine, like sin and sex and the woman he craved ceaselessly. He pushed his hands harder against her thighs, opening her wider, further, wanting her abandon. His dick throbbed painfully against his pants with every thrust of her hips, with every cry that sounded from her lips. He could barely take it. The intensity of his own want for her racked his body, electrifying his blood. He looked up at her, and he very nearly stopped to flip her over, put her on her hands and knees and take her, like a crazed man in desperate need of his woman. Because as hot as she'd been every other time, every other night, right now she'd crossed some kind of line of eroticism.

She was phenomenally passionate.

Her head was thrown back, her neck stretched long and inviting, and her hair spilled in curls over the stairs. Her lips were parted, her mouth forming a perfect *O*. Her arms were extended, taut and firm, almost as if she'd been tied to the railing by her own restraints—her hands that savagely gripped the wood posts, as she rocked her pussy into his face. He kissed and sucked and licked, giving her everything he had, devouring her mouthwatering taste as her cries echoed in the tropical night. Then, because he needed to feel more of her, he slid three fingers inside her tight heat, and kissed her hard, groaning in pleasure along with her.

"*Nate*," she moaned, her eyes squeezed shut. "I'm going to come on your face."

Her scream seemed to rip from her throat. That scream was his name as she came hard on his lips, flooding his tongue with the taste of her release.

Soon, she relinquished her hold on the posts, her body turning limp like a rag doll. He shed his pants, then grabbed a long cushion from the deck furniture, tossed it on the hard wood, so her back wouldn't hurt, and then returned to the steps to scoop up his beautiful woman. He carried her to the cushion, loving the utter contentment in her expression, and the rosy color in her cheeks.

"Was it as good as in your dirty dreams?" she asked, a woozy look on her face, as her lips curved up.

"Hell no," he said, shaking his head, as he positioned her on the soft red material.

She shot him a curious look.

"My dirty dreams can't even hold a candle to the real thing. You are the sexiest woman I have ever known, and I've never wanted anyone so much," he said, settling on his knees between her legs. "Now, get those ankles up on my shoulders so I can fuck the woman I love."

She shivered, her shoulders curling in as she propped her feet on him, giving him another insanely hot view of her body that he treasured. "Is this how you want me?"

"Yes," he said, as he gripped his cock and rubbed the head against her wet center. His muscles tightened as desire thundered through him. "Raise your ass."

She lifted her rear, giving him a better angle. He gripped her ankles and then he sank into her. All the breath fled his chest from that first dizzying rush of filling her. He stilled his moves, imprinting this moment in his mind—the moonlight dancing across her skin, the sweet vulnerability in her blue eyes, the warm air that wrapped around them. And then the pleasure, the absolute endless pleasure that charged through his cells as he thrust.

One deep thrust after another.

Watching her.

Savoring each unsteady breath from her lips.

Thrilling at her hands grabbing onto his thighs.

Loving every second of their connection.

He swiveled his hips, and drove deeper, holding tight to her legs. She arched higher, seeking him out. Her lush body was greedy, eager for contact. Keeping a firm grip on one ankle high up in the air, he let go of the other, dropping his hand between her legs.

She cried out as he rubbed his thumb across her clit.

"God, I love making you feel good," he rasped out as he sank into her again.

"You are pretty fucking awesome at it," she moaned, her eyes going dreamy as her breath came faster, and she purred his name. She was close, nearing the cliff once more, so he gave her what she always wanted. *More, harder, faster.* Driving into her, white-hot sparks ripped through his body. His vision went blurry, and the world slipped away as the pressure in his balls shot sky-high. His spine ignited. His hand curled tighter around her ankle, and he stroked her faster, urging her on until she shuddered once, twice, three times as another climax swept through her. At last, he was free to succumb to the orgasm that tore across his body, lighting up all his muscles and bones, pulling him under into a place he only went with her.

Soon, he rested alongside her as she snuggled against him, fitting perfectly in his arms.

"Mmmm," she murmured. "We do good make-up sex."

"We do good every-fucking-time sex," he said on a soft laugh.

"That too."

They lay on the deck, under the stars, the water lolling lazily against the sandy shore nearby. She turned to him, propped up on her elbow, and brushed a fingertip along his hipbone. Every ounce of contact with her was such a rush.

"I like it better when we get along," she said.

"Me too."

"Let's keep being open with each other."

He nodded. "Yes. No more shutting down and not talking."

"Dirty talking, and sexy talking, and honest talking."

"Sign me up."

"Because I think we make a damn good team," she said, her lips curving up in a sexy grin.

"Speaking of being honest, did I ever tell you what we originally planned to name this hotel chain?"

She furrowed her brow. "No. I don't think you did. It wasn't always The Luxe?"

He reined in a smirk as he tucked his hands behind his head and stared at the stars. "You can't tell anyone, okay?"

"Promise," she said, sounding eager to learn his secrets.

He lowered his voice to a whisper. "Originally, we were going to call it The Sock on the Doorknob Hotel."

Her mouth fell open and she laughed, the kind that must have spread through her whole body as her shoulders shook. "Was The Sex Panther already taken?"

He nodded. "It was. Another option was Bed Barista."

"Oh, that's good," she said, admiringly. "But if that hadn't worked out, you could have tried the Spork of Love."

296 · LAUREN BLAKELY

He snapped his fingers as if to say *aww shucks*. "Or the Tunnel of Chubb."

She pointed in the direction of the villa. "By the way, I hope you don't mind, but I did put your sock on the doorknob. I figured it was the best way to let housekeeping know not to disturb."

"Perfect," he said, wrapping his arms around her, and everything was in that moment as they returned to who they were before, laughing and loving every minute together.

CHAPTER TWENTY-NINE

New York, same day . . .

Ethan cursed.

His boss had just put him on notice. Revenues were down at the Victoria Hotels and it was his job to turn this ship around or else. He kicked the side of the desk in frustration. How hard did a man have to work these days? The answer—too hard. He'd been working his ass off for the last two years, and his boss railroaded him on nearly all his ideas to improve their image. And then, the guy took it out on him. Blamed him for lackluster quarters and poor performance. He let out a long stream of air, the frustration thick in his blood.

Things were supposed to be different. He was supposed to be CEO of The Luxe. He'd worked in this business long enough, he had known that hotel inside and out, and he was sure the top job would've gone to him.

Instead, Nate Harper had won the gig. Nate was younger by a few years, and it ticked him off that the time he'd put in wasn't enough to beat out the young hotshot.

Ethan hadn't stayed on at The Luxe after losing that two-man race. That would have been too hard, so he'd sought out a new job, and grabbed the chance here, thinking he could make a difference. But most days he was banging his head against a brick wall.

He sank down in his chair, swiveled around, and stared out the window of his office building in midtown. He wanted something to change the image of Victoria Hotels. Make it more like Victoria's Secret. Something sexy. Something alluring. Hell, that's why he'd reached out to Casey Sullivan in the first place, trying to strike a deal with Joy Delivered. Victoria wouldn't be the first hotel to include pleasure packs in its rooms. Plenty of high-end hotels around the world included anything from shag bags to condoms to feather ticklers to blindfolds, and such perks had been proven to spread positive word of mouth—but he wanted something no one else had. With the way Joy Delivered's star had risen in recent years, he'd wanted to pair up with that company.

But Casey had given him the blow-off in her messages. Maybe he needed to try something else, another sexy type of product. He turned around, grabbed the phone, and dialed Grant Abbott at Entice. He knew the guy because the Victoria Hotel in Chicago featured an Entice boutique in the lobby.

"To what do I know the pleasure of this phone call?" Grant said, his southern drawl coming through loud and clear from New Orleans all the way to Manhattan.

After a bit of friendly chatter, Ethan tackled the matter at hand. "What are the chances that we can expand our deal with Entice?"

"You know I'd love to do something with you. But right now my energy is focused on this new partnership with Joy Delivered. But perhaps, we can discuss it as soon as that's done."

His spine straightened and his radar went off. There was that name again. What the hell was Casey up to? "What are you doing with Casey?"

"Just launching a new product with them. It's the ultimate pleasure toy on the path to prolonged orgasm," Grant said, speaking in an over-the-top voice as if he were narrating an infomercial.

"Which means?"

"Apparently it's like being licked and fucked at the same time," Grant said, choosing bluntness now. "That's not how we'll be positioning it in our boutiques, but that's what it is and what it does, evidently. Tried it out myself with a lady friend in Hong Kong and it pretty much sent her flying. So there you go."

When the call ended, Ethan flipped open his laptop and hunted through his emails to Casey Sullivan. He stabbed his finger at the screen as if he'd caught her red-handed. Because right there, in black and white in her reply from a few days ago, she'd told him that she was already working with another hotel. His antennae went into overdrive, a memory resurfacing. Hadn't Nate told him on the phone when he'd called to give him the Danya report that he was doing business with her?

What the hell? Had she taken his idea and given it to fucking Harper?

Searching through his sent messages in a flurry, he found his original note to her. Early June. His eyes narrowed and his jaw clenched.

Harper again. Coming out ahead.

If she'd stolen his idea and handed it over to the man who took the job he'd wanted . . . well, he'd find a way to get what rightfully belonged to him.

CHAPTER THIRTY

The Maldives, sunrise . . .

She was stealthy that morning.

Her pink bikini was already on—she'd retrieved it from her villa after the first rays of a bright orange sunrise peeked over the horizon—and her breath was minty fresh. She had her sights set on one thing—destination waterfall. The night before, she hadn't been able to see it in the dark, but it was one of the first things she spotted when the soft peach dawn painted itself on the sky this morning. There, in a little lagoon next to an outcrop of rock was a waterfall, serene and falling softly.

She kneeled next to Nate, naked and beautiful under a sheet. He'd grabbed one from the bed last night and brought it out to the deck so they could sleep under the stars. The sheet slipped down to his waist and she couldn't help but admire the strong muscles in his back and his shoulders as well as the trim taper of his hips. He had a pretty fantastic ass too, so she gave the sheet a gentle tug, revealing a few more inches of that firm, rounded rear that she loved to hold on hard to when he was inside her. He stirred from the movement, turned over, and blinked. Flashing her a drowsy smile, he shielded his eyes from the sun, and said a husky good morning.

"Good morning to you too," she said, matching the wattage with her own grin. "I just decided that kissing you under a waterfall is on my bucket list and we're going to go check that off right now."

"Ah, I see you're enjoying the perks of the best villa on the property. Or I should say, you're about to." He sat up. "Give me one minute."

As he retreated up the stairs and across the deck, she watched him walk, enjoying the view of his backside as he headed into the hut. A minute later he returned, still in his full birthday suit. His eyes raked her over from top to bottom. He scratched his forehead as if something didn't compute. "What I don't understand is why you have on a bikini."

She held her hands out wide as if the answer was obvious. "Because we are about to go in the ocean."

"The way I see it, this whole bucket list thing should be satisfying to both of us. And mine has skinny dipping in the Indian Ocean with you on it, so get out of that right now," he instructed. Then added, "This area of the beach is private. There's no access to the lagoon except from this hut. So, if I were you I'd strip."

She laughed and rolled her eyes, even as she did what he asked, leaving two pink scraps of fabric on the wood floor. "You just love being the alpha male, don't you? Giving me orders."

He wiggled his eyebrows. "I do, and I love all your orders too," he said, then dropped a quick kiss on her lips. His breath was fresh, just the way she liked breath to be in the morning, and all day long, for that matter.

Casey walked down the final set of steps that descended into the ocean. A former swimmer, she would've preferred to dive in, but the water was shallow by the hut. Soon, it deepened and she and Nate swam naked to the lagoon.

Serenity took on a new meaning here in the tranquil water with the sun caressing her skin. The world was calm and not a care was to be had, not a concern existed, and nothing at all could ever go wrong. This was the true escape, and she understood why people wanted to make island getaways for life. This kind of paradise had a way of working a magic spell on you.

When they reached the secluded lagoon, the curving rock ledge shielded them further, hemming them into this private little pool for lovers. The waterfall pattered down the slate, beating out a steady rhythm.

She roped her arms around Nate's neck and pulled him in for a kiss. It was a morning kiss, the kiss of the sun rising and the start of a new day. It was a kiss that held the promise of so much more between the two of them, of a whole future. Of lazy Sundays. Of breakfasts together. Of Saturday matinees, and foot rubs, and baths, and Chinese takeout, and someday, walking a dog together in the park.

She ran her tongue across his top lip, then the bottom, savoring this lingering pace—soft, slow and unhurried. No one was in a rush. They weren't subscribing to a set amount of lessons or expecting only a finite amount of time together, and the kiss said as much. She gave herself over to the delicious sensations that spread through her whole body, warming her inside and out with the tenderness of his touch. Then, he picked up the speed, kissing her harder and deeper, their tongues tangling as the falling water made its morning music. Soon he backed her up so they were under the waterfall. It was like standing in an afternoon summer storm as the drops cascaded over her shoulders, her breasts, her waist. She sighed contentedly as his lips fused to hers.

But then, sometimes easy kisses turn into something more. As he yanked her closer, the evidence was clear in the hard length of his erection—this kiss was primed for much more than first base. "I'm thinking we want to kick the bucket list item up a notch. How about you?"

She nodded, flashing him a naughty grin. "I'm thinking we're on the same page again. But just to make sure, is this how you're thinking you'd like me? In this position?" She turned around, dropped her hands onto a rock that peeked over the water's surface, and raised her backside into the air. He groaned appreciatively.

"Yes. You are reading my mind," he said as he slid his hand between her legs where she was ready for him.

Funny, how she'd intended simply to kiss him in this romantic, blissful setting. But then the two of them had never been very good at stopping at kissing. The first night in New Orleans his kisses had made her want to climb him like a tree. They'd only grown hotter since, and they always led to more.

He rubbed his hard-on against her entrance, and a little whimper escaped her throat from that first heady sensation of him touching her where she wanted him most. In one quick thrust he had them both moaning at the same time, their sounds echoing across the rocks, carried off on the morning breeze along the ocean. The water lapped gently around her as he rocked in and out, filling her.

Even though she was the one bent over with her ass in the air, being fucked standing up in the wide open waters, she still felt possessive of him, of this man who wanted her, who craved her, who seemed to need her desperately. Somehow, she was the one who *had* him. But she also knew they were a perfect match. Perhaps that was why she felt so possessive of him and wanted him as her own for all time.

He took her like he wanted her that way too.

Pinning her to his body, he twisted her hair around his fist, pulling hard, giving him even more leverage to drive all the way into her, which is exactly where she wanted him. Her fingers dug into the rock as she held on tight, the waterfall raining down on them. Like that, the sea turtles somewhere out there and the birds flying by the only witness to their intense pleasure, she rose higher and higher. Her toes dug into the wet sand. Her body tightened as she sought release from the sheer intensity. Concentrating on the sensations that blasted through her body, she rode closer to her climax, and then she shattered—bright, brilliant diamond lights exploding behind her eyelids. In seconds, he chased her there, grunting her name as he came, his body jerking from the aftershocks.

He pulled out of her and then, and as if on cue, they both sank down in the water to their necks, enjoying the pleasant sensation of the ocean covering their bodies. He rained more kisses down on her mouth, her cheeks, her eyes, whispering words of love, words of desire, words of sweet, tender passion. She was a lucky woman. She was a happy woman. In their time together he'd made her feel so good about herself, loving her for who she was, not who he wanted her to be. That's how he'd always treated her, from way back at the start of their friendship on through the here and now.

They played in the water, splashing each other, laughing, darting under the crystal blue waters like dolphins. She was faster and each time she popped up, her hair sleek, she'd laugh at him. "You must've forgotten that I was a swimmer in high school."

"I remember. Did you think I'd forget anything about you?"

Her eyes widened and she clasped her hand over her mouth. "Uh-oh. What if we don't have anything to say to each other? What if we know everything about the other person and there's nothing left to talk about?" Her voice rose in mock fear.

He laughed and shook his head. "I'm not worried about a damn thing when it comes to you."

They swam to the dock, water droplets falling off their naked skin as they climbed the stairs, and then headed inside to get ready for the wedding.

CHAPTER THIRTY-ONE

The Maldives, early afternoon . . .

The chiffon dress fell just below the bride's knees, the ideal length for a beach wedding. The thin straps showed off her strong arms that were already tanned from a few short days here. Casey pinned a white orchid in Michelle's hair, while her other bridesmaid, Sutton, sprayed the loose tendrils that framed Michelle's face.

Casey stepped back, appraised the bride, and clasped her hands at her heart. "You look so beautiful," she said, pushing past the lump in her throat.

"Thank you so much," Michelle said, her expression heartfelt.

"His jaw is going to drop the second he lays eyes on you," Sutton chimed in as they finished the final prep in the villa nearest the beach.

There was a soft rap on the door. Sutton and Casey stared at each other with wide eyes. "It better not be Jack. I'll answer it," Casey said and opened the door a few inches, peering around the wood to find Michelle's brother, Davis. "Oh, you're the only guy allowed in right now," she said, with a bright smile. Davis flashed a quick grin in return, his piercing blue eyes lighting up his face.

"I have something for the bride," Davis said. He held a small box and carefully opened the lid.

Michelle gasped when she looked inside, and brought her hand to her mouth.

"It's mom's," he said softly.

Michelle nodded. "I know," she said as a lone tear slid down her cheek.

"I thought you'd want to wear it. I've held onto it for you for this day."

"I do want to wear it," she said, holding out her hand so Davis could clasp a simple, thin silver bracelet on her wrist.

Sutton grabbed a tissue and dabbed quietly at Michelle's cheek.

Michelle held up her wrist. "I love it."

"And I love you," Davis said, then wrapped his arms around her in a warm embrace. Casey looked away, giving them their private moment.

When he pulled apart, Michelle spoke first. "Are you ready to give me away, but not give me away?"

Both Davis and Michelle laughed, and the touching, tender moment had turned to a lighthearted one now. "No one could ever give such a strong, independent woman away. It is merely my honor to walk by your side on this journey," he said, and it was Casey's turn to steal away a tissue and bat at the tear in her eye. She loved their approach—Michelle wasn't anyone's to give away, but she and Davis had looked out for each other and took care of each other, and it simply felt right for him to be the one to walk by her side at this moment.

They made their way through the resort to the beach, weaving through palm trees and banyan trees, lush and emerald green. The sun was high in the sky, but the breeze that blew off the ocean kept them from sweltering. Soon, they reached the patch of sand where the ceremony was to be held.

Pretty music from a string quartet rose up to greet them. A Brahms Symphony, she recalled Jack telling her, and then he'd made some offhand remark about never catching the end of it the night he and Michelle had gone to the symphony. Casey didn't press him about what he meant, figuring it was a sexy inside secret between bride and groom.

They rounded the final bend in the path to the beach, and the wedding came into view. A canopy was set up on the soft white sand, and Jack stood waiting, looking handsome in beige slacks and a white shirt, as casual as he could ever be. Her heart raced as her eyes landed on Nate, standing next to the groom. God, he was beautiful, and he took her breath away even from this distance. The wedding was small—perhaps twenty people—and they all stood since the ceremony would be short.

"Ready?" Davis asked.

"Never been more ready," Michelle said.

Davis gestured to Sutton, her cue to walk down the white runner spread out on the sand. With flowers in hand, Sutton led the way. Michelle grabbed Casey's wrist, and tugged her close. "You told me last night you were glad I was marrying your brother," she said and Casey nodded as she recalled their conversation. "I want you to know how happy I am that you're my sister-in-law."

"Oh hush," Casey whispered, waving her hand quickly in front of her face to try to quell the tears that welled in her eyes once more. "Now you're going to make my mascara run yet again."

Michelle grinned. "Go. I'm eager to see my soon-to-be husband," she said, then let go of Casey's wrist, and she walked to the canopy, her smile growing ever wider as she neared her two favorite men—her brother, who she adored to the ends of the earth, and Nate, who she loved madly. She wore the yellow dress she'd snapped a photo of herself in a few weeks ago, and she knew, without a shadow of a doubt, that Nate was remembering the time she'd sent it to him, and was savoring the way it fit her in the flesh. She thrilled at the way he looked at her; it told her he only had eyes for her.

"Hi," Nate whispered under his breath as she took her post next to Sutton.

"Hi," she whispered in return.

They both turned their gaze to the bride as the music shifted, and the quartet began playing *Ode to Joy* by Beethoven. Casey had asked Michelle why she'd chosen this piece and she'd responded that the music made her happy. That seemed reason enough, and Casey understood why. The piece lived up to its name, matching the expression on Michelle's face as she walked to the canopy. When they reached the wedding party, Davis let go of her arm, planted a kiss on her cheek and stepped aside to join his wife.

Jack gazed at Michelle with such happiness, such certainty, that she wanted to jump up and down, and dance in circles. She was so damn happy for him.

The officiant began the ceremony. An older man with graying hair and kind eyes, he seemed well suited for his role. "We're here today to celebrate the relationship of Jack and Michelle. Together, they have gathered the most important people in their lives," he said, stopping to gesture to the guests, "to share in their love and their joy."

As the officiant continued his introduction, Casey locked eyes with Nate. She couldn't have wiped the grin off her face if she'd tried, nor could he, as a warm breeze rustled the canopy. She had never expected to be at her brother's wedding having fallen in love herself. But it had happened, hook, line and sinker, and here she was, deep in the throes.

Soon it was time for the vows.

"Michelle and Jack are here to marry each other and begin this next path in their lifelong journey," the officiant said, his deep voice carrying across the coconut-scented tropical air. "Their words, their intentions, their vision, and that love and faith in each other will define and shape their marriage and all their days together. There will be times of conflict and times of joy, and amidst all those times I ask them to remember always that love is a gift, that marriage is a lifelong commitment, and that together they can face any hurdles with a love this strong. I call on them now to give their promise to each other before their friends and family. These are the pledges that will bind them together."

The gray-haired man looked from Michelle to Jack and back. "Please join hands and look into each other's eyes."

Michelle handed Sutton her bouquet of pink roses, then focused on Jack as he clasped hands with her.

"Jack, with this understanding, do you take Michelle to be your wedded wife and to live together in marriage? Do you promise to love her, comfort her, honor and keep her, for better or worse, for richer or poorer, in sickness and in health, forsaking all others and to be faithful only to her, so long as you both shall live?"

Jack nodded. "I do," he said, his voice full of confidence and hope.

"Michelle, with this understanding, do you take Jack to be your wedded husband, and to live together in marriage? Do you promise to love him, comfort him, honor and keep him, for better or worse, for richer or poorer, in sickness and in health, forsaking all others and to be faithful only to him, so long as you both shall live?"

Michelle beamed as she answered, "I do."

The officiant turned to Nate. "May I have the rings, please."

Nate dipped his hand in his pocket, and presented two platinum bands.

"These rings are a symbol of your unending love and a sign of your commitment to each other. A ring is unbroken. May your marriage always be unbroken, too. Now, as you place these rings on each other, you may share your vows," the officiant said, gesturing to the couple.

Jack slid the ring on Michelle's finger, his eyes on her the whole time as he spoke. "This ring is a gift for you and symbolizes my desire and my love for you that grows every day, and will continue to for as long as we both shall live."

Michelle took his hand, placed the ring on him, and repeated the same vow. Then the officiant delivered the words that sealed off the ceremony: "You may kiss the bride."

As her brother kissed his wife before their friends and family, Casey let her tears of happiness fall, and soon the guests were clapping and cheering, and the quartet was playing again.

She felt a hand on hers, then fingers threading through hers, then a voice in the ear. "What if the best man wants to kiss the bridesmaid?"

"She'd say yes."

They kissed too.

CHAPTER THIRTY-TWO

New York, two weeks later . . .

Nate tugged at his tie, wishing he could yank the damn thing off, and shed the whole jacket and suit too, just wear shorts and a T-shirt to his board meeting.

He headed up Lexington as the sticky July heat pelted the sidewalks and the city sweltered under the weight of the sun's punishment. He pushed his sunglasses on the bridge of his nose, and walked quickly around a group of teenagers sucking on iced drinks. Glancing at his watch, he ran a quick review of the day's agenda in his head. In a word: packed. He'd just gotten off the phone with Jack, thanking him for making the necessary European intros that Nate had asked for at the rehearsal dinner. He'd need to make some final calls on that front next. Then, he had a board meeting all day, a Skype call scheduled with his Las Vegas property manager, and finally he'd get to see Casey. That was his reward, and what he longed for most. He'd just returned late last night from a four-day trip to New Zealand, and couldn't wait to have her in his arms again.

But first, he'd promised Ethan he'd grab a cup of coffee. The man had called him that morning and said he desperately needed to run an idea past him. He'd sounded worn thin. Ethan said he was catching up on emails at a diner so Nate had told him he'd stop by for a few minutes. It was on the way to the meeting, and he figured it was the least he could do for the guy. Ethan had been busting his ass. He'd always been a hard worker.

Pushing open the door to Sunnyside Diner, he scanned quickly for Ethan, spotting him in a booth at the back. He had his laptop open, and papers spread across the table.

As Nate slid into the orange upholstered booth on the other side, Ethan did a quick sweep of the papers, grabbing everything as best he could and piling it on top of his computer. "Sorry. I've been working here all morning. I kind of took over the space."

"No worries. You setting up a new office?" he joked.

Ethan scoffed, then shot him a sad smile. "You never know, right?"

Odd response. Nate was about to ask what was up, but the waitress stopped by. "What can I get for you?"

"Just a coffee. Black, please," he said, and she nodded crisply and left. "So what's the story? How can I help?"

Ethan shook his head, and blew out a long stream of air as he shoved a hand through his hair. Damn, this man was the very definition of frayed. "Fucking boss," he muttered. "The guy is relentless and is constantly on me to come up with new ideas, then he shoots them all down. And everything I've brought to him has fallen apart too. Like this deal I had with Joy Delivered. It was all signed and ready to go, and then wham," Ethan said, miming an explosion.

Nate narrowed his eyes, trying to process what Ethan had just said. How on earth would Ethan have a deal with Casey's company? "She pulled it out from under me to go to the Pierson," he added, mentioning the name of another hotel chain.

Nate furrowed his brow. The details didn't quite add up. The Luxe had a deal with Joy Delivered. They were ready to roll out the marketing for the LolaRing. The product had been kept under wraps, along with the specifics of the partnership. The *exclusive* partnership.

"What do you mean?" Nate asked carefully as his spine pricked with an oddly familiar feeling. He almost couldn't put his finger on it. It had been a while since he'd experienced this, but the déjà vu running through his mind was intense.

"She came to me last month to roll out some new product. Said the other hotel chain she'd planned to work with wasn't going to cut it. Not classy enough, she said. But then she yanked it from me a few days ago to go with the Pierson. Hasn't told anyone yet," Ethan said, shaking his head.

Nate clenched his fists under the table, and swallowed dryly. He tried to tell himself not to jump to conclusions. Not to assume the worst. The waitress appeared with a mug and a pot of coffee and poured a cup for Nate. She turned to Ethan. "More for you?"

"That'd be great," he said, pushing his white ceramic mug closer to the waitress, and knocking some papers around in the process. "Look at me. I'm a fucking mess," he said to Nate with a self-deprecating chuckle as he grabbed some of the papers and tried to organize them, then stopped. "Screw it. I just need more coffee."

Nate blinked and tried to clear his head as Ethan took a long drink from his mug. He pursed his lips, keeping his mouth shut, as he worked hard to ignore the rapid-fire fear and anger that stirred in his blood. It was only a business deal; this wasn't the same situation as Joanna, and besides, Casey wouldn't do something this sneaky. She wouldn't lie or play these kinds of games.

But then he'd once believed all of Joanna's lies.

Every single one of them.

Ethan set down his cup. "Can't get too upset about it, I suppose. Even though she promised me the deal. Hell, it was *my* idea. I brought it to her way back before she gave it away to the Pierson," he said, stabbing his finger against a piece of paper in his stack. Nate's eyes followed Ethan's moves, and he flinched when he saw the words in black blaring at him. An email from Casey to Ethan from nearly a month ago, with only a line or two visible since the paper was partially covered up by the computer.

Love the concept! Looking forward to exploring possibilities with you!

It was like being shot back in time. Discovering an email he wasn't meant to see, full of words that subverted him, words that revealed how he'd been played like a fool again.

He swallowed back his anger, and spoke slowly, trying not to show he was reeling inside. "She was doing this deal with you first? It was your idea?"

Ethan nodded. "Yup. She yanked it out from under me though. And hey, I guess I can't blame the Pierson for taking it, right? I hear this toy is supposed to be pretty intense. She told me it feels like being licked and fucked at the same time."

Nate gripped the edge of the table. Blood pounded in his ears as those words echoed loudly, like a cruel mockery of all that was supposed to be private.

* * *

Casey peered at the address on her phone one last time, then glanced up at the street sign. She didn't spend much time in Chinatown, and the streets had names instead of numbers. Baxter Street. This was the one. She turned right, hunting for her destination.

The stores along the block were tiny, wedged next to each other, and addresses on the front of the buildings could be hard to spot. She readjusted her ponytail, so it was high on her head, keeping her hair off her neck. She tugged at her silky, short-sleeved blouse, wishing for the thousandth time that New York and hot summers played nicely together. But they didn't and never would. She still loved this city though, loved the hustle and bustle, and loved the fact that she could track down anything she wanted in mere hours, as she'd done today. That was the reason she found herself walking past Chinese grocery stores peddling odd fruit, then dim sum dealers, then sardine-sized shops that specialized in embroidered robes and dresses. She checked the numbers of all of them, and soon she found the X that marked the spot.

The Fortune Cookie Factory. With a name like that, she'd half expected a Willie Wonka-style establishment, with gears and cogs and conveyor belts that produced the little cookie creations. Instead, she'd arrived at a small storefront, stuffed from floor to ceiling with boxes. The door was open, and the interior was dimly lit. She walked in. No one manned the front counter. She tapped the bell lightly.

Soon, a heavyset woman with short black hair and tired eyes waddled to the counter.

"I'm picking up an order," Casey said.

The woman nodded. "What is your name?"

Casey gave her the name and a minute later the woman handed her a small Chinese food carton with fortune cookies in it. She returned to the blanket of heat in the New York mid-morning, ready to jet back to her office and focus on work before she could give this small little gift to Nate tonight. She hadn't seen him in four days, and was so ready to let him know how much she'd missed him.

When she reached Canal, she raised her hand to hail a cab, but two minutes later she was still standing there, peering down the long stretch of street at occupied cab after occupied cab. She sighed heavily, shrugged, and hoofed it to the nearby subway. As she walked down the steps to the uptown platform her phone rang. Nate's name flashed across the screen.

* * *

Something dark and nasty gnawed at Ethan's gut. It was *that* thing—that creature inside of him—that told him to keep going. Somewhere inside, he knew he was pushing things too far. But that voice of reason wasn't speaking loudly enough for him to hear.

Maybe it was because of his boss. Maybe it was because he wanted things that he didn't have. Or maybe it was just because he was still pissed. He didn't usually resort to these sorts of tactics to get what he wanted, but he was backed into a corner at work, and if he could convince Harper that Casey had fucked them both, perhaps he could swoop in and steal the deal back that was his in the first place. Be the knight in shining armor for her. She'd have no choice but to work with him, as she should have in the first place.

A long shot, but it was the only shot he had. He wouldn't have operated like this a few years ago, but a few years ago he was still on the rise. Now he was on the downhill, and men on the downhill had to fight dirty to climb their way up the summit again.

"Look," he said, "I was totally shocked. I never expected she'd pull the deal out from under me like that."

Nate knit his brow together and stared at Ethan as if he were speaking a foreign language. The silence worried him so he kept talking.

"She's got a good rep," Ethan said, words spilling out quickly.

"She does," he grumbled, finally saying something.

"That's why I was so surprised. That's why I went look-ing for other opportunities. I didn't think she'd screw me over like that. But you know what they say about women in business," he said, with a scoff.

Nate stared at him, narrowing his eyes. He shook his head. "No. What do they say about women in business?"

Ethan gulped. A tinge of red splashed across his cheeks. Then, he sucked down his embarrassment and kept piling on. Truth and lies began to blend. Everything he said felt true because it sure as hell seemed to him that Casey Sullivan had stolen his idea. "I just mean she's kind of a ball breaker. She's tough. She's cutthroat. She goes after exactly what she wants, no matter what."

Nate pushed his fingers against his temple and rubbed. Closing his eyes, he lowered his head, and let out a frustrated sigh. Then he looked up. "Hey man, I need to go. I have a board meeting. Was there something particular you wanted to talk about? I thought you wanted advice on something."

Ethan waved a hand in the air. "We'll talk another time."

Nate rose, tossed a few bills on the table, and turned to go.

Ethan called after him, plastering a smile on his face. "Your money is no good here. I'll take care of the coffee."

"Leave it for the waitress then," he said, then grabbed his phone. Ethan gathered up his papers and exited a few minutes later.

* * *

When Nate left the diner he was seeing red. Dark clouds billowed from behind his eyes. Anger lashed his body, fueled by a latent shame. Fine, he understood on a rational level—though that level was much harder for him to access right now—that this situation was not the same as Joanna sleeping with her professor.

And yet, somehow it had the makings to be precisely the same. Because Casey knew how important trust was to him. She knew that it was the cornerstone of their friendship and the foundation of their love.

He breathed out hard, huffing through his nostrils. He fumbled at his phone as he marched along the crowded avenue, late morning foot traffic clogging the sidewalk. He slid his thumb across the screen to unlock it but the heat beat down, and he missed, his fingers slippery with sweat.

He cursed, and was damn near ready to slam his fist into a streetlamp again as he replayed the conversation with Ethan. Though something felt off about Ethan's take on the events, that email seemed to reveal the Casey had been up to something.

Cutthroat.

Was she truly that cutthroat in business? He flashed back to what Scott had said about her. *Good at business, bad at relationships.*

No, his heart screamed. But his head warned him that he'd been fucked with before, and not to let it happen again. He'd learned his lesson, hadn't he?

His chest felt heavy, and his pulse beat with fury as he pushed his way around crowds of New Yorkers. He jostled past a group of hipsters, barely caring that he nearly knocked into one of them. Tension coiled in his muscles as his brain went wild, racing through the possibility that Casey had subverted their deal. Because of one sentence. One line. One phrase from Ethan.

"It's like being licked and fucked at the same time."

Casey had said that to him the night in London. Said it in the throes of passion the time she came undone courtesy of that toy. That's what rankled him the most. She'd made such a big deal about never using those words outside of the bedroom, but somehow that private description had made its way back to Ethan. The kernel of doubt inside of him ballooned as he turned the corner, heading towards the high-rise building. All rational thought fled his brain, and he was reduced to raw, exposed nerves, and the fear that he'd chosen the wrong person to love yet again.

He reached for his phone once more, ready to call her, to confront her, to ask her what the hell was up, but as he started to dial her number, his phone beeped.

The guy Jack had put him in touch was calling. Crap. Nate answered, not wanting to deal with it, but knowing he had to. He gave the guy the necessary details for the delivery, then hung up. Was he really going to stick to the plan to give this gift to Casey tonight after what Ethan had shared?

When he reached the building he wasn't ready to go into the board meeting, so he parked himself on a brass bench in the lobby, thinking about tonight, and what he'd planned for her. If Ethan was right, he was the ultimate chump.

But then, another voice spoke up. A louder voice. That of his sister in the park, saying you have to make a choice to move into the future.

It was that simple.

That easy.

That important.

He took a deep breath, reminding himself that he wasn't the same person who had been blindsided by Joanna. Casey wasn't Joanna. Nate didn't have to act on this anger. He didn't have to call her furiously and demand an answer. He had made a choice to trust her, and that meant not flying off the handle. That also meant he needed to call her, tell her what had happened, and ask her what she thought. Calmly. Carefully.

He stripped the anger from his voice, he let go of his pride, and he decided to do what they'd pledged to do the night they returned to each other in the Maldives.

Dirty talking, and sexy talking, and honest talking.

It was a time to be honest and to speak the truth.

When she answered, he heard the rattle of a subway train leaving the station.

"Hey! I'm downtown and heading back to work. The connection here is terrible," she said.

What a shitty time to have this conversation. But even so, he had to do it. "Hey. So I just met with Ethan Holmes and he seemed to think you were doing a deal with him, then with the Pierson for your new product. He went on and on about how he pitched it to you and you stole it from him or something," Nate said, and he felt terribly vulnerable saying these words. He felt stripped naked as if he were admitting his fears to her. But he pressed on. "He's crazy, right?"

"What the hell?" she shouted. "He said that?"

Nate shared more of the conversation, keeping his tone even, his voice free of accusation. "He made a few comments that made it seem as if you and he had talked, then he showed me an email," he said, then he stopped himself. He hadn't seen the entire email. He'd only seen a few words. "Actually, it was a line or two about exploring possibilities."

"Oh!" she shouted, seething, her anger coming through loud and clear. "He pitched me on an idea. I didn't look at it right away, and when I finally did I was already doing the deal with you. And, for the record, it was my idea to work with you. I didn't steal it from him. Besides, his pitch was for another product, and his tagline was terrible. But I was going to put him in touch with Good Vibes. That's what I meant by exploring possibilities. On top of that, I'm not even in talks with the Pierson."

"He said something about how it must feel to use the LolaRing. The whole being licked and fucked. It just made me wonder where he'd heard that."

Casey laughed. "It's a freaking cock ring with an oral sex simulator vibe attached to it. It damn well better feel like being licked and fucked at the same time. I don't think it takes insider knowledge to conclude that. Besides, I would never ever try to screw you or anyone else on a deal. You know that, right?"

He inhaled deeply, and a smile dared to appear on his face. He believed her. It was that simple. Kat was right. You simply made a choice to trust, a choice to believe, a choice to move forward. He was doing all three and would keep on that path.

"I do know that," he said, and all that anger and fear faded away. In its place was something better. Something that came from a true and deep faith in another person. Ethan had tried to shake that but he'd been unsuccessful. He would, however, get a piece of Nate's mind after his board meeting.

CHAPTER THIRTY-THREE

New York, a few minutes later...

Casey infiltrated his office easily, making it past the receptionist by claiming a meeting. Hell, if he was going to make up shit about her, she could very well do the same. She marched to Ethan's office, knocked on the open door, and stepped inside. He raised his face from his screen, and the look in his eyes was one of pure guilt.

"Knock, knock," she said in a cool, even tone.

"Who's there?" he choked out.

"The ballbreaker," she said as she walked over to his desk, parked her hands on the wood, and stared him in the eyes. "You thought I was a ballbreaker. You thought I was cutthroat. You thought I screwed you over. Does that about sum it up, Holmes?" she asked, completely in control, even as she broiled inside.

He nodded, like he'd been caught stealing. "Because I sent you the idea," he said, as if he were on the witness stand under cross-examination.

"You did. You did send me an idea. And it was a good idea. It also was not an original idea, but that's okay. I don't require original ideas. But do not act as if your idea was patented. You would not have been the first hotel chain to offer sexy perks in the rooms," she said, rattling off the names of a litany of hotels that featured late-night menus. "Yet, you are acting like you brought me the pro-totype for the next iPhone and I stole it from you because I didn't respond to your email right away. The reality is this —I am a busy woman. I didn't read your email for a week. And during that time, I struck a deal with Nate Harper, a deal I am sticking to. And you had the nerve to try to turn a line—one line—in an email to you into some sort of character assassination of me," she said, pointing at her chest as she continued to deliver her speech, "but here's what you left out. The parts where I said we should find ways to work together in the future. The parts where I said I had an idea for you. You want to know what that idea was?"

He nodded meekly, the color draining from his face. "Yes," he squeaked.

"I know people in business. I know lots of people in the business world. I have good relationships with those peo-ple because I don't screw anyone over. I was going to intro-duce you to my friends at Good Vibes because I liked your idea," she said, savoring the wince on his face when she said Good Vibes. It was the wince of a man who'd been bested, who'd lost out from his own hubris. "But do you think I will now?"

"Umm," he began.

She stabbed a finger against his desk. "That's right. The answer is no. And it's not because I'm cutthroat. It's not because I'd do anything for a deal. It's because I care about the people I work with and the products I sell. And you, Ethan, do not. But maybe I will reach out to the Pierson. Maybe the Pierson would like to carry The Wild One. Because from what I know about management at the Pierson, they don't play these kind of bullshit games." Then she paused, took a deep breath, and hit him hard with her final words. "By the way, do you know what they say about *this* woman in business?"

He shook his head meekly.

"I'll tell you what they say. That I'm fair and honest. And I'll tell you what I say to people who aren't. And it's this. You lost out. Because no one fucks with me, my company, or my family."

She turned on her heels and marched out.

* * *

Five hours later, the board meeting ended and his Skype call was finished, and Nate couldn't wait to track down that slimy fucker and give him a piece of his mind. Admittedly, there'd been a moment in his meeting when he'd doubted his ability to judge people, but then he reminded himself that he hadn't let Ethan far enough into his life for the man to do true harm. Ethan wasn't a best buddy who'd turned on him. Ethan was no Bryan or Jack in his life. He was merely a colleague that Nate had tried to give a small bit of help too, and the guy had turned out to have one hell of a chip on his shoulder. Nate was not going to beat himself up over having had a few drinks with him in the past.

He was, however, going to let the bastard know not to pull that shit with him or Casey ever again. The elevator shot him down to the lobby, and he tapped his foot, anxious for the doors to spread open. When he reached the lobby, his eyes were treated to his favorite sight.

"Want to know what I've been up to?" Casey asked invitingly, as if she had a naughty secret.

"I do."

"I paid a visit to Mr. Holmes," she said then proceeded to narrate in fantastic detail, acting out the priceless moments of her encounter with Ethan. "And then I marched out, and it was awesome," she said, and the expression on her face was one of pure victory.

"That's because no one messes with my badass woman," he said, then pulled her in for a quick kiss. "And to think, I was just going to take care of that myself."

Her eyes widened for a moment, and she turned starkly serious. "You don't mind that I did already?"

"Why would I mind? We are a team, aren't we?"

"We are," she said, her grin returned, lighting up her face. She was magnetic when she smiled. My God, had he ever stood a chance at resisting falling in love with her?

"Hey, was that our first big test?" he asked.

"You mean besides the time that we split up and were so damned stubborn we could barely admit how we felt for each other?" she said playfully.

He nodded. "Yeah, besides that one."

She laughed. "Then I'd say it was and we passed with flying colors."

"Damn. We're good together."

"Want to go get some Chinese takeout and drip hot candle wax between my breasts?"

He yanked her closer, giving her the answer in his instant arousal. "Always. But I need an hour. There's something I have to do. I'll meet you at your place."

She dropped her lips in a pout, and he whispered in her ear. "Wait for me. I want you good and ready."

"I'm always ready for you."

* * *

Later that evening, he knocked on Casey's neighbor's door. The dark-haired plastic surgeon answered and flashed a quick smile. "You all set?"

"I am. I'll be back in three minutes," he said, and handed Khashi a large, wrapped object. The man set it down in the entryway of his apartment, then shut the door.

Nate adjusted the gym bag on his shoulder, then rapped his knuckles on Casey's door. When she opened it, his heart thumped hard against his chest. There was nothing inherently unique about her outfit tonight—she had on a short skirt and a tank top, with her hair high in a ponytail. It didn't matter. She was always stunning to him, and every time he saw her she took his breath away. He thanked the lucky stars that he had a sister like Kat and a friend like Jack, because those two had talked sense into him when he'd needed it most and made sure he didn't miss his chance with the woman he adored.

"I have a gift for you. It's a big one," he said, dropping his bag on the floor.

Her eyes lit up with excitement, the sapphire blue in them sparkling brighter. "Where is it? What is it?"

"Do you trust me?"

She parked her hands on her hips, and cocked her head to the side. "What kind of question is that? Haven't we already established twenty million times over that I do?"

"Then I need you to put on this blindfold," he said, reaching into a side pocket of his bag and brandishing a black silky piece of fabric. "Consider this sensory deprivation. I'm not sure we ever had that on our original lesson plan. But it's on our new curriculum."

She arched an eyebrow, looking doubtful. "Okay. I'll do it."

He took her hand, led her to the couch, then asked her to sit down. As she settled in, he pressed the fabric over her eyes and tied it behind her head. He grabbed her phone and popped her ear buds into her ears. Then he called up her newest playlist, and turned up music so she couldn't hear.

When he returned to Khashi's apartment, the man handed over the gift and Nate thanked him. He grabbed a hammer from inside his gym bag, along with some nails, and set to work.

* * *

Casey blasted an upbeat song from her friend Jane Black, the music distracting her from whatever Nate was up to. She didn't know if she'd find him naked doing a striptease when he took off this blindfold. She considered that image for a moment. She liked that image a lot. But a striptease wasn't his style. For now, she'd simply have to wait patiently.

Soon, she felt his fingers on her cheek, his soft touch that melted her. He removed the ear buds, unfastened the blindfold and let it fall to her neck. She drew a sharp intake of air, then blinked several times. She was sure she was seeing things. There was no way *that* could be on her wall. She pointed, repeatedly, opening her mouth, but no words came out. She was like a fish trying to breathe above water.

Her collection had grown, and her wall of kisses now featured a man and a woman, caught in a rainstorm, gazing at the sky as big, buoyant raindrops fell. She stood and whispered, as if she were in church, "Is that it?"

He nodded, a huge grin in his face. "It's the Miller Valentina you wanted."

With quiet, careful steps she walked to the wall, raising her hand when she reached the painting, but not touching it, merely coming close. Her fingers tingled, and she held her breath. Astonishment unfurled inside her as she gazed at the work of art she had longed for that evening in London. The piece that she'd craved, but had lost out on because she couldn't resist stealing away for a private moment of bliss with this man.

"How?" she asked, and her voice was comprised purely of wonder.

The corner of his lips quirked up. "Jack's been working with some European companies investing in high-end items, like art. He made some calls to Sotheby's and found out who'd bought the painting. I called the guy, and made him an offer."

Her eyes widened and excitement took off inside her like a rocket. He had done this. He'd really done this. "I want to kiss it," she said, staring at the painting in awe. "But I want to kiss you more. This is the most amazing thing anyone has done for me." She cupped his cheeks in her hands, and locked eyes with him. His stunning amber eyes were full of love. "You gave me a painting."

He nodded happily. "I gave you a painting," he echoed.

"But it's not just any painting. It's *The Big Love*."

"That's what you've given me," he said softly, reverently, and she melted from head to toe, her skin sizzling, her heart igniting, her body shouting and cheering with a gleeful kind of abandon.

"I have a gift for you too, but it might seem kind of tiny now."

"Size doesn't matter," he said, and her eyes drifted to his pants.

"I beg to differ. Your size does matter, and it's just the size I want."

"Well, *that* size matters. Obviously."

"Stay here," she said, and walked to the kitchen, grabbed her box of fortune cookies, and brought them to Nate.

"Aren't we supposed to have these after dinner?"

She gestured for him to move it along. "Dessert comes first."

He opened the box, and found the two fortune cookies that she'd special ordered. "They're just fortune cookies," she said, suddenly feeling like her gift was tiny. She hadn't known that he was bringing her a work of art tonight. She'd simply intended to give him a sweet little something.

That was all. "But I had them specially made. Open them."

"Both?"

"Yes."

He took out the first one, cracked it open, and removed the strip of paper. "*Now is the time to try something new,*" he said, reading off the fortune. He looked at her, crinkled his brow, then snapped a finger. "That was your fortune the night we had Chinese. After I blindfolded you."

"Among other things," she said, gesturing to her breasts.

He smiled widely. "I'll happily do that again. And if memory serves, you wanted to give me a tattoo right here," he said, tapping his fingers to his chest.

"I did, and I still do. And if you open the other one too you'll find out what it would say if I inked you."

He snapped open the second cookie, letting the next fortune fall out. "*Your fondest dreams will come true this year,*" he said, reading out loud. He set down the cookies on the coffee table, and she wrapped her arms around his firm waist and tipped her chin up to look at him.

"Remember how you thought our fortunes were mixed up? You had the fortune '*now is the time to try something new,*' but you said it was mine?"

"I remember."

"But I don't actually think they were mixed up after all. I think the right fortune went to the right person. You did learn something new. You learned to trust again. With me," she said, and a flurry of pride and joy spread through her chest that she had been the one who could show him that love and commitment didn't have to turn sour.

He brushed the back of his fingertips against her cheek. "I did learn that. You showed me that."

"And my fortune was that my fondest dream will come true," she said, leaning into his hand, to the tenderness of his touch.

"So I guess that wasn't for me? It was for you?" he asked quietly. "Why?"

"Because my dream was to have a love like this," she said, her heart bursting with joy. Though she'd told him countless times how she felt, she still believed that moments like this, that words and gestures and actions, were the foundation of any great love. And that's what he was to her. He'd shown her that she didn't have to change for any man, that the right man would love her for who she was.

"Did it come true?" he asked softly as she ran her fingertip across his chest, as if she were imprinting him with those words. Tattooing him as she nodded, and wrote on his skin. *Your fondest dream will come true.* She had marked him in her own way.

A quiet tear slid down her cheek. He pressed his lips gently to her skin, kissing it away.

"Do you have any idea what it's like to fall in love with your best friend?" she asked.

"As a matter of fact I do. I know exactly what that's like."

"What's it like?"

"It's like the big love."

EPILOGUE

One year later . . .

A new Miller Valentina was for sale, and Casey intended to win it this time. Not that she'd lost out technically on the last one. She'd won, and she'd won big. Even so, she had her sights set on her favorite artist's latest work. She practically bounced in her chair with excitement because it was next on the evening's agenda at the sale of modern art at Sotheby's in New York. They sat in the front row. Nate had arranged with the auction house in advance for her to have these premiere seats. He'd told her it was a special gift to her to celebrate one year of being in business together.

It had been a busy year, and the partnership their companies struck had been a smashing success. The new product had delivered a fantastic return on investment for Joy Delivered, and for all its launch partners, from Sofia's to The Luxe and even to the loose-lipped Grant Abbot at Entice, who'd remained a solid business associate, especially because they'd connected recently about renewing their deal, and then got to chatting about Ethan. Grant had mentioned he'd talked to him once and had perhaps said more than he should about their partnership before it launched. Grant had a habit, it seemed, of opening his mouth too far, but Casey wasn't going to kick him to the curbside for that. She simply reminded him of the importance of privacy.

As for Ethan Holmes, he'd tucked his tail between his legs and had gone home to live with his parents after Victoria Hotels let him go due to a nervous breakdown. She was glad he was getting help for his issues, and that was all she thought about the man who'd tried to drive a rift between Nate and her.

Nate threaded his fingers through hers. He must have sensed her nerves, but also her coiled desire to nab the prize. "It's up next," he whispered, and she squeezed his fingers.

"Ouch," he said playfully as if she'd hurt him. She squeezed harder in response, and he planted a quick kiss on her cheek.

"And for the next item this evening we have the newest Miller Valentina," the auctioneer said as his assistants escorted the painting to the front of the room. Casey nearly groaned with lust for the painting. She wanted that beauty badly. "I shall start the bidding at—"

Then he stopped, brought his finger to his lips, and gazed at the ceiling. "Wait. That's not quite right."

Casey furrowed her brow. Auctioneers were always poised. This guy sounded as if he'd been thrown off his game.

"No. That's the wrong item. Take it back," he shouted, shooing away the painting dramatically. His assistants obeyed. Casey's jaw dropped and she turned to Nate. "What was that all about?"

He simply shrugged and held up his hands.

"Now bring out the correct item," the man said, and a few seconds later, one of the assistants returned with a small maroon box.

Casey pointed and whispered. "Now that's definitely not on the catalogue tonight."

The auctioneer flipped open the box, and it was almost like being blinded. The stone was so bright.

"Our next item is a vintage halo ring, set in a hand-crafted platinum band with an inlay of diamonds, and this gorgeous 2.5 carat stone. I start the bidding at—"

Nate raised his paddle. "—I'll take it."

The auctioneer pointed at him. "Sold! To the gentleman in the front row."

Then it hit her. It had happened so quickly, and she hadn't been expecting it at all, but her heart was beating out a wild rhythm in her chest as Nate clasped the box, dropped down to one knee, and took her hand in his. "Casey, I was crazy about you long before I even kissed you, and that's because you have the kindest, most caring heart I have ever known. I still can't believe you're really mine, but somehow the dream isn't ending, and every moment with you is more wonderful than the last. You make me laugh, you make me happy, you make me want to be better every day for you. You've been my best friend, my lover, and now I hope you will continue on this journey with me as my wife," he said, holding open the box, as her lower lip quivered and her heart danced. "Will you marry me?"

"Yes," she said as tears streamed down her cheeks, a wholly necessary side effect from this cocktail of bliss and pure happiness she was having right now. She held out her hand, and he slid the ring on her finger. She held it up, stunned by its beauty. Then she locked eyes with him—with this man she'd never expected to become her partner for life.

And he'd become the love of her life.

He returned to the seat next to her, and tipped his forehead to the podium where the auctioneer was beaming. He'd clearly been in on it. "And now, we have a painting from Miller Valentina," the man said.

"You better bid on it," Nate said in a sexy whisper. "You know how I like it when you go after the things you want."

"I know you do. And I'm going to make sure I get it."

"You will."

The bidding began and a few minutes later she had a new painting, and a promise for a lifetime of love. She had everything she'd ever wanted and more.

THE END

Check out my contemporary romance novels!

The New York Times and USA Today
Bestselling Seductive Nights series including
Night After Night, *After This Night*,
and *One More Night*

And the newest installment, the standalone
romance *Nights With Him*, also a New York Times and
USA Today Bestseller! (Michelle and Jack's romance)

Caught Up In Us, a New York Times and
USA Today Bestseller! (Kat and Bryan's romance!)

Pretending He's Mine, a Barnes & Noble and
iBooks Bestseller! (Reeve & Sutton's romance)

Trophy Husband, a New York Times and
USA Today Bestseller! (Chris & McKenna's romance)

Playing With Her Heart, a
USA Today bestseller! (Davis and Jill's romance)

Far Too Tempting, an Amazon
romance bestseller! (Matthew and Jane's romance)

Stars in Their Eyes, an iBooks bestseller!
(William and Jess' romance)

My USA Today bestselling
No Regrets series that includes

The Thrill of It
(Meet Harley and Trey)

and its sequel

Every Second With You

My New York Times and USA Today
Bestselling Fighting Fire series that includes

Burn For Me,
(Smith and Jamie's romance!)

and *Melt for Him*
(Megan and Becker's romance!)

ACKNOWLEDGEMENTS

Thank you so much for everyone who helped shape this story including Violet Duke, Kim Bias, Tanya Farrell, Jen McCoy, Gale and Kelly Simmon. Thank you to Sarah Hansen for the gorgeous cover, to Helen Williams for fabulous graphics, to Kelley for the daily grind and keeping track of so very much, and to Jesse for making the books. Thank you to KP for all her wisdom, to Lauren McKellar for her word tune-up, and to Kara for her eagle eye. Thank you to the talented bloggers, passionate readers, and outspoken advocates of books and sexy. Thank you to Laurelin and CD for being my girls. Thank you to Little Dog, Big Dog, Husband, Kids and Family of Awesomeness!

CONTACT

I love hearing from readers! You can find me on Twitter at LaurenBlakely3, or Facebook at LaurenBlakelyBooks, or online at LaurenBlakely.com. You can also email me at laurenblakelybooks@gmail.com.

Printed in Great Britain
by Amazon.co.uk, Ltd.,
Marston Gate.